WINGS OF DECEIT

A SENECA JAMES MYSTERY

RUTH J HARTMAN

To my husband, Garry. Always supportive!

Contents

Chapter One

I couldn't find Winifred anywhere. My cat was hiding from me. Usually, she tried her best to rush out the door when I was ready to leave the Majestic Monarch's butterfly farm, but today, there wasn't a whisker or orange tail in sight.

But I couldn't take time to locate her. Today, I was providing a butterfly release at the wedding of Devan Keller and Kinley Snare. I had everything in my truck, ready to go. I was even dressed in something nicer than my usual farm garb, which was normally a T-shirt and old jeans. Today, it was casual black pants, and I had on a nice blouse. Our rural town wasn't much for dressing up. If someone did, everyone noticed.

I glanced behind me. Obviously, Winifred wasn't going to come out to say good-bye. She'd be in a snit when she realized I'd left and she didn't get her customary cuddle. I grabbed my purse and headed toward my kitchen door. "Okay, then, I'm leaving now." I held still, waiting for any small mews of delight at Winifred getting away with something, or the scratch of her claws on the floor.

Nothing.

"Fine. I'll see you after the reception." With an aggravated huff, I shut and locked the door behind me, then got in my truck. I always looked forward to butterfly releases. Especially at weddings. What a great way to help celebrate the joyous occasion of two people getting married.

My vehicle bumped along the gravel drive, finally reaching the country road that took me to Sweethearts Chapel, an out-of-the-way wedding venue on the south edge of Maple Junction. The building had been around for decades, the outside covered with beautiful stones, while the inside had long wooden church pews made of pine. And of course, the building wouldn't be complete without the lavender and cream stained glass windows.

Several people were already milling around the front entrance, which stood open, as flowers were unloaded from the Precious Posies van, owned by Betty Rollins.

I parked, then checked on my monarch butterflies to make sure they were doing all right. They were currently housed in a mass release box, kept closed with an orange ribbon, but were quite safe. I gingerly picked up the decorative box. A few were fluttering around, but not wildly, and that was probably due to the bumpy short ride to get here.

I peered through the clear sides of the box. "All right, you beauties, I'll see you again in a bit, right at the beginning of the reception. Once the bride and groom tug on the box's ribbon, you get to take flight." I set the container back down on the passenger side floor of my truck and closed the door gently.

Footsteps came from behind me. I turned. "Oh, hey, Evie."

My cousin, Evie, ran my café, Painted Wings. Our chef, Murray Grimes, was catering the reception, and Evie was serving. "Hey, yourself. Are your painted beauties ready to take flight?"

"Yep, they're all set." I glanced at my truck. "It's warm out. I'm going to lower a window partway for some breeze. It's best for them to stay cool. They're okay in their box for a bit, but..."

"You're a good butterfly mom, Seneca."

"Thanks. I try."

"As well as a great cat-mom. How is Winifred today?"

I scowled. "I wish I could tell you. I couldn't find her before I left. Probably passed out in a closet somewhere. I hate leaving when I haven't been able to check on her."

Evie patted my shoulder. "I'm sure it's like you said. Winifred's napping in some hiding place, and you'll see her when you get home. Kitties are great at hiding, right?"

"Yeah, they are. She'll be mad for sure, having missed out on something.

But I didn't think a wedding would be the best place for a cat to roam around. Plus, she chose to wear a white butterfly costume today, a Checkered White Butterfly. I wouldn't have wanted her to outshine the bride by wearing white as well."

Evie laughed. "I can just imagine her prancing down the aisle in her little white butterfly costume. Making sure everyone's attention is focused on her. You should make her a veil to go with it." She pointed toward the chapel. "I'm serving afterward and will have to slip out as soon as they say their I do's, but I can't wait to see Devan and Kinley's wedding. Those are two sweet kids, right there."

"Yeah. They are. I'm so happy for them."

"Well, better get back to the reception area. Murray was frowning when I left, and I'm sure he'll wonder where I am."

"Murray always frowns," I pointed out.

"Right, but I don't want him to growl, so I better get back there."

"I totally understand that growl." I waved. "See ya later."

I was so fortunate to have Evie and Murray in the café. Evie was as sweet and efficient as they came, and Murray made the best food ever. His only flaw, that I could see, was that he tended to frown and scowl a lot. But those of us closest to him knew he was a cream puff, down deep. Not that I'd ever say that to his face. I might get growled at. And I got enough of that from Winifred when she was moody.

After leaving one truck window open halfway, I headed toward the chapel. Voices reached me from inside. Some I didn't know, a few I recognized right away. When I entered the building, Cody, our town sheriff, my best friend—and hopefully, maybe someday more than friends?—was standing just inside the doorway.

I bumped his side with my shoulder, something we'd done since we were kids. He was so much taller, my shoulder didn't come close to reaching his.

He glanced down. "There you are. I've been waiting for you. You're usually early for stuff like this. Did something happen?"

"Some*one* happened." I tapped my shoe against the floor.

"Who? Are you all right?" Cody was always sure I was in some sort of danger. To be fair, with two previous murders in town, there'd been times I had been, so I couldn't really fault him for being concerned.

"Winifred."

"Oh, I see." His shoulders relaxed. "What did my favorite cat do this time?"

"I was ready to go, and…you know how I like to see that she's all right before I leave the house? I try to find her for cuddles before I go?"

He smirked. "Yeah, I know this about you."

I ignored his comment. "I couldn't find the silly cat. Not in any of her normal hiding places. And I looked in every single place I've ever found her when she was hiding. Plus a few new ones I thought she might have tried out. But there was no sign of her."

"I'm sure she's fine." Cody nudged my shoulder. "You know how she can be. And how she seems to like to make you hunt for her."

"Yep. You're right about that."

A few more people drove into the gravel lot, then parked. I squinted against the sunlight to view them. "Hey, have you seen Edward yet? He's supposed to be here and help me with the butterfly release."

Edward Peffley was my new assistant. He'd only been working for me a little while, so it was still too soon to know if it would work out. I liked him; he was polite and followed directions well. At least he tried to. I'd discovered that he had a cow if he had to touch something, as he termed it, icky. I should have made it clear during his interview that when working on any kind of farm, there was usually ick involved.

However, that never bothered me, so I hadn't talked about it. Since he was a nice guy, I really hoped we could work it out, because finding a replacement for Annie, my first assistant, hadn't been easy.

And two older gentlemen, Sid Fairgate and Norman Gates, had tried it for a while until I gently kicked them out. It had taken me more time and effort to explain things to them, and to do the work myself, mostly while they watched, that it wasn't worth it. I did like the two old codgers, and yes, they wore that moniker proudly, and I was glad that at least we were all still friends after I'd told them I didn't need their services any longer.

I wasn't sure they cared all that much, since they were both retired and didn't even need the money. They'd just been bored and had wanted something to entertain them as they followed me around while I did their jobs for them.

As several people entered the chapel, I glanced at my watch. "I hadn't realized the time. Are you going to sit or stand near the back for crowd control?" I pointed at Cody's sheriff uniform.

He snorted a laugh. "This chapel won't hold enough people to need crowd control, but I will sit in the back row in case I get called out."

"Mind some company? I have to dart out as soon as they say, 'I do.' Then, when everyone comes out back for the reception, we'll do the monarch butterfly release."

"Dart? Really? Can I watch?"

"Stop it." I smacked his arm.

He lifted his hands. "Hey, just trying to have fun where I can."

"Why is it always at my expense?"

"Because you're too much fun to tease."

"Lucky me."

When several more people entered the chapel, I followed Cody to the back pew. We took our seats, earning a glare from an older man I didn't recognize who was seating guests. I was generally a good, law-abiding citizen. With the sheriff as my best friend, I had to be.

But life was too short to obey every single teeny tiny rule by a church volunteer that made no difference in the long run. His volunteer job may have been to seat people where he wanted them, but that wasn't my plan. Or Cody's. The older man huffed out a breath, then turned and led some more people to where he chose to put them.

Suddenly, a huge cloud of flowery perfume nearly overpowered me as a tall, fifty-something woman passed by me. My throat tickled and my nose itched. I covered my mouth, avoiding a coughing fit. Why did this always happen when I was in a crowd of people? It wasn't so bad if I was at home and sneezes or coughs came over me, even though I got the stink-eye from Winifred at the loud explosions.

Cody leaned close. "Are you okay?"

I swallowed hard, then cleared my throat, hoping nothing loud, obnoxious, or embarrassing happened. "Uh, yeah. Just…ack…that lady's perfume."

"It did seem like a lot." He rubbed his nose. Was it getting to him, too? Then he glanced up at the woman. "Wait. Do you know who that is?"

I reached into my purse for a cough drop, hoping it would help keep me from coughing or sneezing from the sickly-sweet stench. "Not sure. She kind of looked familiar." I quickly unwrapped the lozenge, relieved when the cherry-flavored disk did its job.

"That's Yolanda Steele."

I frowned as I thought for a second. "The one who owns Steele Enterprises?"

"That's right. It's been years since I saw her. Even then, it was just a glance. From what I know of her, she rarely comes into town."

Come to think of it, I hadn't seen her for years, either, and had never spoken to her. When I was little, my grandmother had mentioned one time that Yolanda was a piece of work. Gram never said what she meant, exactly, but at the time I'd decided it wasn't a compliment. From then on, I knew I never wanted to be a piece of work either. "Is she some sort of recluse?"

He lifted one shoulder in a shrug. "I guess so. When her husband was alive, he wanted to move back here after they married, since this is where he was born. I've heard she considers Maple Junction to be beneath her standards and doesn't like to leave her property and fraternize with the common folk unless she has to."

My eyebrows shot up. "Common? You mean like us?"

He snickered. "Might as well own it."

"I have no problem with that. I'm common through and through. And proud of it."

"Same here. That's why you and I are a good fit."

I knew he meant fit as in friends, but wouldn't it be great if it were more?

I watched as Yolanda was escorted to the front pew and seated by the guy who'd given me the scornful look. She'd taken the usher's hand and held hers slightly higher than his as if she were royalty. When she'd walked by me before, I'd been so overcome by her perfume, I hadn't taken in her attire.

It was hideous.

Her hat had an impossibly wide brim that would have poked someone in the eye if they'd gotten close enough to her. From the brim hung a sheer veil, so her face was recognizable. Since we could see her, maybe the veil was a pretense, something to separate her from people she had no desire to converse with. In her free hand, she held a tiny clutch purse, not big enough to hold a set of keys. But I doubted Yolanda ever drove herself anywhere, so why would she need those?

Her long gown was dark red, the color of blood. Sparkling diamonds, rubies, and sapphire rings on her fingers were so big I wondered if her hands were tired from wearing them. And the spiked heels on her sandals—easily six inches—looked pointed enough to stab a person in the heart if Yolanda could indeed kick her aging leg that high.

Movement from my left made me turn that direction. It was Gretchen Thompkins and Tonda LaSalle, both in their early twenties, who watched Yolanda, their eyes wide and mouths gaping open. Maybe they'd never seen her before and didn't know who she was. Yolanda did make quite the spectacle when compared to everyone else at the wedding and how they were dressed. And no one besides her appeared to act as if they were a queen.

A few rows ahead of them, Marla Tiegs, another twenty-something, elbowed her friend, Camry Baker, next to her and pointed at Yolanda as she passed by them. Camry's mouth dropped open as she stared at the older woman. Marla giggled as she pointed at Yolanda.

Several other people in attendance watched Yolanda, either staring, pointing, or whispering. I noticed Liza Loring whipping around as Yolanda passed by, giving the older woman a glare. What in the world was that about?

The wedding guests must have been as surprised as I was to see the rich, powerful woman out and about among the lowly serfs. Or maybe it was only about her clothes, that were so very different from what we all were used to seeing. Either way, after today, I doubted anyone would see Yolanda again for a very long time, since she so rarely appeared in public. Once every few decades seemed to be her limit.

Quick movement came from a few rows ahead. Tonda had her phone out.

Was she taking Yolanda's picture? Why? Did she know her? Or did she just want a photo of someone who looked so out of place? I hoped the picture wouldn't end up on social media with some rude hashtag below it. As much as I also stared at the older woman's outfit, I never liked when someone posted pictures of other people online with the sole purpose of making them look foolish.

The more I took in all the people in the chapel, the more I noticed they had their full attention on Yolanda. I frowned. That wasn't how it was supposed to be at a wedding. At least, if I imagined having my own someday…Well, that was way in the future, if at all.

But shouldn't the wedding itself be what guests should pay attention to? Especially to the bride and groom? I was sure Kinley, Devan, and their parents had spent lots of time and considerable money planning the flowers and bridal attire to make it the perfect day for both. It was a shame that one guest had taken the focus off that.

Yolanda must have had a connection to someone in the wedding party to leave her huge mansion at the edge of town if she truly was a recluse. Just the fact that I'd never spoken to her before and had lived in town my whole life told me that.

I'd driven by her mansion before, the tall iron gates that surrounded her property appearing ominous and foreboding. Plus, the home stood on a high hill, rising above the rest of Maple Junction as if judging the residents of the town. I shook my head. But none of that was my business. I was here for a wedding. Wasn't I doing the same thing others were, as I stared at Yolanda instead of taking in the chapel around me? Time to switch my focus back to why I was here.

As I glanced around, I took in the lovely pink and mauve flowers at the front, the white runner down the main aisle floor, and that the chapel had filled up while I'd sat talking to Cody and checking out everyone else. On top of the weather being perfect for the reception beneath a large tent that would follow the ceremony, the chapel, and the way it was decorated, was enchanting.

When music began to play, I turned to view the doorway to the chapel, as first one bridesmaid, then another, slowly paced down the aisle. The young women were very pretty. I bent over farther to see the aisle better. Would they have a flower girl as well? Not every wedding had one, but I always looked forward to a smaller version of the bridesmaids trooping down the aisle in a tiny dress, tossing flower petals on the aisle runner.

However, there was no little girl in sight. Maybe Kinley didn't have any relatives who were the appropriate age to be a flower girl. I settled back against my seat, ready to enjoy the ceremony.

From behind me, someone in the hallway gasped loudly, then laughed. Why were they laughing at a wedding? I hoped the bride wouldn't be upset by it, thinking it was about her on her special day. But no one else walked down the aisle yet. It must be time for Kinley to enter with her dad.

Sure enough, the wedding march began, and I stood along with everyone else to wait for Kinley's entrance. I glanced at the open doorway. There she was, looking radiant and joyful in her flowing white gown. Suddenly, she peered down. Her eyes widened. Then, she giggled.

Laughter from around us erupted, but I couldn't find the reason why. What was going on?

Suddenly, my heart lurched in my chest as I spotted my very own Winifred, with her tail held high and white butterfly costume sparkling as the sun shone through the lavender and cream stained glass windows. And Winifred was—as Evie had joked—prancing right down the aisle.

My loud groan was covered by the laughter, so at least I wouldn't be embarrassed by that. But my cat sauntering along the aisle runner in front of the bride… This was not good. Not good at all. It might be a banner day for Winifred, but how was I, as her cat mom, going to live down the teasing from this? People already made jokes about me dressing my cat in butterfly costumes every day. But this was so much worse.

Ready to grab Winifred and end the spectacle she was making, I took a step toward the end of the pew, but Cody grasped my arm. I whipped around. "What?" I whispered. "Didn't you see—"

He smirked. "I saw her, all right. But to do anything about it now might spoil Kinley's walk down the aisle. Don't worry. We'll get Winifred after the ceremony. It'll be okay."

That cat! My face heated as I sat down when the rest of the crowd did, to watch the wedding take place. How had Winifred ended up here at the chapel? She didn't know how to get here and, besides, her little legs were too short to run that far even if she had. But Cody was right. I wouldn't want to do anything to draw further attention away from the bride and groom. Better to let it play out and hope Winifred didn't do anything even worse.

Then it dawned on me what might have happened, how she ended up here. I'd left my truck door open to go get the butterflies to put in there before I left the farm. Had Winifred already snuck outside when I'd stepped out earlier this morning, then jumped inside? She'd done that in the past, hoping for a spur-of-the-moment joyride. When I was headed to see Cody or run an errand, it wasn't as big a deal, but a wedding? A lot more trouble. Especially when she took it upon herself to become a member of the wedding party.

Once Winifred had gotten into my truck and ridden here with me, it would've been easy for her to climb out and enter the chapel, since I'd left the truck window halfway open for the monarchs once I arrived.

I was mortified. But had to give my fluffy child credit. She was cunning, clever, and too smart for her own furry good. When Cody tapped on my hand to get my attention, I nodded to let him know I was okay.

Thankfully, once Winifred had made her way to the front of the church, she didn't sit down beside the bride, or bat at the long trail of her dress. Instead, she jumped up on a pew near the front. I could see the tip of her tail move in slow arcs, which only meant one thing. She was circling before lying down to take a nap. At least she'd stay out of trouble that way.

I hoped.

I tried to focus on the people now standing up front. One of the two groomsmen looked familiar. Had I met him before? I couldn't place him, but would ask around later. In a small town like ours, someone was sure to know something about him.

The pastor stood in front of the couple and looked ready to begin, but he first gave a side-eye to Winifred, blinked, then shrugged. Maybe it wasn't the strangest thing he'd ever witnessed at a wedding. I was sure pastors heard and saw much more than I could ever fathom.

I relaxed against the back of the pew, determined to enjoy the wedding. But later, Winifred and I were going to have a long talk about her inappropriate behavior today. And how wearing white while preceding the bride down the aisle was the worst.

Chapter Two

As soon as the pastor announced the newly wedded couple, I rushed from my seat and darted—yes, darted—out the main doors and to the parking area. Time to get the monarchs for their release.

When I got to my truck, Winifred sat on the hood, washing her front paws. How had she beat me out here without me seeing her? I eyed the chapel behind me. No need to worry about that now. I didn't have enough time to drive her back home. She'd have to stay.

"Listen, kitty, we'll have a longer discussion later, but for now, you got your way. You have to stay here with me until I leave."

She closed her eyes in contentment and purred, obviously pleased with herself for such an amazing stowaway experience in my truck. I retrieved the butterfly box from the front seat floor, then reached beneath Winifred's tummy.

She growled, reminding me of Murray when he was irritated, which was often.

"Sorry, kid, but you need to come with me."

Her hiss sprayed the back of my hand.

"Thanks a lot." I wanted to wipe it on my pants, but couldn't while holding her in one hand and the monarch box in the other. She squirmed to get down. "Winifred, it's either come with me to the reception, or get locked in the truck. With the windows closed this time. And it's going to be hot today. Your fur would wilt. You know how much you hate having a bad fur day."

Her body sagged over my arm in apparent defeat.

"Good choice. Okay, let's go."

A car pulled up beside me. It was Edward, my assistant. I wanted to shout, "Where have you been?" But refrained. Instead, I forced a smile as he climbed out of his car. "Hey Edward. Ready to help me with the butterfly release?"

He bobbed his head twice. "Yes, quite ready."

He was wearing a tuxedo.

I angled my chin toward his jacket. "I'm pretty sure I told you to dress nice but casual?"

His eyebrows lowered. "This is nice but casual. Casual would have been what I wear to help you at the greenhouse."

"Then what in the world would dressed up be?"

"My newer tuxedo, of course. This one has been in my closet for years."

"Of course it has," I muttered under my breath.

"Mother told me I should wear the new one, but I told her what you said about casual."

I watched him for a few seconds, trying to fathom what his homelife must be like, still living with his mother while in his forties.

With a start, I realized I'd been standing out here way too long. "Listen, it's nearly time for the butterfly release. We need to hurry to the reception, okay?"

"Right behind you."

Out past the chapel was where the reception was going to be held. A giant white tent covered the large area where guests would be served food and could dance. For the butterfly release, I'd stand just outside of the tent to one side, so the monarchs could fly straight up or to the side. There were always a few who veered back beneath the tent, but I'd make sure they were all out by the time the reception was over. Kinley and Devan would stand with me. They'd be the ones to untie the box so the butterflies could rise into the air.

I speedwalked toward the tent. I would have handed Edward the butterfly box so I didn't have to juggle both it and my cat, but he might have considered that too icky. And there was no way I'd hand him Winifred. His tuxedo might have ended up in shreds because she despised most people aside from Cody, Evie, and me. Then Edward's mother would have been upset about the appearance of his nice but casual attire.

We reached the area where I was going to release the monarchs. A podium had been placed there, laced in long ribbons in the wedding colors. I set the box on the podium, motioned to Cody, who was standing beside the food table, then handed Winifred to him when he reached me. She was only too glad to snuggle against his chest, while batting at his sheriff's badge on his shirt. Evie and Murray were there, ready and waiting for the guests to line up soon for food.

Voices rose as the small crowd emerged from the front entrance of the chapel, then ventured to the tented area. They filled in places at tables to wait for the newlyweds' arrival.

When the couple entered, a cheer went up. Winifred, still in Cody's arms, buried her head into his chest. He scrunched her closer and whispered something in her ear. My heart nearly melted at the sight. He loved her like she was his own.

Something poked me in the side. I jerked, then looked at Edward, who was pointing toward the box. "Aren't the couple supposed to open that now?"

He was right. "Yep." I moved to the podium and adjusted the microphone lower so I could speak into it. "Welcome, everyone, to the celebration of Kinley and Devan." More cheering. Poor Winifred. "They've requested a monarch butterfly release today as a symbol of their new beginning together as husband and wife. So if you'll give them your full attention, we can wish them the best by watching the monarchs take flight."

Chairs were moved, and people murmured as the newlyweds made their way to the podium.

"Thanks, Seneca," Devan put his arm around his new wife.

Kinley clapped. "Yes, this is awesome."

"You're more than welcome. Ready to meet the monarchs?"

They both nodded.

"All right." I held the box out to Devan and placed it in his upturned palms. Then I turned to Kinley. "If you'd like to undo that ribbon at the top, the magic will happen." It wasn't magic, of course, but was so amazing and special, it lit up my heart each time. I knew for many people here, this would be their first experience watching a butterfly release ceremony.

Kinley winked at her new husband, then reached out and gingerly tugged on one end of the ribbon. The top opened. Orange and black beauties fluttered out and up, into the late afternoon sunlight. They went in all directions. Most flew upward, but a few, like I'd guessed, floated into the tent area, delighting the guests.

Applause for the butterflies followed. Laughter floated across the small sea of people as a few monarchs settled on the tables, small flower arrangements, and even on some of the guests' shoulders, hands, or heads. I loved how people reacted to the tiny painted flying flowers. It truly was a special feeling to be chosen as a landing spot for a butterfly.

Winifred now had her head buried in Cody's armpit from the delighted sounds the guests were making. But Cody took it in stride like he did everything else. I was so fortunate to have him for my best friend. As I glanced at the newly wedded couple, my mind wandered to the what-ifs. Would there ever be a day when Cody and I might—

"Seneca?"

I whipped around. Evie was furiously motioning me to the serving table. She must need help. I glanced at Edward. "All right, your job will be to keep an eye on the monarchs."

He pressed his fingertips against the front of his tuxedo jacket as if in self-protection from what was to come. "What do you mean?"

"If you see some near the opening, try to gently shoo them outside. We don't want anyone to accidentally step on one when the dancing begins in a little bit. But remember, don't touch their wings, they're very fragile."

His eyebrows knitted together. "I'll do my best."

"That's all I can ask." I sure did miss my former assistant, Annie, who was so in tune with the butterflies, she asked them if they'd slept well the night before. But I would give Edward a chance. He hadn't been with me very long, and I was in desperate need of the help.

When I got to the serving table, I saw the long line of guests who were ready to chow down. I didn't blame them. Murray's culinary skills knew no equal in Maple Junction. My stomach growled. No, I'd have to wait to eat, since Evie and Murray needed my help to serve. Besides, Murray was a master of planning meals. There was always enough food for everyone, with some leftover at the end of the event.

I stepped behind the table, tugged on disposable gloves like the ones Murray and Evie had on, and began dishing out food to people in line. Once the three of us got into a rhythm, it seemed to go smoothly. When the line dwindled and people had retaken their seats, the atmosphere turned even more festive.

I watched Kinley and Devan at the head table with their parents, families, and the rest of their wedding party, enjoying the feast. I was so pleased those two had gotten married after having broken up not that long ago during a murder investigation. There'd been two murders in town recently. Hopefully, there wouldn't be any more.

Evie took a step back from the table. I joined her as we watched to make sure everyone had what they needed.

Murray pointed in the direction of the parking area. "Heading out to my van to get some refills of a couple things."

"Need some help?" asked Evie.

"Nope. You girls stay here and take a break." He walked out of the tent and around the side of the chapel, which led to the parking area out front.

I turned toward Evie to say something, but she seemed a million miles away. She was staring toward the head table, but she wasn't smiling. "Evie, are you okay?"

She jumped. "What? Um…" Her face reddened.

"What's going on?"

"I…" She pointed toward the table but lowered her hand.

"Honey, is something wrong?" I grabbed her hand, which had gone ice-cold.

"I'm fine. Well, not fine, exactly."

I shrugged, not knowing what that meant. But I wished she'd tell me, because now I was really getting concerned.

She pointed toward the table again. "Do you recognize the guy to the left of Devan? That groomsman?"

I moved a little to one side to see him better. "You know, he does look familiar, but I can't place him. Who is he?"

"We went to high school with him."

I checked the guy out again. Then, a memory sparked. "Wait. Is that…"

"Yep, it's George Marshall."

"He looks great. I didn't recognize him with slightly longer hair and the beard."

Her eyes sparkled. "I know."

Then I also remembered that Evie had dated George in high school until his family moved away. "Ah, still got the hots for your old boyfriend, then?"

She smacked my arm. "Not hots. Well…" The redness in her cheeks slid down to her neck. "I mean…he's so…"

"Yeah, you're right about that. He's gorgeous." I elbowed her gently. "Have you talked to him today?"

"Not yet. I want to. But—" She indicated the table. "I am working, after all."

"True, but if you get an opportunity to, oh, I don't know, dance, maybe…"

Her eyes widened. "You think he might ask me to dance? He hasn't even looked this direction. He might have forgotten me. I mean, it has been several years, you know."

Music, a slow number, started up. A few couples got up and headed to the dance floor.

"Now's your chance, Evie, if you want to talk to him. He'll be busy otherwise, having pictures taken and being a groomsman. You know how long those photo sessions can take."

"But he hasn't come over to ask me, and I…"

"But you can ask him."

Her face paled. "What?"

"You. Ask. Him."

Her earrings swung as she shook her head quickly. "I couldn't."

"Why not?"

"Because…I just couldn't."

"Because you're the girl?"

"Um, I guess." Evie glanced over my shoulder, then back. "All right, Seneca. I will if you will." She lifted her chin toward something behind me.

"If I will, what?" I whipped around. Cody was headed toward us, still carrying Winifred.

It was my turn to widen my eyes. "You want me to ask Cody?"

She crossed her arms. "Yep. That's the deal. You go first."

"But…" This was my own fault. However, Cody and I were friends, so it wouldn't be that weird, would it? I faced Cody but didn't make direct eye contact. "Uh, hey there."

He didn't say anything.

"Um, thought maybe…would you like to dance?"

He remained silent. My heart plummeted. What was going on? Why wasn't he answering me? If he was trying to tease me again, it wasn't going to work.

Then, he chuckled. "Oh. You're asking me? I wasn't sure if you were asking Winifred. You know how much she likes to do the bunny hop."

I laughed and was flooded with relief that everything was okay. "Yeah, you got me. Why don't we all three go?"

"Sounds like a plan." He pulled Winifred closer to his chest.

As I took a step to follow Cody, I gave Evie the stern-eye that our grandmother used to give us if we did something bad when we were little. Evie would know exactly what I meant.

She swallowed hard. "All right. Here I go."

I stepped into Cody's one-armed embrace as he held Winifred next to his chest with his other arm. Thankfully, my cat seemed to enjoy it, instead of growling or struggling for Cody to put her down.

When I turned my head, I was pleased to see that not only had Evie asked George to dance, they were now caught up in what appeared to be animated conversation. Evie's grin was the biggest I'd ever seen. Great. Maybe something good would come of their meetup.

As we danced, someone brushed by me. I turned to see Yolanda marching toward a room at this end of the chapel where there were restrooms and areas for brides and their wedding parties to prepare for the ceremony. Was she leaving already? Or just taking a break. I shrugged. None of my business, since I didn't even know her. Although I was sure she'd be the talk of the town in the days to come, as everyone speculated on why she was here.

When the song ended, Evie and George approached us. I glanced down to see they were holding hands. Wow. That happened fast. Maybe George had been thinking about Evie all this time, too?

Evie gazed adoringly at the guy next to her. "You guys remember George from school?"

Cody shifted Winifred to his other arm and shook George's hand. "Yeah, hey, how are you? Good to see you again."

"Doing well, Cody. Good to see you too."

With a happy sigh, Evie gazed up at George. "He was just telling me that he's moving back here. And he's the new pharmacist at the drug store."

That would be welcome news for Evie, who hadn't dated much since she and George split up. And definitely nothing serious. "That's great." I took Winifred from Cody's arms. After holding her on one side and holding me with his other arm for the dance, he was probably going numb by now. "Glad to see you again, George." I tilted my head. "I didn't remember that you were close to either the bride or groom."

"Devan is my cousin. A few years younger, but we've always been close."

It never ceased to amaze me all the connections between people who lived, or had lived, in town.

George glanced at Evie. "I need to get my notes so I can give a toast to the happy couple. I meant to stick them in my pocket, but forgot. I'll grab them and be right back."

"Sure." Evie's gaze followed George as he left the tent and headed toward the back door of the building. Her chest rose and fell in a long, drawn-out sigh.

I sidled closer to her. "Reconnected, have we?"

Her blush encompassed her from her neck to her forehead. "Yep." Her grin was wide. "I can't believe he's here. And that he's going to stay. It's…" Her fingers pressed against her collarbone. "I can hardly wrap my mind around it."

"I'm happy for you. And so is Winifred." I picked up my cat's paw and gave a wave to Evie, making her laugh.

"So am I," said Cody. "Good for you." He winked at her, then gave a brief glance toward me. Wait. Did that mean something? What did it mean? My heartbeat sped up. Did our dance bring out some feelings Cody might have had for me, like it did for Evie and George?

But the thoughts took a back seat when the father of the bride tapped his champagne glass to get everyone's attention. Several toasts followed until it was time for George to give his.

Devan stood up and glanced around the room. "Hey, anybody seen my groomsman?"

Everyone laughed.

But George had been gone longer than I'd expected. He said he'd be right back. When I looked at Evie, I could tell by her expression that she was worried too.

Evie frowned. "Do you suppose he got lost?"

Cody lifted one eyebrow. "It's not that big of a place."

"I know, but..." Her gaze drifted toward the back of the chapel building. If I knew Evie, she was worried that George had changed his mind and didn't want to spend more time with her. I had serious doubts that was why he hadn't returned yet. But it did seem odd that he'd been gone so long, knowing he was due up soon to give his speech.

I handed a now sleeping Winifred back to Cody. "Listen, Evie, why don't you and I go see what's taking so long. The reception will be over soon, and we'll need to clean up. Besides, I think Edward will also need help corralling any remaining monarchs left in the tent."

When I pointed, they both turned. Edward was standing on a chair near the back of the tent, waving a napkin at a butterfly that was perched on top of a pole, too high for Edward to reach.

"Yeah, let's go." Evie grabbed my hand and squeezed it hard, the tension rushing through her hand to mine.

"Don't worry, Evie. I'm sure everything is okay."

From behind me, I heard Cody say, "Well, Winifred, it's just you and me again."

I was glad my cat loved my friend so much. It made my life easier. Evie and I walked the short distance to the building and entered. Even though I'd been here before, I wasn't as familiar with it as Evie was, since she and Murray had worked at a few weddings here when I wasn't attending. I followed her down a short hallway, and we turned right into a long, narrow room.

She stood just inside the open doorway. "Um, George? Are you in here?"

A shuffling sound came from just around the corner inside the room, where a large cabinet blocked our view.

"George?" Evie stepped closer to the sound.

And screamed.

I raced to stand by her and nearly screamed myself. Because lying on top of some old tablecloths was Yolanda Steele, her eyes open and mouth agape, but she didn't seem to be moving.

And standing next to Yolanda, with a pillow in his hands that hovered a few inches above Yolanda's face, was George.

Chapter Three

The next day, I hurried to Painted Wings as soon as possible. Even though I'd told Evie she should take some time off if she wanted to spend the time with George after yesterday's tragedy, she said she'd be there as usual, that it would help keep her mind off what might happen with George if she kept busy. Although I wasn't much of a waitress, I was determined to get her day started as best I could.

Cody showed up right when Evie opened the doors for customers. Even though she loved Cody like a brother, the sight of him in his sheriff uniform seemed to give her a jolt, under the circumstances. I went to Evie's side and took her hand, trying to keep her calm. It wasn't working very well. But she had an enormous reason for being upset. She'd just found George again, and he'd been discovered standing over a dead body, holding the murder weapon. I couldn't blame her.

Cody walked toward us. "Wanted to let you know that after everyone left, Bud and I called Arnold Wellings to come take care of Yolanda's body."

Arnold was the town's funeral director. The strange older man rarely said anything, which kind of freaked me out, living in a town of otherwise mostly friendly citizens.

Bud Olsen, Cody's deputy, did his job okay, but was a little daft. Still, Cody liked him and depended on him, so I tried not to say too much. It wasn't a job I would want, so I was glad to have Cody and Bud, who were willing to make sure our town was safe.

Evie, who was now clinging to my arm, disengaged herself and began wringing her hands together. "Cody, what do you think? I mean, I know

George was standing there holding a…well, he didn't kill her, okay? He really didn't." Her breath hitched. "He—"

Cody held up his hand. "Right now, we're looking into everyone who was there. But I have no reason at this point to assume George had anything to do with it. He explained why he happened to be there. Wrong place, wrong time. My only qualm is, none of us have heard from him in all these years. How much do we really know about him now?"

Evie let out a sob. "But I know him." She pressed her hand over her chest. "In here. He hasn't changed from the sweet guy he always was. I know he hasn't."

I wrapped my arm around Evie's shoulders. "It's going to be okay." Not only was she upset over George being found in a questionable situation, but Evie had been the one that townspeople had pointed fingers at when a man had died recently in town. No wonder she was wired so tight. I'd also been in that same situation, so I understood. Plus, I hadn't had emotional ties to the person I'd been suspected of killing.

I looked at Cody. "So you said you spoke to George?"

"Yes. Since he was at the scene. And had been holding the murder weapon."

She started to speak, but Cody shook his head. "It's standard protocol, Evie. Naturally, we had to speak to George. Just like we did to everyone who was at the reception."

Before I could ask about the pillow and why George might have been holding it, Cody took out a small notebook and read something from it. "When I spoke to George, he insisted he held the pillow because it was lying over her face when he walked in. He wanted to remove it, hoping she'd be okay. Nothing more than that. He, of course, had been concerned to find her that way. And hadn't even had a chance to start CPR yet when you entered. But, according to him, you, and Seneca, Yolanda was already dead anyway."

It did make sense. I hoped what Cody said was true, because I didn't want the guilty person to be George. I liked him. And wasn't sure Evie would recover if she'd just found the love of her life again, only to have him taken away by murdering someone and spending the rest of his life in jail. My heart ached at the thought of them not getting to rekindle their relationship.

Cody hung his head. "Another bad part was talking to the bride and groom about a dead body when their reception wasn't even over yet."

Murray emerged from the kitchen area, wiping his hands on a dishtowel. "Cody, I'm sure that didn't go over well with the rest of the wedding party. And telling Devan and Kinley not to leave town when they had arranged to leave the state for their honeymoon?"

"I know. I felt terrible about that. But I couldn't very well let them leave when a person had been murdered right after their wedding. Trust me, I didn't like doing it, and I'll get them out of here as soon as I can. In the meantime, they'll have to...uh...carry on with...things, uh, somewhere here in town until then."

Carry on with things? The thought of wedding nights and the particular activities involved caused heat to rise up my face. I'd been married before and had experienced a honeymoon. But it wasn't just me who'd reacted.

Every other person in the room either turned red, snickered, or had raised eyebrows. I needed something to diffuse the situation, and fast. Winifred, who'd just strolled in through the doorway, provided that. I hurried to get her and picked her up.

Evie latched onto the provided diversion. "Doesn't Winifred look cute today in her monarch butterfly costume?"

"Yeah, I decided that her wearing her white one and walking down the aisle in front of Kinley was long enough to have it on."

One side of Cody's mouth rose. "I have to admit, it was funny."

Murray, who rarely even smiled, let out a snort. "Glad I got to see it before we had to leave to finish setting up the food. I doubt that's something I'll ever see again."

"Don't bet on it." I sighed. "You never know with this one." I lightly jiggled Winifred in my arms, causing her to narrow her eyes at me. When she fidgeted in my grasp, her butterfly wings moved as if in flight.

"So, back to George," Evie pressed her hands over her cheeks. "I'm so worried that—"

Cody shook his head. "Don't worry. I have to check everyone out, you know that."

She looked up at him. "I'll try."

"I'm not focusing on him right now, okay? I'll keep an eye on him and check out his story, like I will everyone else who was there. But for now, I believe what he told me."

"All right. Thanks, Cody."

"No problem." He patted her shoulder. "Just wanted to give you guys an update. I need to go, but I'll check in later." He turned and made his way toward the door.

As soon as he'd gone, Evie clutched my hand, even though I was trying to hold onto Winifred. When my cat growled, I put her down and focused on my cousin.

"Seneca, what are we going to do? I need your help to find out who did this so George won't be in trouble. I just connected with him again. I don't think I could stand it if something happened and he had to leave town, or..."

"You heard what Cody said, that he's not focusing on George right now."

"Yes, I did. But I also know how scared I was when some people thought I'd committed murder before. I don't want George to feel that way, you know?"

I nodded. "Sure, I get it. And of course, I'll help you."

"Count me in too." Murray tapped the countertop. "If you think this highly of George, then he must be a good guy in my book. I trust your judgment, Evie."

"Thank you." She brushed a tear from her cheek. "I know it seems sudden, this attraction between him and me."

"But you were close before, so it's not new, is it?" I rubbed her shoulder.

"No, it isn't. It's like all those feelings rushed back as soon as I saw him. And he said it was the same for him. We...I guess it's like we took a break and are back to where we were when he had to leave town. Just a few years older."

I thought about Cody and how I was attracted to him now. My first marriage had been a disaster. Even though I saw Cody nearly every day, and we were close, there were still those lingering feelings of wanting more with him that I couldn't quite get past. "Don't worry, Evie, we're going to figure all this out. Why don't we think about who was at the wedding and what they might have said or done that needs extra attention?"

She gave a single nod. "Yes, you're right. We'll look at this objectively. Or at least try to."

"That's the spirit," said Murray. "I'll get orders ready for the few people who've already popped in. Why don't you two take a minute to go over all that? You can fill me in later."

I gave Murray a grateful smile. "Thanks. Yes, good idea."

I motioned Evie to follow me to a far table, where we took our seats.

Evie watched a couple more customers come in the café. "Gosh, I don't feel right sitting here when I need to be working."

"It's fine, Evie. It will only be for a couple of minutes. It's not busy yet, and Murray has it under control. You can be sure he'll wave you over if he needs you."

We both turned toward the counter. Murray did indeed have it taken care of, motioning everyone to form a short line down the middle of the main aisle between tables, efficiently taking down what they wanted to eat or drink and rushing back to fill their requests. The man was a marvel.

I put my forearms on the table and clasped my hands together. "Do you remember anything at the ceremony or reception that seemed a little off?"

Her eyebrows lowered as she thought. "I did notice that Tonda had her phone out and held it up as Yolanda walked by."

"Yeah, I saw that too. It seemed weird to me, since I assumed they'd never met. I wondered if Tonda was doing it just to have the picture and make fun of what Yolanda was wearing later on."

"That's possible." Evie smoothed her hand down the front of her blouse. "She was dressed differently than anything I'd ever seen someone wear around here. Not that it was wrong. Just noticeable."

"Exactly."

Evie glanced toward the counter, then back. "I'd never even met the woman. But I'd heard about her. Her elusiveness. How she rarely left her property."

"Same here. I did see her when I was a kid, and I was with Gram one time, who hadn't thought very highly of Yolanda. She pointed her out to me, but that was my only time seeing her until Cody reminded me who she was at the wedding."

Evie's lips curved up briefly on one side. "Leave it to Gram to say exactly what she thought."

"Right." I grinned, then sobered. "I also noticed Gretchen pointing at Yolanda, then whispering to Tonda."

"Why do you suppose they'd be so interested in her? She's a lot older than them and it seems unlikely that they'd have anything in common with her. It could simply be that they thought she looked weird, but who knows? There must be a reason, though. Maybe we should start with those two. See what's up with them."

"Exactly what I was thinking. It's as good a place to start as any."

The door opened, and a group of four older women came in, talking loudly and laughing.

Evie let out a breath. "Sorry, but I need to help Murray. He's already got a line of customers to wait on and will need me for a bit in the kitchen."

"No problem. You go ahead."

"But that will leave you checking this out on your own." She frowned as she stood. "That's not fair since I'm the one who asked you to look into it in the first place."

I got up from my chair and pushed it back toward the table. Then I heard a growl. And since furniture didn't normally make those noises, I knew who had. I bent down to grab Winifred, but she darted out from the table and out the open doorway. I shrugged, then turned to Evie. "It's not a problem. Not my first time, remember?"

She released a breath. "Yeah, I know that all too well. You saved me when I was on the bad end of people and their pointing fingers. You're good at this, Seneca."

"I don't know about good, but after two other murders, I do have some experience in tracking down clues. Unfortunately."

Evie gave me a quick hug. "Thank you. I feel so much better knowing you're going to check things out." She hurried toward the growing cue of hungry people and took her place next to Murray behind the order counter.

Now that those two were working, I needed to think about the rest of my own day. I'd already checked on my butterfly larvae in my greenhouse and still needed to go see how my adult monarchs were doing.

As I headed toward the door, ready to go out to my milkweed fields where the adult monarchs hung out, someone uttered George's name. Snippets of conversations from the ever-growing line of café customers warred for my attention. But the overall impression was that they were all talking about the murder. And how George, someone who was a stranger to some in town since he'd been gone for years, was the most obvious person they suspected of smothering Yolanda Steele.

I glanced at Evie, whose shoulders were slumped. She had to be hearing the same things I was from the crowd. I hated that she had to deal with the gossip while worrying about George, too.

That settled it. Evie needed my help, and I was ready to dive in. My monarchs could wait a little longer. First, I needed to check into who Evie and I had discussed. I'd start with Tonda.

And I knew where I'd probably find her. At the grocery, where she was a cashier. It just so happened that Winifred needed some canned cat food, so at least I had a valid excuse to stop in there.

Chapter Four

I knew from experience that spying on, uh, observing those who might be in question about a murder, was a good way to go. Often, I caught people saying or doing things they wouldn't have if they knew I was skulking, um, hanging around.

Later that afternoon, when I entered the grocery, I was relieved to see Tonda busy with a customer. She didn't seem to notice me rushing past her checkout station. I speedwalked to the cat food aisle. Might as well stock up on Winifred's food while I was here. I tended to let her food supply get too low. Way Low. As in, a few times, I opened the cabinet and was met with an empty shelf glaring back at me. Then, I'd turned around, and Winifred was glaring too. And she added a hiss for good measure.

I grabbed a small, empty blue grocery basket sitting on the floor nearby, probably left by a shopper who'd changed their mind about needing an item, and stacked can after can of salmon, her current favorite, into the plastic container. When I'd relieved the store of every can of her favorite brand, I lugged the basket, cans clanging against each other, closer to the checkout aisle.

When I got within a few feet of Tonda, I saw she was talking to Camry. This might be useful. Maybe they'd talk about the wedding since they'd both been there.

With no one else in line, Camry relaxed against the counter, appearing to settle in for an extended gabfest with her friend. While that might be convenient for the women to talk, it would also give me a good opportunity to listen to them while crouching behind a nearby endcap.

With a glance behind me, I saw no one else was around. Good. I could wait here and hopefully not attract attention to myself while listening to their conversation. While that might sound as if I was some sort of expert, I wasn't. But this being the third murder in Maple Junction and me having been unintentionally involved in each one, I was starting to get the hang of investigation. Not that I wanted it to be my new career or anything.

As the young women talked about their newest shoe purchases, which didn't interest me in the least, I noticed what was stocked on the endcap I was hiding behind. Chocolate. Now, how was that fair? Along with pizza, it was my favorite food. Not that I ever put chocolate on pizza, and not that there would be anything wrong with that. But for me, chocolate was impossible to resist.

Hoping the other two would continue their conversation without noticing me, I grabbed one of the bars and tossed it into the basket. When it hit the metal cans, they shifted, causing a loud clank.

I held in a gasp, hoping my loud heartbeat wouldn't be audible to anyone but me. I could barely see Tonda and Camry as they stood on either side of the checkout counter. But I was now crouched down, and they were looking somewhere above me.

Tonda had whipped around just as I lowered all the way behind the endcap. I was now perched uncomfortably in a squat position that only cats could achieve without yelping in pain. But I wanted to stay here long enough to hear something useful. My calves were screaming. I wished Tonda and Camry would start discussing the wedding.

When I glanced to my left, the chocolate caught my attention again, as if beckoning me closer to grab another bar. I shrugged. What was one more? In my house, there was no way it would go to waste.

I picked up another one, this time, placing it carefully into the basket. I was relieved when it didn't announce its presence with another annoying rattle. No use letting the women know I was here. It was lucky enough neither had walked over here to see what the noise had been.

I must have been staring at the chocolate bars on the shelves for too long because my stomach growled, and it was loud.

Stop that!

I placed the basket on the floor as quietly as a plastic container full of metal cans could be accomplished, and wrapped both arms tightly around my middle. Maybe I could suppress the intestinal protests that longed to escape into the grocery store for all to hear.

When nothing came of my innards making themselves known, I shuffled forward a few inches—again causing my calves to yell—and peeked around the corner of the shelves of chocolate delight.

Tonda was holding out her phone for Camry to see something on the screen. Too bad I couldn't see it too, but if I were to stand up, groaning as my muscles spasmed, and limping toward them, it would blow what little cover I had.

Tonda pointed at the phone. "I can't believe she wore that to the wedding. And why would an old cow like that even try to look attractive anyway?"

Camry glared at the phone. "Old people. Who knows what they might do?"

I frowned. The way they talked about old people and old cows could be someone, well, my age. I was a few years older than they were, but to them, I might seem ancient. Wait, had she taken a picture of me at the ceremony? I wasn't the most beautiful person out there, but I did at least attempt to look presentable when attending something like a wedding. And I wasn't a cow.

"What was her name again?" asked Camry.

"Yolanda Steele."

I perked up. This might be something I could use. And it wasn't my picture they were making fun of. Win-win.

"Why did you take pictures of her?" Camry lifted her chin toward the phone.

Tonda laughed. "Didn't you see what she was doing at the reception?"

"Nope. Must have missed it." Camry narrowed her eyes. "What happened?"

"She danced with the groom, Devan. He's young enough to be her son. Or grandson."

Camry gasped. "Eewww. I'm glad I didn't have to see that."

"It was gross. I can't imagine touching someone that much different in age than me. It would be like touching a dead person. We should ask Gretchen about that since she works at the funeral home. I wouldn't touch someone that old. Unless it was my grandfather or something. Even then, I wouldn't want to dance with him."

"Did Devan seem like he was having fun dancing with the old hag?"

"He was kind of smiling, but I couldn't tell if he was just being polite or not. Yolanda scowled the whole time."

Camry harrumphed. "I just don't get women like her. It's no wonder she has no one in her life besides people she pays to work for her."

Tonda tapped the screen on her phone. "Why would Yolanda have even been at the wedding? Did she know someone there?"

I leaned forward a little to hear them better, but nearly lost my balance. I smacked my hand against the floor to keep from tumbling into the aisle completely.

A shuffling noise came from behind me. I whipped around to see some tennis shoe-covered feet. As I gazed upward to the face, it belonged to an older gentleman. He had a scowl.

"Young lady, what are you doing down there?"

I glanced quickly at Tonda and Camry, but they were still lost in their own conversation and hadn't seemed to notice me or the gentleman. "I'm, uh…" I shrugged, not wanting to say much in case either of the women recognized my voice.

"Do you need assistance to regain a standing position?" He peered down at me over the edge of his half glasses.

"No, thank you."

"Are you planning to simply sit there all day, taking up space and becoming a literal stumbling block for some unsuspecting shopper?"

Why wouldn't he just move along and mind his own business?

His bushy eyebrows lowered. "Say, where did you get that shopping basket?"

I looked down at the small plastic enclosure, now filled with tiny cans of kitty delight and a couple of chocolate human delights, too. I pointed toward the front entrance where the shopping carts and baskets were kept.

He glanced in that direction, then peered down at me again. "But it's blue."

I checked my basket again. By golly, yes, it was blue.

He bent at the waist and narrowed his eyes. "I'll have you know that I like the blue ones."

"Um, okay."

"Do you see me carrying a blue one, young lady?" His small basket was fire engine red.

I shook my head.

"And do you know why that is?"

What was with this guy? Why did he care about the color of the shopping basket, anyway? "No, I don't," I whispered, still relieved that Tonda hadn't come around from her station behind the checkout counter.

"The reason I do not have my coveted blue basket is that you got the last one."

Surely he wasn't expecting me to remove my purchases and make a trade with him, blue for red.

He huffed out a breath and stood up straight. "Well, I never…I shall let you get away with it this time, but in the future, leave the blue ones alone." He stomped away and headed toward the fruit and vegetable aisle.

I let out a breath. Thank goodness he was gone. What a nut. I stopped and listened, realizing the conversation between Camry and Tonda had stopped.

Uh-oh. Had they heard the man berating me?

Seeing that my cover might be blown, I stood and approached the counter. Camry had gone, and Tonda was talking to someone on her phone. She didn't appear to have heard my conversation with the man, so maybe I'd gotten away with spying on her and her friend.

Still, I hoped I hadn't missed anything they said while the crazy dude had my attention. I was relieved that it was a slow time in the grocery, at least here at the checkout area. Thank goodness, only one person passed by me while I camped out on spy duty with my supply of sustenance for Winifred and me.

I placed the basket on the counter and waited for Tonda to finish her call and realize she had a customer waiting.

She pointed toward the basket. "Some things never change, huh? Your cat is going to starve if you keep forgetting to buy her food."

"She's far from starving." But the mom guilt crept in, like it always did. However, I wasn't going to let that spoil my chance for talking to Tonda alone, the whole reason I'd come today. Well, that and the tiny cans of salmon. "Hey, did I see you talking to Camry Baker?"

"Yep."

"She seems nice. I don't know her very well."

Tonda shrugged one shoulder as she ran each can individually over the scanner. It was an annoying habit she had when I had several small items that could have been input into her register quicker. But I kept those thoughts to myself. It would only lead to more snarky comments about me being a bad cat mom. And I'd heard quite enough of those over the years.

"Camry moved here last month from Ohio." Tonda stacked the cans on the other end of the cash register. "We get along pretty good. Makes Gretchen mad, though."

"Why is she mad? Doesn't she like her?"

"It's not that exactly. Camry is okay to be around."

I watched Tonda. She wouldn't meet my eyes. Ah, I saw what was happening here. "She's jealous of the time you've been spending with Camry? Because you found another friend."

"Yeah, I guess. It's dumb." She placed the cans in a plastic bag, one at a time, stacking them in rows. Didn't she realize they'd all tumble toward the bottom of the sack once I picked it up?

"You're right. It's dumb. But it's girls. That's how it works sometimes."

Her gaze met mine. "I don't like it, but I want to spend time with all my friends. I like doing stuff with Marla, too. Wish they'd get along better so we could all do more things as a group."

"You don't all hang out together?"

"Sometimes, but it doesn't always go well. It's like when the four of us are together, it won't work, you know?" She bent over her counter to look past me. Was she checking to see if any customers were waiting? Or was she worried that somebody might overhear us?

"I'm sorry to hear that."

She shrugged again. "It's okay."

I wanted to change the subject and get more information. "Hey, I saw you at the wedding. Did you have a good time?"

She snorted a laugh. "Weird that you'd ask. I was just talking to Camry about that."

"You were? What did you think about it?"

"We thought it was wild that Yolanda Steele was at the wedding. Hasn't she been hiding in her palace for like, decades? She's like some weird recluse who only comes out into the sun every so many years. Maybe she's a vampire."

I wasn't going to address the vampire theory. And I started to say it wasn't a palace, but compared to other houses, here, it sort of was. "I must admit, I hadn't heard of her being around town in a long time. I don't think she gets out much since her husband passed away."

"Then it's strange she even showed up at the wedding." Tonda edged my bag of cat food cans toward me, then held out the two candy bars. "Want me to leave these out? Figured they might be for the road."

My mouth dropped open. "I'm not going to eat two candy bars before I even get home. For Pete's sake, I only live five minutes from here." My stomach growled again. Traitorous internal organ. "Fine, leave one out. Just one. The other can go in there." I pointed to the bag.

With a smirk, Tonda did as asked. I stuck the chocolate bar in my purse and gave her my credit card.

As I lugged the clanging sack toward the store exit, I wondered why Tonda and Camry were so interested in Yolanda, someone I doubted they'd ever even met.

And why had Yolanda even been at the wedding in the first place?

Chapter Five

I'd come into Painted Wings the next afternoon for my daily drink that Murray always had ready for me. I stood close to the counter. The café was filling up. Something that Evie, Murray, and I always welcomed. I waved hello to Angel Bales and Connie Sellers, who were grabbing seats at a table near the back of the café. Angel was Cody's cousin, and she and Connie owned the local Quilt Shop.

Mike Larsh, with his ever-present paperback, sat at a corner table close to the counter. And Gretchen, a few feet away at the other end of the counter, harrumphed a couple of times while she ordered her food. Her face was a confusion of wrinkles on her scrunched brow and turned down lips.

I moved closer. "Hey, Gretchen. What's up?" I already had a hunch that she was upset about Tonda spending time with people besides her, but I'd wait and let her tell me if I was right. Too often, I blurted out what I wanted to know instead of allowing others to tell me what was going on. I tried to do better at keeping my mouth shut, but wasn't always successful.

Gretchen huffed out a breath loud enough for Murray, behind the counter, to return her frown. She rolled her eyes at me. "Friends. Who needs them?"

Ah, so I'd been right. I propped one hip against the side of the counter. "Well, I do, for one. I think everyone does. Why would you say that?"

She paid Murray when he brought out her food, then turned to view the café. "Just because."

That wasn't going to tell me much. "Want to talk about it?"

"With you?" She gave me the side-eye, reminding me of Winifred when the store had been out of her favorite brand of catnip, and she had to settle for the kind that made her feel only mildly giddy instead of super spectacular.

I could take offense at Gretchen's slight, that maybe I didn't measure up to the task, but decided it wouldn't help matters any. "Sure, why not?"

She turned to face me fully, her eyes narrowed as if sizing me up. We'd never been close, but had known each other for years. Did she have something against me that she might not trust me to listen? "To be honest, Seneca, death seems to surround you. The first one in your greenhouse. The next one right here in your café. It's creepy. What is it with you and dead bodies, anyway?"

She'd always made a point of bringing that up when previous murders had occurred. And she'd been right. But it stung to be constantly reminded of it.

I placed my hand on my hip. "They surround you, too, Gretchen, considering you work for our local mortician. I'd say you deal with death a whole lot more than I ever do." Or ever would. At least I hoped so.

Gretchen huffed out a breath. "Fine. I'll give you that, I guess. But at least mine is because of my official capacity. It's my job being assistant to the mortician. The fact that people keep dying wherever you are is creepy and just plain weird." She studied the café again, then gave a quick nod. "All right. If you want to listen to me vent, I'm going to sit at the table over by the back window. But I warn you, you might not like what you hear."

She took off in a rush, leaving me to trot just to keep up with her. Obviously, she was very upset about her friend issue. But at least she gave me the green light to go and sit with her. That was something.

When I reached the table, I waited for Gretchen to choose her seat. She claimed a chair right by the window where the sun streamed in. Winifred would have done the same, since cats loved to be warm and lie in sunbeams. Maybe Gretchen needed some solar therapy. It sure couldn't hurt with the mood she seemed to be in. Taking short breaks in the sunshine when it was nice outside always lifted my mood.

I sat opposite her, then sipped my drink, waiting while she took a bite of her sandwich, a BLT that I happened to know was amazing. But then, everything Murray made was remarkable.

When she'd had a little to eat, her shoulders relaxed. Perhaps she was a person who did better when her stomach wasn't empty. Again, like Winifred. And, I had to admit, also like me.

Gretchen moved her food aside, reached for a napkin on the table dispenser to wipe her hands, then focused on me. "See, you might not remember since you're so much older, but sometimes girls don't always get along."

My left eyebrow rose slowly. I might not remember? I was only a few years older than she was. But I let that go since she was upset, and from prior conversations, I remembered that she'd never had much of a filter anyway. The way Gretchen had told everyone in town during a previous murder that I had bodies piling up at my farm confirmed that. She'd made it sound as if I had some despicable hobby of collecting corpses. Ick!

She propped her elbow on the table and her chin in her hand. "See, it all started when Camry moved to town. She's okay, I mean, she seems nice, and everyone likes her. I just…" She shook her head.

"You were disappointed to not spend all your time with Tonda? Is that it?"

Her eyes widened as if shocked I might understand. "Right. Tonda has been my best friend forever. And then, somehow, because Camry and Marla work in the same shop, Marla got included in with things the rest of us were doing. So we went from two people to four, real fast."

I felt for her. It was hard enough fitting in. But when there was a person you'd thought of as your very best friend, and assumed they felt the same, then things changed; it did hurt. "I understand. I do."

"Really?" She blinked. "You do?"

"Of course. Believe it or not, it hasn't been that long since I was your age." I took a sip from my straw.

"Huh. I always thought you were like, I don't know, in your late forties."

I nearly choked on the drink and reached for a napkin when I felt a cough coming on. Then I swallowed a few times before I could speak. "For your information, I'm only twenty-seven."

Her eyes widened. "Really? Well, my bad." She waved her hand as if making me a couple of decades older was no big deal.

I purposefully forced my thoughts away from the snarky comment I longed to give, and instead waited for her to continue. Finding out anything I could about Yolanda's murder was way more important than my pride. Even though it was irritating to let it go without making a comment in my own defense.

Gretchen drummed her fingers on the table. Mable, one of our resident octogenarians who sat at the next table, turned and gave us a stare. Odd that Mable heard it, since I usually had to yell for her to hear what I was saying. With a glance at the rapidly-filling café, and a check of my watch, I realized I only had a little bit of time before someone else would need our table. Plus, I needed to get back to my butterflies.

And Edward was supposed to be cleaning out the larvae pens now, but he was still trying to get past the icky factor. I supplied him with disposable gloves for his work, but the facial expressions he wore made it clear how he felt about touching them, even with his hands covered. Pretty soon, I'd need to go check on him and make sure he was coping okay.

I pushed my nearly empty drink to the side. "Is there something about Marla you specifically don't like? I mean, aside from the fact that you don't appreciate her hanging around."

"Marla seems like she's not always being up front with people."

"You mean she's lying about things?"

"That's the vibe I get sometimes. I can't believe Tonda doesn't see it. But she tells me to just chill and give Marla a chance. I've tried. I really have. But Marla and I are just way too different, I guess."

"What do you mean?"

"Well, you know how I'm really quiet and don't always say much?"

Was she kidding? She talked to everyone and anyone, about everything. I'd witnessed it. But her expression was one of sincerity. She really believed that about herself. "Um, yeah. Sure."

"Marla is the opposite. She talks constantly. And she doesn't watch what she says. Just blurts out whatever is on her mind."

In my opinion, Gretchen had just described herself. But it wasn't always easy for a person to see themselves as others did. "What kind of things does Marla say?"

"She makes fun of everyone." Her face reddened. "Especially me."

"Like what?"

"Like that, I don't always dress in the latest fashion. That my hair is straight and I don't wear much makeup. Stuff like that."

"I think you look fine, Gretchen. Besides, everyone is different. What a boring place it would be if we all did everything alike."

"I guess. I just get tired of hearing how I should change everything about myself. It gets old."

"I'm sure it does. I wouldn't like it either."

"Thanks for saying that, Seneca."

"Well, it's true. No one likes to have someone pointing out things to them all the time. You're right. It would get old. Was there anything else you wanted to tell me about Marla?"

"Let's just say…" She glanced to her left and right, then back to me, "that I don't trust her."

"You don't?"

"Nope. Not even a little."

"Why do you feel that way?"

"For one, she's messy. I mean, a total slob."

I frowned. That didn't seem that off to me. Maybe a little odd, but weren't we all? "What else don't you trust about her?"

With a second look around the café, she then edged closer to the table, motioning me to lean toward her as well. "I saw her following Yolanda around. At the reception. It looked like…"

"Like what?"

"This may sound crazy, but it seemed like Marla was stalking Yolanda Steele."

"Stalking?"

She curled her fingers like they were claws. "It was like I was watching a wild animal stalk something. The look on Marla's face was… It scared me. And, I know lots of people in town are talking about the murder a lot. That seems to happen when someone dies."

"Yeah, it sure does."

"But when Marla talks about it, it's like she's obsessed."

"You mean with murder?"

Gretchen thought for a few seconds. "No. I think just with this murder. Yolanda's."

I bent even closer, not wanting to miss a word. "Does Marla know her?"

"Yeah, I guess she must. Why else would she be so consumed with talking about a lady that old and following her around? Unless Marla was lying, which I also wouldn't put past her. As far as I'm concerned, that girl is conniving."

The distrust from Gretchen for Marla was huge. The only time I used the word conniving about someone was when they'd treated another person in the worst possible way.

Gretchen crossed her arms over her chest. "There've been times when the four of us were out doing something together, and Marla would start spouting off about Yolanda. Just out of the blue. Like she couldn't wait to get the words out."

"What does she say?"

"That the old lady has so much money, she probably uses it instead of firewood in her fireplace and wouldn't know the difference or care."

I jerked. Marla appeared to have deep-seated resentment for Yolanda. It occurred to me that to know if Yolanda had a fireplace in her house, Marla might have been inside at some point. "Do you know if Marla has visited Yolanda at home?"

She shrugged. "I don't know. She makes it sound like she has. Either that, or she's just bragging, which wouldn't surprise me in the least. She always has to make herself seem better than other people. Like she deserves things that the rest of us don't."

"Deserves? Like what?"

"Marla talks about money a whole lot. All the time. It's not like the rest of us have a lot of extra funds lying around. I'm not sure why she'd think we'd want to hear her go on and on about it."

"That's weird."

"Besides that, she drinks. A lot."

I raised my eyebrows. "She does?"

Gretchen's phone buzzed from inside her purse. She reached into the pocket to get it. A smile formed on her face. "It's Tonda. She wants me to stop by the grocery to see her. I better go." She stood suddenly. "Thanks a lot for listening, Seneca. I'll see you later."

She grabbed her purse and rushed from the café. I glanced down at her side of the table. She hadn't even finished her sandwich. Getting the text from Tonda seemed to have made her day.

Poor Gretchen. Trying to find the right friends wasn't always easy.

With a glance at my watch, I realized I needed to get back to the greenhouse and check on Edward. I grabbed the trash and tossed it all in a nearby trashcan so Evie would have one less thing to do when she wiped down the table for whoever would have it next. Then I walked outside and toward my greenhouse.

Was it possible Marla and Yolanda had some sort of history no one else knew about?

Chapter Six

When I entered Precious Posies the next morning, it was with relief. With Betty Rollins on my suspect list in a previous murder, I was so glad it turned out that she hadn't done the deed. I liked her and was glad things were back to normal in her shop.

On an earlier visit, I'd purchased a small spider plant, who I'd named Ingrid, as my excuse to get Betty to talk about the person who'd been killed. Even though I'd gotten the plant as a ruse to be in the shop, I'd come to love her cheery green spikes and colorful ceramic pot. I'd made sure to purchase a plant that was kitty-safe, even though I had Ingrid hanging above my sink, where my cat would have to work really hard to get at her. But knowing Winifred, she'd give it a try.

Today, I was hoping to buy a sister for Ingrid. It also gave me a similar reason to stand and chat in the flower shop, to see what I could find out about Marla.

When I approached the order area, Betty came out of her back room, wiping her hands on a small towel. "Seneca, good to see you."

"You too." I pointed to the huge display of Lilies. "These are gorgeous."

"Thank you. I think so too. How can I help you today?"

"Remember Ingrid?"

Her eyes crinkled at the corners. "How could I forget? How's our girl doing?"

"She's being a nice, polite plant."

"Just what I wanted to hear."

"But, I think she's lonely."

Her eyebrows rose. "Oh?"

"She needs a sister."

"Ah, I see. Does this new family member need to look like Ingrid?"

"Well, she wouldn't have to, but if you have another spider plant, that would work great since she wouldn't be harmful to Winifred if she got ahold of her leaves."

"You know, I just happen to have one that would make Ingrid happy."

"Perfect."

She grinned. "I'll be right back."

"Thanks." I perused the beautiful roses and philodendron plants Betty had on shelves near the front door. She was a master of putting textures and colors together for the ultimate display to please the customer's eye.

At my farm, I didn't have to do any of that. The amazing black and orange Monarchs did it for me, just by being who they were. And that was good, because I didn't possess the decorating gene that some people had, like Evie. She had decorated Painted Wings in a butterfly theme, along with muted shades of orange and black subtly blended into the décor. If I'd tried to accomplish something like that, it would have looked like the area around Winifred's dish once she'd demolished her wet food and left splatters of it smeared on the floor.

As I waited for Betty to return, the entrance door opened. It was Camry.

"Hi." She waved.

"Hi, there. I heard you'd started working here. How's it going?"

"It's okay."

"Well, it's good to enjoy what you do."

"Sure, I guess. If you like being stuck inside a small building."

I thought of Edward, and his ick-factor. At least he seemed glad to have his job with me at the butterfly farm.

Camry walked to a back room. When she returned, I noticed she wasn't carrying the purse she'd brought in with her.

"Just starting work today?"

"Yep. I have the later shift this week."

"It's kind of nice to have a varied schedule sometimes." Although mine was pretty much like clockwork, that was how I was wired, so it worked for me. Besides, Winifred never let me sleep in anyway, so getting up early was for the best.

Camry's eyebrows lowered. "Yeah, but I hate to miss out on my evenings with my friends. Marla has the early shift this week, so we only see each other in passing here at work. We're roommates, too. It made sense to share a space and the rent."

"That makes a lot of sense. Especially if you're not always there at the same time."

"Right." She stepped to the computer, tapped some keys, and gave a nod. "There. All clocked in." She glanced behind her, then back. Was she making sure we were alone? "I mostly like working here but…"

"But what?"

"It's a little boring. It'd be nice to find a job with some excitement."

If Camry wanted an exciting job, she better learn to mountain climb or deep sea dive, although neither of those could be done in rural Indiana. "Maybe a different job will open sometime down the road. You never know."

"True. But life is short." She frowned. "Think of that lady who was just killed."

"Yolanda Steele?"

"Yeah, that's the one. Breathing one minute, gone the next." She glanced at a clock on the wall. "Uh, I better get to work now. See you later."

"Yeah, see ya."

Camry trotted off to a room to my left.

Steps sounded from the back area, but Betty didn't reappear. It was Marla.

Maybe I could find out her impression of the wedding while I was here. "Hi." I waved. "How are you?"

She jerked, as if she hadn't expected me to speak to her. "Okay, I guess."

I waited, but nothing else was said. I shrugged. Quite a difference between the two roommates. At least Camry was outgoing and somewhat pleasant. Even though Gretchen had said the two were friends, maybe it was a good thing they weren't always sharing space in the apartment.

As Marla stepped near the counter, I tried again. "I noticed you were at

Devan and Kinley's wedding. Did you have a good time?"

"They had a nice spread at the reception. The drinks were good, not watered down like some places I've been to. And the wedding was okay, I guess." She rolled her eyes. "Honestly? It was fine until that weird old hag came prancing down the aisle."

I knew who she meant, but asked anyway. "Who was that?"

"Yolanda Steele. I can't stand her."

"Did you know her well?" It would be surprising if she did, considering how most people in town either had never talked to her or only on an occasion or two over the last several years.

"Well enough. But it couldn't be avoided. Believe me, I had no choice."

I was ready to ask another question, but Betty stepped out of the back, holding what had to be Ingrid's twin. The plant was even in a similar pot, with the same colors, but in a varied pattern.

At seeing Betty, Marla slipped out of the room, going to where Camry had gone. Was Marla afraid she might get in trouble if seen talking to a customer instead of working? Maybe she didn't like working here either and thought it was boring, like Camry did. It could've been just their age and longing for something different, but at their age, I was thrilled to be working with Gram and the butterflies.

Betty placed the spider plant on the counter between us. "Do you think this one will work?"

I bent down to study the plant more closely. "I love her already."

Betty grinned. "Wonderful. And does she have a name?"

"I'm thinking, Imogene."

"Imogene and Ingrid. Perfect."

"Thanks for going to the trouble to find a plant so similar to Ingrid. I appreciate it."

"No trouble. You know how much I love finding plants and matching them to their people."

"Yeah, I do. You're good at it."

"Well, thanks." She reached down below the counter and found a small box for Imogene to ride home in. "How are things going at your farm?"

"Pretty well. Lots of talk, of course, at the café about what happened at the wedding."

"I'm sure. It was so awful. I heard about all of it since I was there with the flowers. Normally, I'd leave after delivering them, but Kinley's parents invited me to stay for the ceremony and reception."

"Your flowers were amazing. They made the wedding and reception even more beautiful."

She smiled. "They light up my day every time I see any of them."

"I get that. Same for me with the butterflies."

"Maybe that's why we're friends, right?" She processed the credit card I handed her for the plant, then handed it back to me with my receipt.

"Exactly." She and I weren't close, but I did consider her a friend. And I wouldn't mind getting to know her better in the future. "You may have heard I have a new part-time employee at the farm, Edward Peffley."

"I did hear something about that. How's it going?"

I shrugged. "Okay."

"Just okay?"

"It's taking a little longer than I'd hoped." I held up one finger. "But I do like him. And he's willing to work, so that's something." That couldn't have been said about Sid and Norman when they'd made feeble attempts to do their jobs for me, so I needed to keep a positive attitude about Edward.

"Yeah, I understand. It's not always easy finding people who mesh with you right away."

I glanced toward the area where Marla and Camry had gone. I hadn't been able to hear anything from them working in that room, so hoped they couldn't hear us either. "Are things going smoothly with your employees?"

She bit her lower lip. "Um, I wouldn't say smoothly. There's an issue of not always showing up, or coming in, but quite a bit late."

"That's annoying. And a time waster for you."

"You're right. It is."

"Edward has a problem with handling anything icky. So that has made things interesting."

Her mouth formed a one-sided smile. "We don't have the icky factor.

However…" She glanced toward the other room, then back to me.

"Is there a problem?"

"Both girls have been skittish and moody. Especially Marla. I've caught them a few times arguing with each other when they should have been working."

It sounded as if Marla might be the worst of the two, according to Gretchen. "I'm sorry to hear that. It makes running a business difficult."

"True. Sometimes it does. We're hanging in there, though." She wiped a tiny speck of dirt away from the counter. "Did you know they live together?"

"Yep. Camry mentioned that."

"I'd always thought Marla wanted to live alone, but Camry must have convinced her to allow her to move in."

"That was nice of Marla. I noticed she was at the wedding." I looked to my left at the door where the young women were. "I know what happened at the service was very traumatic for all the guests and the wedding party. It was traumatic for me too, because my cousin, Evie, is dating George Marshall. Who is innocent, by the way?" I wanted to toss that last bit in there. Betty was known for telling customers newsy items when they entered her shop. If she could put in a good word for George, then all the better.

"I'd heard that about Evie's new boyfriend. Glad to hear he's not guilty, though, of using that pillow for bad purposes."

I wouldn't elaborate that Evie and George weren't exactly new, but renewed in their relationship. "He feels terrible. Was just removing that pillow to see if Yolanda was all right. Which, of course, she wasn't."

"Have you heard who might have done it? Killed Yolanda?"

"No, not yet."

"Just thought with you and Cody and your relationship…" She winked. "Well, you know."

Would people never tire of spreading the false news that Cody and I shared a passionate kiss? Or that we were now involved? Though I wished it was true, sadly, it wasn't.

Time to change direction. "Are Marla and Camry handling what happened with Yolanda all right? I noticed they were sitting a few rows ahead of me during the ceremony."

"It's definitely caused some problems here at the shop."

"Really?"

"Yes. I'd mentioned they'd been arguing here at work?"

I nodded, waiting for her to continue.

"During one of their arguments, I overheard them. Marla said she hated Yolanda more than anyone in the world."

That seemed over the top. "Did Camry agree?"

"She didn't go as far as Marla had, but did say that it didn't bother her at all that Yolanda was dead." Betty glanced at the ceiling, as if thinking. "I don't remember who, but someone told me they saw Camry standing outside Yolanda's mansion one day."

I stood up straighter. "Do you know if that happened before or after Yolanda's murder?"

"Not sure."

"I wonder what Camry was doing there."

"According to the person, just staring at it."

"That's weird."

"I thought so too, at first, but let's be honest, it's quite a sight to see. No other place like it in Maple Junction. It's so huge, it's nearly overwhelming to look at. I've never been inside, but have driven past lots of times on my way across town."

"You've got that right. It sure dwarfs every other house and building."

From behind me, the main door to the shop opened. Betty waved at her new customer. "Sorry, I better get back to work, Seneca. It was nice to see you. I hope you enjoy Imogene."

I smiled. "Thank you. I have no doubt she'll be a great addition to our family."

As I walked toward the door, the squeak of a rusty hinge came from the other room. Then the door clicked shut. Had it not been all the way closed before? I glanced across the room. Had the girls heard our conversation?

Somehow, the fact that they, especially Marla, might have heard us talking bothered me more than a little. There was a murderer roaming around, after all. And I wasn't sure who I could trust.

Chapter Seven

I was in my milkweed field the next day, making sure my adult monarchs were doing okay. They were more than okay. They were thriving. Even though I saw them every day, I never tired of their fluttering orange and black wings. The way their flight was more like floating through the air than flying. Their tiny antennas tickling my skin when one of them landed on the back of my hand as I cleaned out their milkweed fields.

Every day, I thought of my grandmother, so thankful that she'd left me the butterfly farm when she passed away. Even though I missed her terribly, the chance to take care of the legacy she'd left behind was what spurred me on, day after day.

I watched the monarchs for a few more seconds. "Good job, you guys." I moved closer to a male monarch and held out my hand, thrilled as always when one of them climbed onto my wrist, showing that they trusted me. Like they understood I was taking care of them, trying to keep them safe, and giving them a good life. I grinned. The monarch turned in a semi-circle and faced me, his tiny front legs moving the slightest bit, as if he wanted to dance. "You, my good man, are so incredibly handsome."

"Why, thank you!"

I yelped and whipped around, my heart thudding hard. I knew, of course, that Mr. Monarch hadn't answered, but was relieved to see Sid and Norman standing close by. Well, maybe not relieved, since they usually made my stress level rise, but at least I wasn't losing it by hearing my butterflies talk.

How had the two men snuck up on me? Usually, they talked nonstop and clomped their feet when they walked. That hadn't gone over well when they'd worked for me for a short time, since butterflies didn't like a lot of sudden movement when they rested on milkweed stalks.

I lowered my hand to the milkweed, waiting until the butterfly rose slightly into the air before settling in the milkweed patch. Then I turned back toward the men. "Good morning, guys."

"Morning, Seneca," Norman beamed at me. He elbowed Sid. "See? She was talking to me when she made the handsome comment."

"Nope, it was definitely to me." Sid narrowed his eyes as he looked at me. "So, which of us was it?" They both stood up as straight as they could, giving wide grins and flexing their eighty-year-old muscles.

"Um…" I didn't want to hurt their feelings by telling them that the compliment had been about a winged orange creature. Instead, I held in a giggle. "Why, both of you, of course."

They guffawed at each other, obviously quite proud of the way their day was going. Then, they compared arm muscles, arguing about who was more manly.

I glanced at the rake in my hand, knowing if I didn't get back to work soon, I'd get behind, which I hated. These two guys had cost me a lot of wasted time when they'd temporarily been my help—and I used the word help, lightly—after my first assistant, Annie, had left for med school. It was best to get down to business with them.

"Hey, guys." I waved to get their attention away from their muscle comparisons. "Was there something I could help you with today?"

"First of all," Sid held up one finger. "I'd forgotten what a long journey it was just to get back here."

"Yeah." Norman glanced down at his feet. "My dogs are really barking." He tapped his shoe on the ground. "And pretty sure I feel a blister forming from the long haul. Remind me, Sid, to stop at the drugstore and get some bandages for my toes."

Sid waved his hand at his friend to end his whining. "Seneca, we wouldn't have bothered to make the trip out here, but we got tired of waiting for you to come into the café. It seems like you're in there a lot of times when we are, but you never showed up today. I can only drink so many milkshakes while I wait for something." He rubbed his tummy. "Might regret all that dairy product later today, though. And may have to spend some quality time in the bathroom." His eyebrows lowered when his stomach gurgled loudly.

I blinked. Did I really need to have a visual of what might happen to him later? No, I did not. It was probably a good thing Edward wasn't present to hear this conversation. His ick monitor would have gone through the roof.

Norman tilted his head. "And I'm pretty sure I cleaned Painted Wings Café out of French fries. That Murray guy glared at me when I asked for refills for the third time. Can you imagine? I mean, isn't the customer always right?"

I sighed, trying to imagine Murray's expression when Norman kept coming back for more, for free. It wouldn't have been pretty.

"It was the fourth time you wanted refills," pointed out his friend.

He shrugged. "Okay, you're proving my point. Murray should have been more accommodating. Glad that his fries were so well-liked, so he could make more for us to eat. Because other people were ordering them too."

This conversation was going nowhere fast. I needed to get the two men to tell me why they'd stopped by, even though the journey for them had been torturous.

I glanced toward my house. I could easily see the roof from this short distance, as it sat on the other side of one of my barns. It wasn't a long journey, except for when Winifred wanted to follow me. But her furry legs were so short, I'd have to give her credit for that one. She had to take ten steps to my one, just to keep up.

I resisted rolling my eyes, but just barely. "Yeah, sorry about your, uh, journey. To come all the way back here, there must have been a reason you traveled so far, right?"

"You're right. You see," Norman lifted his chin toward his friend, "we encountered some information which might be helpful in your investigation."

I jerked. "My…" The murder had just occurred. How did they know I was already on the trail of whoever had committed it? Sure, I was starting to talk to some people, but it wasn't like I had a banner out in front of my farm announcing I was tracking down a killer.

"That's right, Seneca." Norman wiggled his eyebrows. "We know how you operate. We worked for you, in case you forgot."

"Trust me. I haven't forgotten." I was still recovering from the time lost while showing them what they should have been doing, while not getting my own work done, then, in the end, having to do their work as well. They'd usually been wanting to take naps or get another snack from the café instead of work. And while naps and snacks, especially Murray's creations, were amazing, they didn't get all the chores completed that needed to be done.

Sid crossed his arms over his chest. "With us having watched you, witnessing the way you chased after suspects, we thought you were the right person to come to with our findings."

That got my attention. "Findings? You guys know something about who might have murdered Yolanda Steele?"

Norman pointed toward me. "We have a winner. That, my little lady, is why we've trudged out here today at the risk of our own health." He stared down at his foot. "Yep, definitely have a blister forming on my big toe."

I laid my rake on the ground and moved closer. "What did you have to tell me?"

Sid glanced behind him, as if worried someone might overhear. The only ones close by were the butterflies, and I doubted they cared one way or the other. "It's about that animal person."

I frowned. Animal person? Did he mean like at a circus? "Who're you talking about?"

"You know, the man in town who does things to animals."

"Does things?" I nearly laughed at what all that might imply, but held it in. In Maple Junction, that could only mean a certain thing. "You mean a veterinarian?"

He pointed at me. "That's the guy."

"Dr. Cummings just retired, so he's not there much anymore." I figured with their ages, they might know the older veterinarian.

"No, the young one. Wet behind the ears. Probably doesn't know a whisker from a tail."

"Oh, you mean Drew Paulson." I wouldn't acknowledge his whisker tail comment. I knew from watching Drew with my cat that he was a good veterinarian.

"Yep." Norman brushed something from the front of his shirt. "That's the guy."

"What about him?" I snuck a look at my watch. Darn, I really needed Norman and Sid to tell me whatever it was so I could finish up my work.

Sid's brow furrowed. "What do you mean?"

"You wanted to tell me something about Drew? The animal person?"

Norman tilted his head toward his friend. "Seneca, I think Sid is having a reaction from milkshake overload. He may not be thinking clearly right now."

"I have dairy brain." Sid pressed his fingertips against his temples.

If he'd had a ton of milkshakes, his brain probably did feel like a block of ice sat on it. Not enjoyable. Stabbing pains, a headache, and icy teeth all rolled into one unpleasant sensation.

Norman watched Sid for a few seconds. "Since he seems indisposed for now, his brain encased in chocolate ice cream, I'll go ahead and tell you what happened. He and I were standing in the park, minding our own business, of course."

"Of course." I crossed my arms over my chest.

"And that Dr. Drew guy, he was upset."

"What about?"

"We don't know. But he was on his phone."

"His face was red," pointed out Sid. "Like he might explode." At the word explode, he covered his eyes with his hands, as if fearing the same thing might happen to him at any second.

Norman nodded. "Yep, that's right. The doc's face was super red. Like a vegetable. Anyway, the animal doctor was shouting at somebody on the other end…"

"…of the phone," added Sid, who pressed his hand to the top of his head. Was he trying to make the after effects of all the milkshakes disappear by doing that? It wouldn't work. He'd just have to wait until the awful sensations went away by themselves.

"All right." I peered over my shoulder at my monarchs again, hoping I could get back to them soon. I angled around toward the men. "The times I've been around Drew, he seemed calm and accommodating. I take Winifred in there, so I've seen him several times." I wouldn't bother telling them that Drew was not, and never would be, my cat's favorite person. But since he invaded her personal space and checked the area under her tail she'd rather not have looked at, I didn't blame her.

Norman raised his hands, palms out. "All we can tell you is what we saw and heard. That he was yelling and was very angry."

"And his face was red," reminded Sid. "Don't forget that part."

"Got it." I held up my hand. "Thanks for the information."

Norman looked at his friend, then at me. "Should we report in with any other sightings or findings?"

"Yes, that'd be great. Thanks so much for your help, guys." Boy, that sounded off, considering they were never very helpful when they were my employees. But I did appreciate any information I could get about the people of Maple Junction, since yet another murder had been committed. Never in a million years would I have believed there'd be a murder in our tiny, quiet town. And now there'd been three!

Sid and Norman stayed where they were. I'd hoped thanking them would be the opportunity for them to make the super long trek down the short path and past my house, since our business, at least in my opinion, was done.

I raised my eyebrows and gave a smile. "Was there anything else?"

Sid rubbed his head again. "Still got that funny sensation from all the ice cream."

Norman tapped his friend's shoulder. "Oh, I know what will help that go away."

"You do?" He dropped his hand to his side. "What is it?"

"You need to eat a bunch of fries, like I did. Those will soak up all the ice cream in your system. Come on, let's go see if Chef Murray McGrumpy has made any more yet." He waved. Bye, Seneca."

"See you guys later." I picked up my rake, then watched them trudge back down the path, complaining with each step about the treacherous terrain—dirt and a few small rocks—and the dangerous wildlife—butterflies and a couple of chipmunks—and the blisters forming on their feet.

I believed they'd overheard Drew having a conversation, but it was hard to imagine that the kind veterinarian had yelled at somebody or had been so upset that his face had turned the color of ripe beets.

However, I'd only been around Drew a few times. Was there a different side to him that wasn't the nice guy everyone thought he was?

Chapter Eight

I dropped into Winifred's doctor's office the next morning, sure that my cat would be thrilled not to be included this time. I spotted Penny's car in the lot outside and a couple of others. Did one belong to Drew? I hadn't been around him enough times to have noticed what he drove.

Just to be safe, I'd keep my voice down when talking to Penny about him. No use angering anyone in my cat's physician's office when all I was trying to do was get answers. Hopefully, the information Norman and Sid had given me was correct. Even though I still found it difficult to imagine Drew being that angry on the phone with someone, after his kind treatment of Winifred.

When I dropped into the office, I always liked to have a valid reason for going there instead of just popping in to be nosy, which I was, but I didn't want it to be so obvious. As I walked into the building, Penny was standing in her reception area, but not near her desk. Instead, she stood with her back to me, talking on her cell phone. No other pets or their parents were in sight.

At first, I was going to sit and wait until she was finished with her call. But when she mentioned Drew's name in a worried tone, I decided to stay quiet and listen. I stepped quietly and stood partially hidden behind the tall divider between her area and the waiting room.

"That's just it. I don't know." Penny tapped her foot. "When he first came here, Drew was so friendly, so calm. He even reminded me of my dad in that way. Now he's, well, he seems different. So moody. Sometimes it's like he's a different person."

Was there truth to what Sid and Norman had told me? That Drew had been shouting at someone on his phone? If it was true, he'd done a complete turnaround, from kind and gentle to gruff and loud. I could understand why Penny was concerned.

She shook her head even though whoever she spoke to couldn't see her. "You don't get it. I…I'm not sure I can work with him. He's changed so much since he first got here."

I gripped the edge of the partition. Was Penny thinking of leaving the practice? She'd hate doing that. And I'd hate not seeing her here.

"He treats me… Let's just say I never know what he's going to say. He's been disrespectful to me. But I'm even more concerned about what he might say to our pet parents. Dad built this practice over decades, and people love him." She made a sound like a cough, or maybe a light sob." It would break my heart if we lost patients because of Drew and had to shut down."

My heart ached. I loved Dr. Cummings. And was getting to know Drew. I liked him at first. Had he really changed that much?

Penny turned slightly. I took a step back, but she didn't seem to have noticed me yet. Her knuckles turned white as she clutched the phone tighter. "I don't know what will happen. This is the only job I've ever had. It's all I know. What would I do if…"

I wanted to help Penny. Not that I could change whatever was going on between her and her new boss, but she and I had become friends.

"I'm not sure how long I can last. I think he's going crazy, I—"

The door opened behind me. I spun around. It was the mail carrier. She walked past me, placed the mail on the edge of the counter, then waved at me and left.

Penny huffed out a breath. "Listen, I have to go. I'll let you know how it goes." She ended the call, set her phone on a nearby table, and turned. "Oh! Seneca. I didn't know you were here."

"I just got here." I pointed toward the door. "Uh, along with the mail carrier." I hated to lie, but didn't want Penny to think I'd come in simply to listen to her conversations. I'd come in to see Drew, but also to speak to Penny since she always knew everything that was going on in the office.

Her shoulders relaxed. "Um, sorry, I was busy when you got here."

"No problem."

She glanced at her computer screen. "Do you need an appointment for Winifred? I hope she's okay."

I waved my hand. "She's great."

"Good, I'm glad. I always like seeing her in here. Though I'm sure it's not her favorite place to be."

"I really don't like going to the doctor either, so…"

"Right. Same here." She moved in her seat. "So how can I help you today?"

"I wanted to get some of that high-powered catnip. Um, for her, not me."

Penny giggled. "Can you imagine what human catnip might do to people? It might make them downright crazy." Her smile disappeared as her mouth fell open.

"Penny? Are you all right?"

"It's…" She glanced behind her and back. "Drew. Lately he's been…"

I waited a few seconds, hoping she'd finish her thought. When it seemed she wasn't going to say more, I went on. "Is he here today?"

"Yes. A pet parent dropped off their cat to be spayed, so he's monitoring her after the surgery. Did you need to speak with him? I can go back and tell him you're here."

I looked past Penny to the hallway that led to the rooms Winifred hated most, where she had her yearly exams. "I can wait until he's finished back there. It's not an emergency."

Even though I didn't have a ton of time to spare and needed to get back to my own work, it seemed more important to check out things here after speaking to Sid and Norman. And the fact that Drew only had one furry patient right now hopefully made it a better time to interrupt his day.

Penny motioned me closer. She moved her chair forward and focused on me. "First of all, I wanted to thank you for helping me before…when some people thought I was a murderer." She swallowed hard, obviously upset at the memories. And who wouldn't be?

I cringed, remembering I'd been one of those people at first. How I'd wondered if she might have been guilty of killing another person. "You don't need to thank me, Penny. You already have. I was only worried about you. I'm just so glad it all worked out like it did."

"Thank you. So am I." She pressed her fingertips against her collarbone. "It was such a stressful time for me. Things got better for a while, but…" She glanced behind her again.

"Is anything else wrong, Penny?"

"Well, it's…"

I lowered my eyebrows. "Is it Drew? Is he all right?"

"No, things are not all right. I don't know what to do. About him."

She watched me for a few seconds. "Seneca, you were so caring and sensitive when I needed to talk before. I was at a loss as to what to do. And you were there when I needed a friend. That day you took me out to see your monarch butterflies, well, you have no idea how much that helped me. How much it meant to me."

My heart warmed. "I'm so glad I was helpful to you."

"Because of that, I feel more inclined to tell you about the changes in Drew. I'm getting very concerned about the way he—"

A door opened to one of the clinic rooms, and Drew stepped out. His head was bent over his phone as he tapped something onto the screen. His eyebrows were drawn together, and his mouth turned downward. Once he finished his text, he headed our way. I waved, getting his attention, and he startled.

"Seneca. Hi. I didn't realize you were here. Did Winifred have an appointment today?" He glanced at Penny's computer, where I assumed they kept their schedule for the day.

"Nope." I held up the tiny package of high-volume catnip Penny had given me. "Winifred loves your particular brand of catnip, and she's been good lately, well, sort of good… So I thought I'd reward her with this."

His eyebrows were still lowered, and he stared at the catnip as if confused. Then, he gave a slight shake of his head, as if trying to wake up. "Yes, glad Winifred likes it. It's a big hit with all the kitties. If I get a particularly, um, spicy cat in here, the catnip usually helps get their attention so I can do the exam."

"Spicy? Yeah, that describes my cat, all right. Hyper and moody all rolled into one."

Penny flinched. Was it my use of the word moody, the same term she'd used to describe Drew on the phone?

His phone pinged. "I need to read this text, excuse me." He stepped into the waiting area, fully absorbed in the message.

Determined to change the subject, I set my purse on the edge of Penny's desk and crossed my arms. "Did you happen to go to the wedding? I don't remember seeing you there." I didn't need to say whose wedding, since those weren't a weekly occurrence, but when we had one, it was all people talked about for a while.

"No, I didn't. Dad and I went to a bed and breakfast for the weekend. It's a favorite place of his where he used to go with my mom. Was the wedding nice?"

"It was. Except for, of course…" I waved my hand. Even though the ceremony was beautiful, a murder always seemed to put a damper on things.

Penny tilted her head. "Did something go wrong? I hope everyone is okay."

Obviously, Penny hadn't heard the awful news. "Um, there was another murder."

Her mouth dropped open, then she closed it. "I hadn't heard anything about it. But then, we were out of town, and I haven't been busy with many patients and their pet parents since we got back." Her eyes widened. "Who was it? I mean, who died?" She grasped her hands together tightly, her knuckles forming ridges. Her face paled, like she was preparing herself for the news.

I checked behind me, making sure only Drew had entered the waiting area. He stood alone, still tapping furiously on his phone.

I leaned down a little closer to Penny. "It was Yolanda Steele."

She gasped. "How terrible. I'm kind of surprised she was out in public, to be honest."

"That's the general consensus, since most people in town either don't know who she is, um, was, or it's been a very long time since they saw her."

"If I can ask, how did she…"

"She was discovered in a back room of Sweethearts Chapel. She'd been asphyxiated. With a pillow."

Penny swallowed hard. "My goodness. That's…" She pressed her fingertips to her lips.

"Yes. Really awful."

Her gaze snapped to mine. "And you said you were there? At the wedding?"

"That's right." I couldn't get rid of not only the image of Yolanda lying dead, but George holding the murder weapon as he stood above her.

"You were so good at discovering who the guilty person was in the murder before. Are you…?" She held her palms up, in the I don't know position.

"I am checking into things, yes."

Penny tapped her finger on her desk as if to emphasize her point. "I know for a fact how good you are at that, Seneca."

My face heated. "I'm not a professional or anything, that's Cody."

"And he's wonderful. But so are you."

"Well, thank you." I was grateful Penny thought so, but wasn't sure about my chances of figuring out who this killer was. Sure, I'd assisted in two other murders, but was that just a fluke?

She scooted her chair closer to her desk. "Can I do anything to help you? Since you helped me so much before?"

"If you happen to hear anything about it, anything you think might be useful, I'd sure love for you to let me know. Does that work?"

"Yes, that works. Consider it done."

"Consider what done?" Drew stepped up beside me.

I jumped, not having realized he was finished with his text. I glanced at him, then Penny.

She started to answer, then seemed to change her mind. She looked at me, her eyebrows raised.

I guess it was up to me. "I was filling Penny in on the wedding. About what happened. You were there, right?"

"Not the wedding, but the reception only. I've gotten to know Devan a little bit lately, as I've needed him to do some part-time jobs for me at my new place. I'm not much of a fixer-upper."

"Yeah, he's a good kid. I've used him for things before, too."

"He invited me to the wedding, but I didn't want to impose, since I'd never met the bride and am still fairly new in town. But I did agree to go to the reception, at his insistence."

Penny looked at Drew. "I didn't know any of that. That you were there. Or that someone even died."

Drew's head jerked. "I told you all about that, Penny."

Her eyes widened. "No, you didn't." She held up her hand. "It's all right. You're not required to tell me anything."

"I did, too, tell you." He stomped his foot, startling me. "I gave you all the details that Seneca just did. Why are you making things up?"

"I didn't…" Her cheeks turned pink.

"I don't understand you, Penny." He closed his eyes briefly. "Actually, no one lately is making any sense. And Yolanda… Something happened. I…" He placed his fingers to his temple, as if he was getting a headache.

Taking a chance that I might get snapped at, I looked at Drew with concern. "Are you feeling all right?"

He dropped his hand to his sides. "Why wouldn't I be feeling all right? Do I seem off to you somehow?" His expression was one of challenge, as if daring me to answer.

"I'm sorry. I don't mean to pry or cause trouble. But…"

"But…" He moved his hand in a circle, obviously impatient and aggravated.

"When you were with Winifred, and even just speaking to me the other times we met, you were always kind and calm. But now, you seem a little upset about something." I held up my hand. "Again, sorry if I'm way out of line here. I'm just concerned."

Penny caught my eye and mouthed, "Thank you." I was sure she'd rather I said what I had so she wouldn't have to, Drew being her boss, and all. How difficult this must all be, having her dad retire, getting a new veterinarian, and now, Drew seeming to change his personality overnight.

His shoulders sagged, and he rubbed his hand down his face. "Seneca. I'm sorry. And you too, Penny. I shouldn't have said what I did. It's just that I keep thinking about that wedding reception."

I stepped closer. "What about it? Besides the obvious, of course."

"Something happened. I know something about what happened to that woman."

"You do? What is it?"

"That's just it. I can't remember. She was there. Someone died. I was there and…"

Drew had been in the room when Yolanda died? That would mean he'd been with her before George had shown up, and certainly before Evie and I discovered the scene. Was he saying he'd been the one to kill her?

Quickly, Drew stepped away from Penny's desk and rushed down the hallway to the room he'd come out of before.

I stared at Penny. Her eyes were wide.

"What do you think he meant just now?" She pointed behind her. "Surely he didn't mean…"

I shook my head slowly. "I honestly don't know. He doesn't seem himself, though, apart from what he just said. Like it's something that's affecting him in every way. Am I reading that right?"

Penny sighed. "Yes, you're right. It's in everything he says and does. It's what I was talking about before. He's so different, and I don't know what to do about it. He says some of the strangest things."

There was something going on with Drew. Did it have anything to do with what happened to Yolanda at the wedding? And had he had a reason to kill the older woman?

Chapter Nine

I stopped into Mr. O'Hurley's hardware store for the third time this week. Why couldn't I seem to keep things on hand I needed at the farm? Probably because I wasn't always as organized as I should have been. Kind of like running out of canned cat food. Much to Winifred's chagrin.

Mr. O'Hurley was also a great source of information since he talked to nearly everyone in town at some point or another, and loved to tell one and all every detail he heard. Whether completely true or not.

Recently, he'd been telling people about my supposed passionate kiss with Cody, spreading that little nugget to everyone he saw. I corrected him, that there hadn't actually been a kiss, so I hoped he was now amending that story and setting people straight.

"Seneca, hello!" Mr. O'Hurley waved at me from behind his counter.

"Hi. I ran out of—"

"Let me guess." He held up his index finger. "Duct tape?"

"Yes, you got it."

He clapped once. "Ha, I knew it."

If he knew it, I wish he'd suggested it when I was in here last time. Maybe he could be my personal secretary and keep me on track.

"Say." His eyes narrowed. "Did I ever tell you about the time we had a groundhog move onto our front porch? But then, when he had babies, we discovered it was a girl?"

I might have to rethink having him as my secretary. "Why, yes, you sure did."

He sagged in disappointment against the counter. "Oh. Well, anyway, can

I get you anything other than duct tape today?"

"No, that should do it." I stepped closer to the counter. Now that he wasn't going to talk about Mrs. Groundhog, I wanted to see what he knew about Yolanda's murder. "Hey, wasn't that a lovely wedding with Devan and Kinley? Apart from the murder, of course."

He waved his hand. "Of course, that part wasn't pleasant, not even a little bit. However, the wedding and reception were quite breathtaking. I'm so thrilled that Devan and Kinley were able to get over their tiff and get married."

"Me too. They really are sweet." Devan worked for Mr. O'Hurley. It was nice to see they had a good relationship,

He clutched his hands together over his chest. "Seneca, have I told you about the day I married my sweet wife?"

I forced a smile. I'd heard that one at least four times. "Why yes, you have. It sounded like a wonderful day."

"It was. The best. I keep it in my mind"—he tapped his temple—"and my heart"—he patted his chest—"every day."

While I was glad I wouldn't have to hear the specific details of the ceremony again, and the mishaps with his wife's veil that fell into the bright red punch at the dessert table, it was still sweet the way he talked about his wife and their life together.

"By the way, have you talked to anyone else about the wedding?" I knew he'd be brimming with details, but I hoped to give the impression that I was asking casually. No use giving him another thing to spread around about me, that I was overly nosy. Even though I was.

"Everyone and his uncle has popped in here, most who attended the ceremony and reception. Let's see." He glanced at the ceiling as he pondered my question. "Just this morning, Liza Loring came in for... Now let me think. Why was she here?" He tapped his chin with the pencil in his hand.

I held in a sigh, not too interested in anyone else's purchases but mine. "Did Liza have anything to say about Devan and Kinley's wedding?"

"Oh!" His eyes brightened. "Why, yes. She thought Kinley's dress was lovely. And that the food was amazing. She also commented that the cat wearing the tiny wedding dress was a nice touch. Quite whimsical."

It still wasn't what I was hoping for. And I wouldn't correct him by saying it was my cat who'd pranced down the aisle in front of the bride. That would really give him new information to tell every customer who stepped inside his shop. "By any chance, did Liza mention, oh, I don't know, Yolanda's murder?"

He snapped his fingers. "You know, now that you ask, she did talk about that. She didn't say it directly to me, but was speaking on her phone when she was over there,"—he pointed to the far corner—"browsing for new hinges for her bedroom door. I think she's hanging crooked. Um, I mean, her door is. If Liza was hanging crooked, there'd really be a problem." He wiggled his eyebrows.

I bit my lip, hoping not to laugh at Liza's expense. It wasn't her fault how Mr. O'Hurley chose to phrase something. And he didn't seem to mind my nosiness. In fact, I thought he thrived on mine, and I was sure, other customers', since it made a nice opportunity for him to talk. If he were ever to retire, I wasn't sure he'd be able to stand not hearing everyone else's business all day long. I pitied whoever bought the shop from him someday. It might be part of the deal that Mr. O'Hurley got to hang around every day just for fun.

"Well,"—more chin tapping—"during Liza's conversation…now of course I had no way of knowing the party on the other end of the call."

"Of course."

"But Liza says she was surprised Yolanda was there that day."

That was no surprise, since I, along with everyone I'd spoken to, felt the same way. But maybe Liza had a different take on things. We weren't close, but I knew her fairly well, since she did have the awful misfortune to have to work for my ex-husband in his law practice. "Did she happen to say why she was surprised?"

"Liza said that Yolanda Steele had no right to be in town, much less at a pleasant venue like a wedding."

"No right?" I blinked. "Did she say more?"

"Let me think…"

The door opened, and a woman and her young toddler-aged son entered.

"Oh, hello, Mrs. Cranth," Mr. O'Hurley focused on her and the little boy. "What can I help you with today?"

She waved his offer away. "Thanks, but I think I just need to browse for a bit. Timmy needs to let off some steam. You know how little boys can be. All energy. So hyper."

Mr. O'Hurley's eyebrows rose. "Um, sure. Go right ahead."

Would a hardware store be the right place for a little guy to have access to? I thought of all the sharp objects that a toddler might think were toys, but shouldn't be played with.

From behind me, I could hear Mrs. Cranth. "Timmy, put that down. You'll poke out your eye!"

Mr. O'Hurley kept watch on the new arrivals. After watching them for a few seconds, he rubbed his temples, then looked back at me. "Now, where was I, Seneca?"

I didn't particularly want to have this conversation now, with Mrs. Cranth and her little person in the store, but I'd started the process, and might not get him back on this train of thought. May as well plunge ahead.

I leaned closer, intent on keeping my voice low. "I'd asked if Liza had said more about Yolanda, about why she didn't have the right to be at the wedding." But with the noise Timmy was making, crashing around with some tools, and hopefully not poking out his eye, or cutting off any appendage, I doubted his mom would have overheard us anyway.

"Ah, yes, I remember now. Liza said she knew things about Yolanda. That the older woman should have known she wouldn't get away with it, and that she, Liza, was thrilled the old bat—her words, mind you—"

I crossed my arms over my chest.

"—that the old bat got what she deserved. And"—he held up his hand—"that it was a shame it took so long for it to happen."

My mouth had dropped open somewhere along the old bat comment. I closed it. "Um, 'That's really…"

Rapid footsteps came from behind me. Timmy appeared next to my leg, holding up a very sharp, large, dangerous-looking knife. My eyes widened.

"Hey, buddy, maybe that's not the best thing for you to have?"

His mother rushed up to us and snatched the knife away. She thrust it at Mr. O'Hurley.

He peered down at it. "Are you wanting to buy this?"

"Of course not. Please put it where my son can't reach it."

I happened to know that he kept those higher up on shelves. Timmy's mom would've had to have gotten it for him.

Mr. O'Hurley jerked, seeming unsure as to how to answer. Finally, he set the knife on the counter, away from the edge where little hands could reach it, then forced a smile.

Did the mother really blame Mr. O'Hurley for having sharp, pointy things in his store? It was a hardware store, after all. I wasn't a human mom, but I was a cat mom, and tried to keep Winifred out of things that might harm her. But I wasn't going to say that to Mrs. Cranth, especially not with the sour expression she now wore.

She grabbed Timmy's hand and propelled him toward the door. "Come on. Let's go find someplace to play where you'll be safe."

Once they were gone, Mr. O'Hurley's shoulder sagged. Surely he was relieved they'd left his store. "Not that I ever want anything to happen to a little tyke, or anyone else who wanders into my establishment, but I don't think I should have to be a babysitter to them when the mother is right there. Am I wrong?"

"You're not wrong. That was careless of the mother. And of course, I know you'd never want any harm to come to anyone."

"Thank you. I appreciate that." He tilted his head. "You know, now that I think of it, with how you were inquiring about Liza. She did say something else."

"Really?" My ears perked up.

"Yes, it was just as she was checking out. She indeed purchased a set of hinges for her bedroom door. Bronze-plated, old-fashioned looking. I personally prefer the gold-colored shiny ones, but that's just me."

I waited, hoping he'd get on with whatever was so exciting to tell me.

"Anyway, Liza asked me the strangest question."

"What was that?" I pressed closer against the counter.

"She asked if I had any job openings."

"Really? Did she know of someone who was looking for employment?" I shuddered, hoping it wasn't Sid, Norman, or both back on the job hunt. I pitied the person they'd end up working, or in their case, loafing, for.

"Nope. It was for her."

That was odd. She'd worked for my ex-husband, Payne, for several years. In fact, she'd been with him longer than he and I were together. Poor woman. Maybe her question wasn't so odd after all.

"Wait a second." He tapped the counter with his knuckle. "Am I remembering correctly that Liza works for none other than your own ex-husband?"

I closed my eyes for a second. "Yes, that's right."

"Well now, isn't that interesting?"

Oh no. I braced myself for what was next. Because when Mr. O'Hurley found a fact interesting, whatever the subject matter was, it would become his newest story.

He relaxed against the side of his counter and crossed his arms over his chest. "Seneca, let me ask you, what does the good sheriff think about him?"

"What do you mean?" Cody couldn't stand Payne, but I wasn't about to say that out loud.

"Does Payne know about the tantalizing kiss between you and Sheriff Cody Bales?"

I inhaled deeply, then let it out, hoping to find the right words without sounding rude. "As I believe we've discussed before, there was no kiss, tantalizing or otherwise, between Cody, uh, Sheriff Bales and myself. So there's nothing for Payne to know. Besides, we're divorced, so not sure he'd even care. That is, if it'd happened. Which it definitely did not."

One eyebrow rose. "That's not at all what I've gleaned from other people, Seneca."

Not wanting to, but unable to stop myself, I asked, "What have you heard?"

"Only that Payne has professed his undying love for you and wants you back. If that's the case, then I can see where he might be opposed to you kissing another man. In public, from what I've heard."

A low groan escaped my lips. Hopefully, he hadn't heard that. While the near kiss had happened in public at an auction, there'd been no touching of lips. But other auction attendees had certainly taken it upon themselves to stretch the truth and call it a kiss, along with terms such as tantalizing, passionate, and the one that made me most uncomfortable, titillating.

"You know, Seneca, it's perfectly fine to have romantic feelings for more than one person."

"Oh, no, I don't…"

He looked at me sternly. "But there comes a time when you must choose. It isn't fair to leave one man hanging, as it were."

My face heated. "Listen, Cody and I aren't a thing, and didn't share a kiss or anything else. And Payne and I are divorced. End of story." I gave a little foot stomp, hoping to emphasize my point without sounding rude.

He gave a slow smile. "My dear, life is a journey, and love happens at stops along the way. You may have a long stay, such as a marriage, or a short exciting one, such as…" His eyebrows jiggled up and down.

Oh brother. This was getting way too deep for me. "Okay. Thanks so much for your…advice."

"My pleasure. Always happy to help a damsel in distress." He narrowed his eyes. "Now that we have that straightened out for you, I wonder what will happen with Devan and Kinley?"

I wasn't sure I wanted to know, but with his expectant expression, I asked anyway. "Is something supposed to happen with them?"

"Why of course. They are honeymooners after all. And being stuck here in town and not able to go off alone somewhere…"

I didn't want to think about those two, their honeymoon, and what they may or may not be doing.

Grabbing my duct tape from the counter, I said goodbye and hightailed it out of the store before Mr. O'Hurley could give me any further advice on my love life, or lack of it, or speculate about people on their honeymoon. I had to stop thinking about Cody that way. But I really didn't want to.

Chapter Ten

I had no desire to see my ex-husband, Payne, but since his office was where Liza spent her days, it's where I needed to go later that day. On the way there, my truck sputtered, as if it knew where we were headed. Maybe it remembered the way Payne used to gun its motor when he drove it, and never filled the tank with gas until the truck was gasping, down to its last fumes.

I laid my hand on the steering wheel. "It's okay, Monarch Mobile. I'm planning a very short stay there. Believe me, I don't want to go there any more than you do."

When I arrived at the office of Payne James Attorney-at-law, I parked in the too-familiar lot, recalling when, in the beginning of our marriage, I used to drop by at lunch time and take something for Payne to eat. That was when I still liked him and didn't realize what a scumbag he was. While it might be nice to relive the good times, it wouldn't be worth it to experience what came later.

Now, I could barely stand to be in the same universe as the man. Too bad we had to share a small town too. Running into him occasionally was inevitable. And today, very likely. I had a tiny hope that he might not be in. I didn't see his car, but he often parked behind the building.

I got out of the truck, gave Monarch Mobile's hood a reassuring pat, then forced my feet to walk the short distance to the entrance. I pushed the glass door open and entered the receptionist's area, where Liza's desk was. Just being inside the building where my ex worked made a shudder run across my shoulders. But if speaking to Liza led me in any way to Yolanda's killer, it would be worth my discomfort.

When I stepped farther into the semi-darkened interior, I expected to see Liza. But a quick check around the front room showed that I was alone.

Maybe Liza was in another room. Or in the musty basement where Payne insisted on keeping old records in ancient filing cabinets. There were times when Payne had talked me into going into that dungeon to file things before he had a secretary. I felt sorry for Liza, having to work down there now.

I glanced around. Maybe I should leave her a note saying I was here, instead of interrupting her work. I eyed a pad of paper on her desk. When I picked it up, a piece of partially crumpled paper slipped out and fluttered to the floor. Payne was a stickler for neatness, which made his musty, dusty basement even more vexing. I'd hate for him to get snarky with Liza if he found it lying on the floor.

I bent and picked it up. Just as I was ready to slide it back into its place in the pad, some words caught my eye.

...worthless, pile of refuse. Not worth the space you take up...

Had I read that right? The handwriting was tiny, so I held the page closer and squinted to make sure. A second look confirmed that's what it said. I also noticed some holes in the page, where words had been, as if a pen had pressed so hard that the paper had ripped. Had that been done by the writer or the person who received the letter?

The fact that it was on Liza's desk told me it must be either for her or Payne, since she opened all his mail for him. I could understand Payne receiving it, since most people didn't like him. It might not be the first angry note he got from a person.

But what if it was for Liza? I'd always found her to be a usually nice person. What had she done to make the writer of the letter so hateful and angry?

The squeak from a door came from my left. I gasped, stuffed the letter back into the pad, and took two steps back before Liza appeared from what I remembered being the door to the basement.

She halted. "Oh, Seneca. You startled me."

"I'm sorry. Didn't mean to."

She brushed something from her hair. Dust? Cobweb? "When I'm in the basement, I don't know what's going on up here." She glanced to the main door and then to me. "Oh no."

"What's wrong?"

"I'm supposed to keep that door locked if I'm not on this floor. Payne will—"

I held up my hand to stop her. "Don't worry about that. Believe me, I won't be telling him anything."

She nearly wilted. "Thank you." She brushed at some small wrinkles on the hem of her skirt. "Now that we're both here, what can I do for you today?" She walked to her desk and looked down. At first, I thought she might notice the small corner of the letter sticking out from the pad when I'd stuck it inside in a hurry. Instead, she tapped her computer mouse, bringing her screen to life. "Did you have an appointment with Payne today? I don't see one here."

"No, I didn't." I checked behind her at Payne's closed office door. He usually only shut it if he was leaving the office or was in conference with a client. Since I hadn't spotted cars out front, maybe he wasn't here. Was I in luck, and he wasn't in? "Actually, I came to see you."

"Me? Um, okay, sure." She placed her hands on her desk and clutched her fingers together. I could hear her foot tapping quickly on the floor beneath her desk. Was she nervous to see me?

I'd always liked her, okay, but she was a little flighty. I'd been surprised when Payne had hired her, with him being so picky about the people he associated with, but maybe it was a situation like I found myself in recently. That reliable help was hard to find.

"Is this okay?" I pointed to one of the chairs on the opposite side of her desk, placed there for when clients needed to sign papers or give Liza their information.

She waved her hand toward the chairs. "Of course. Please have a seat."

"Thanks." I laid my purse on one chair and claimed the other.

"Why did you want to see me?" Her eyes widened as she let out a slight gasp. "Wait. I heard about the murder at the reception where you did the butterfly release. You don't need Payne for legal advice, do you?"

"No, thankfully, I don't." At least, not this time. Payne was still the only lawyer in town after mine had been killed not too long ago in my greenhouse. If I ever did need legal advice again, I might have to see him in that capacity, but not today. I sat back against the chair. "I happened to be in Mr. O'Hurley's shop earlier and—"

"Hold on. Let me guess. Mr. Looselips told you what I said. About Yolanda?"

I'd try to ignore the looselip comment, even though Liza had hit the nail on the head. "He did. He told me that you hadn't thought she had the right to be at the wedding."

Liza didn't answer. Was she going to ignore my comment? Tattle on me to Payne? Toss me out of the office for being too nosy? While it wouldn't help me gather information Liza might have for me, having any of those scenarios happen would only serve to keep me far away from Payne's office. Not altogether negative.

Instead, she clasped her hands together on her desk. "Since Mr. O'Hurley is probably telling everyone who walks into his shop what I said, and which now, of course, I wish I hadn't, I guess it won't hurt to tell you now."

I gave her an encouraging smile to continue.

Liza angled a little to one side to see around me. Was she looking out the windows to view the parking area? "What happened with Mr. O'Hurley was this. I went in there to buy something, but also to ask if he had any job openings."

Job openings for her? My shoulders slumped. That wasn't what I was hoping she'd tell me. I'd assumed she been asking for someone else who was looking for work. But since that was where we were, I'd go with it. If we talked about that smaller situation, maybe Liza would feel comfortable telling me about Yolanda afterward. I forced myself to sit up straighter.

"It seems strange, having this conversation with you, Seneca, since you and he used to be married."

I didn't want to discuss Payne, but would under the circumstances. "It's all right. Go on."

"You may not know this, but my dream had always been to go to college and law school."

"You want to be an attorney? That's wonderful."

"I do. Um, I did. Things changed. Too much has happened, and I can't see past it to get where I want, where I used to want, to go." Her mouth turned down at the corners, and she glanced at the floor.

I could see by her expression that not being able to go to law school was a sore, painful subject. My grandmother always encouraged Evie and me to go to college or get some training to do something we loved. No matter what that was. Her enthusiasm and positive attitude had rubbed off on me, because quite often, I found myself in the role of champion of people's goals for the future. "Liza, couldn't you still pursue that? You're still young. I'm of the opinion that it's never too late to go after your dreams."

"No, that ship has sailed, I'm afraid." Her face fell. She blinked rapidly as if overcome with the need to cry.

"I'm so sorry, Liza. It's hard when something you thought would happen doesn't work out." Like my having been in love with Payne, then having my marriage crumble. I was suddenly very glad Payne wasn't here right now.

She grabbed a tissue from the edge of her desk and dabbed at her eyes. "I've…I've come to terms with it after all this time. I need to move on. To something else. Something different, that won't remind me daily of what I could have had by now if my plans had worked out."

"So you don't want to work for Payne?"

When she shook her head, her blonde bangs brushed across her forehead. "No, I don't." She studied me for a few seconds. "Hey, you wouldn't happen to have a job opening for me, would you? I bet it's lots of fun working on a farm."

I refrained from rolling my eyes. While I adored what I did, farm life wasn't always fun. It was just hard work. I couldn't imagine Liza, with her long, manicured nails, perfect hair, and latest style of clothing, even wanting to do some of the chores I did. It could get very dirty and messy even on the best days. I was having a hard enough time with Edward not wanting to touch certain items in my greenhouse. Liza might be even worse. "I'm so sorry, but no, I don't."

She shrugged, then tossed her used tissue into a nearby waste can. "Well, it was worth a try, I guess."

"I know you said you don't want to work here anymore. Has Payne done something to…" I grimaced, not wanting to finish my sentence. My ex was known for being a womanizer. A major downfall of our marriage. And a fact I found out way too late.

"No, nothing inappropriate."

I let out a breath, glad that at least it wasn't what I'd been imagining. "The two of you just don't mesh at work? I mean, that happens. It's not always easy for two strangers to find common ground enough to be successful working partners."

Liza grabbed some papers on her desk and stacked them neatly, as if needing a productive task to accomplish. "That's about it. Maybe we've worked together too long. I don't know. Just ready for a change. I took this job when I still thought I'd graduate from college and go to law school. I wanted to be involved in a law office to further my knowledge of it. Plus, when applying for school, they always like to see how involved you might already be in that field. Now that I see it's not going to work out, I no longer want to be here."

I felt bad for Liza. To have her dream crash all around her, and to not see any way of making it work. And the older a person got and hadn't achieved what they'd hoped to, the worse it felt. "That makes sense."

"It does?"

"Sure. Why stay in a place when you no longer see the point of being there?"

"I appreciate you saying that. Thanks, Seneca. It helps when people understand. I know you said you don't have any openings, but if you hear of anything somewhere else, you'll let me know?"

"You bet I will." Now that we'd had that conversation, I was ready to dive into the other matter. "So, about what Mr. O'Hurley told me you'd said, about Yolanda Steele."

Her eyes widened as her face turned red. She placed her hands on her cheeks. "When will I learn not to have double expressos before I talk to people? It seems to speed up my speech, and I pop out with things I wouldn't otherwise say. And for some reason, I find myself talking about things even more when I'm on the phone. Mr. O'Hurley couldn't have missed what I said in that small hardware store."

"Hey, I get it about caffeine, believe me." I placed my hands on my knees while I waited for her to go on. Even though Payne didn't seem to be around, I wanted to get this finished and then race out the door before he caught me in here. The less time I spent with my ex, the better.

She ran her hand through her hair, as if agitated. "You see, my problem with Yolanda goes way back. To when I was a freshman in college. She caused trouble for me."

I thought about their ages. The two women couldn't possibly have known each other as classmates. What was the connection? "What happened? How did she…"

The front door opened behind me.

"Seneca?"

I closed my eyes. Oh no. It was Payne. I'd stayed too long.

His footsteps sounded from behind me until he appeared to my left. Not wanting to have to look up to him any more than usual with our height difference, I quickly stood.

"What are you doing here?" He pointed to Liza's desk. "Did we have an appointment?"

Liza pointed toward her computer. "I already asked her that. She said no."

Payne narrowed his eyes at his secretary. "Isn't there some filing you need to do in the back room?"

She pushed her chair back and stood. "Yeah, sure. Nice to see you, Seneca." She gave me a small wave and left us alone in the room. I really wished she could have stayed, but Payne was her boss. If he told her to go do something, she didn't have much choice.

"I didn't have an appointment, Payne. Just came by to see Liza."

"What in the world would you have to discuss with my secretary? Don't you have enough to do at that ridiculous bug farm you spend so much time at?"

I decided to ignore his comment, having heard it, or something like it, numerous times over the years. "I just wanted to talk to her. Girl talk. But then, I guess you wouldn't know about that, right?"

He snorted a laugh. "I can't imagine two people with less in common than you and Liza."

I could. Payne and me. I picked up my purse and slung the strap over my shoulder. "Anyway, I need to be going. Things to do."

"Ah, yes. The ever-present, ever-time-consuming butterflies."

I stood up straighter. "That's right. And I need to go see about them now. So, if you'll excuse me?"

Payne reached out his hand toward me, but the glare I gave him must have been enough to change his mind, because his arm lowered to his side. "Yeah, guess I'll see you around, then."

I didn't answer. Because I couldn't think of anything that would have sounded even halfway polite. Besides, I was getting the same reaction I'd had since the day he and I split up—a combination of feeling ill, and that I might break out in hives any second. Or kick him someplace painful.

My feet seemed to feel the urgency to get away from him, as they carried me to the door and out to my truck. My heart didn't slow to its normal beat until I'd left the parking lot and driven a mile down the road. Thankfully, my truck didn't sputter this time. Maybe she was glad to be speeding away in the other direction, too.

I really wished I could have finished my conversation with Liza. But I'd keep checking her out. Some of the things she'd told Mr. O'Hurley were too inflammatory to ignore.

As soon as I returned to my greenhouse, I heard vehicle tires on the gravel drive. But it wasn't a customer headed to Painted Wings. It was Cody. I placed my purse inside the greenhouse, then waited just outside the door for him.

"Hey," I said when he walked over.

"Hey, yourself." But he wasn't smiling.

"Cody, is something the matter?"

He rubbed the side of his face, something he did when confused. "I was driving down the road just now. I saw you turn out of Payne's business parking area." His eyebrows rose.

I waited for an actual question, but none came. Even without that, I knew what he meant. He wanted to know why I'd been at Payne's, given our terrible history and the fact that I loathed him. "I was talking to Liza."

He blinked but didn't say anything.

"There were some things I needed to ask her and…" I lifted my shoulders, hoping I wouldn't have to say anything more about her.

"Seneca, I'm sure there's a very good reason you were at the office of a man you hate."

I crossed my arms over my chest.

"And as far as I know, you and Liza aren't really friends. Am I right?"

"Cody, it's nice to see you, but I am behind on my work. Could you maybe just say what's bothering you?"

He stepped closer and placed his hand on my shoulder. "I think I know why you were there. And while I appreciate your interest in helping me find Yolanda's killer, it's police work."

"But—"

He lowered his arm. "Hey, I'm not trying to sound bossy."

"You are. A little."

He stared at me. "I just don't want you to get hurt. There have been two previous murders where you were put in danger, remember."

"Trust me. I haven't forgotten."

"So you'll be careful?"

"Careful. Yes. I promise." I wouldn't, however, promise to stop checking out people who I thought might have had something to do with the murder.

He gave me a quick hug. "That's all I can ask. Just concerned. Okay? I'm kind of fond of you, and all." He grinned.

"I'm kind of fond of you, too."

"All right. Just wanted to check in with you. Anything you need to tell me?"

I held up my hand. "Nope. All good here."

He studied me for a second, then leaned closer and gave me another hug.

Wow, I couldn't remember ever getting a second one before.

"See you later." He headed back to his vehicle, gave me a wave, and left.

As soon as he drove back down the drive, I realized my body had gone warm all over. If a hug from the guy I liked did that much to me, and he didn't necessarily see me as more than a friend, maybe I shouldn't let him hug me so much.

No, I wouldn't ever give those up. Because the more time I spent with Cody, the closer to him I wanted to be.

Chapter Eleven

At lunchtime the next day, I entered the café as Winifred wandered in behind me, with her tail held high, waving slightly from the tip, like an orange flag on a pole. This gave her an appearance of importance. Which, I was sure, was how she felt about herself at any given moment. The wings of her Swallow Tail butterfly costume shimmered beneath the fluorescent lights, giving her that special feline sparkle that humans only wished for.

She rubbed her stubby nose against the hem of my jeans before sauntering over to sit beneath an empty table and wash her front paws. If she stuck to her normal kitty bathing routine, her back paws would be next, then her face, and finally her hind quarters—the cat position that always made me think of a musician playing a cello.

I stopped to say hello to Angel Bales and Connie Sellers, who co-owned an adorable little shop where they did quilting, sewing repairs, knitting, and crocheting. Basically, all things I never had hope of being proficient at.

Those two ladies were so talented. I'd watched their nimble fingers produce works of fabric art that I could only dream of creating. I'd known them both for most of my life, especially Angel, who was Cody's cousin. As much time as I spent with Cody, I was often invited to their family get-togethers, so I knew them pretty well.

Next, I stopped to say hello to Karen Blain, all dressed up in a professional pair of black pants, a light gray sweater, and dangly black earrings. Karen had always been careful with her appearance, but since snagging the manager's position at our local bank, she really stood out. I was so happy for her, having gotten her new job recently. She'd been through an awful lot and deserved some good news.

I loved our customers. I glanced around the café and smirked. Well, there were a few prickly ones, but that didn't matter. We were all members of the same community, so we knew all about one another. But I rolled my eyes as I thought about everyone's questions about me and Cody. And the kiss that never happened. At times, there was a little too much interest.

But with another murder having taken place, I'd take all the help I could get in discovering who killed Yolanda Steele. Even if it meant spending a little time with those I found to be annoying.

As I walked toward the order counter, Evie was serving customers on the other side of the café, so could only respond to my wave with a brief nod. Murray, stationed behind the counter holding my daily drink request, pointed with his chin to something behind me, instead of any kind of greeting. But that wasn't uncommon.

"What's up?" I took a sip from the straw of my drink.

"Our old dude over there."

I lowered my eyebrows. "Who?"

Murray angled his chin again. "Johnny Overmeyer."

I turned and saw what Murray meant. Johnny was sitting at a table in a far corner, waving his arms wildly at me, like some teenage girl at a concert, hoping the lead singer would notice her.

I glanced at Murray. "Better go see what that's about before all that moving around causes him to tip over on his chair."

"Good plan. He looks like he's having some sort of fit."

I hurried toward Johnny, afraid that his theatrics might attract too much negative attention from those around him. He really did appear to be having some kind of spasm, but his wide grin at least put my mind at ease that he wasn't in serious danger.

When I reached his table, he pointed to the empty chair next to him. "Hello, Seneca. Won't you join me?"

I didn't have much more time to be here today, but he seemed insistent to speak with me. With reluctance, I sat next to him and placed my cup on the table. "Hey, Johnny. Good to see you. What's going on?"

He slid his plate to one side, which still held a half-eaten hamburger, then wiped his hands with a napkin. "Seneca, thanks for coming over to see me."

"No problem." What choice did I have? If I hadn't ventured over here when I did, I wondered if he'd start waving his legs as well as his arms, then maybe morph into jumping jacks. Yeah, that would have gotten everybody's attention.

Johnny leaned close enough that I got a whiff of onions. Ick. "There's something I've discovered that you need to hear."

"Okay. What did you want to tell me?" I hoped it was news about Yolanda's murder, but with Johnny, it could be anything. The time he told me how long it took to tweeze his thick white eyebrows was at the top of the list. He'd spent over five minutes describing each eyebrow, how they were different from each other, and how much it hurt to tug out the poor little hairs that refused to cooperate and lie down against his skin.

He glanced left and right as if we were two spies and he was giving me a super-secret scoop of information. "As you know, I used to be in the insurance business."

I'd heard many stories of his insurance escapades. To be fair, they were escapades to Johnny, but to me would have been mind-numbing. A few of his former co-workers sounded bizarre, but it would have made his job more interesting, I had no doubt.

He placed his flannel shirt-covered elbows on the table and steepled his fingers together, his knuckles large and lumpy. That was probably from arthritis, like my grandmother had. "I still have contacts in the insurance world, you know."

Johnny made it sound like he had a connection to the mob. Hopefully, that wasn't true. But with three murders happening close together in our tiny town, would a mob infiltration be all that strange? I gave myself a mental shake. This was no time to start bringing in even more weird scenarios than what we were already dealing with. "All right. Did somebody in that, um, world, tell you anything interesting?"

"You bet they did. Martin Shaffer, who took over my post—although I'd be doing the job differently than he is and most certainly better, but that's not the point—gave me some mighty useful intel."

Trying not to smile, I bit my lip. Johnny, with his bright blue eyes and thick white hair, was adorable at eighty, but even more so when he was worked up about something.

He lowered his hands to his lap. "See, I've known this for a while, but because of certain events, those being the recent wedding and reception, this information now takes on a much broader meaning."

I narrowed my eyes, trying to follow his logic. "So, because of the wedding, something happened with a customer's insurance?" I hoped there weren't any issues with the service providers who'd worked at the wedding. There'd been times I'd witnessed bridezillas or their mothers causing a scene and threatening to make trouble for providers of the flowers, food, or music.

He let out a sigh, blasting me with more onion scent. "Seneca, you're not getting this."

"Apparently not." I sat back as far as I could in my seat and crossed my arms over my chest.

"What I'm trying to say is about the bride's father."

"Wiley Snare?"

He pointed at me. "That's the guy."

"Something happened with Wiley's insurance?"

"Now you're getting it."

I still didn't feel like I was, but it often took Johnny a while to get to his point. And I didn't want to contradict him and get another scolding for not completely grasping his meaning. Plus, the more he talked, the stronger the likelihood that he'd take an alternate verbal route to wherever his fascinating tale longed to go.

Johnny's eyebrows rose. "According to Martin, Wiley is having horrific financial issues. He had to drop his life insurance because he couldn't make his payments."

"That's awful." I felt for Wiley. When money was tight, some things, like insurance, were the first to hit the chopping block. "I'm guessing things are especially hard for him after paying for a wedding?" As expensive as those were, it seemed there were always pesky over and above expenses that weren't planned on.

Johnny's bangs fell over his forehead when he turned his head. "Indeed. Although a man loves to see his children happily wed, the financial woes can cause serious issues."

"I can imagine. There seems to be a lot of things that go into getting a couple married." Even the butterfly release that Devan and Kinley wanted had a cost that the parents would have paid for. It wasn't a huge amount paid to me, but once all services of the wedding and reception had been accounted for, the total would be a hefty bill.

I didn't know much about that, however, since my wedding to Payne had been very simple and low-key. Too bad our marriage hadn't been. It was more like volatile and high pressure. "So what did Martin Shaffer say about Wiley?"

"According to my source—"

Since Johnny had already told me who the source was, wouldn't it be easier just to say the guy's name?

"—Wiley tried everything to convince the company to keep him on even though he couldn't pay the premiums."

I frowned. "I can just guess how well that went over."

"Like the proverbial lead balloon. Management told Martin to kick Wiley out. Drop him like a hot potato." He made hand motions as if he were quickly dumping something unpleasant onto the floor.

I waited for him to add more trite sayings, but none were forthcoming. "So they dropped his insurance, and apparently, he's having financial issues. Is that what you wanted me to know?"

He spread his hands. "Isn't that enough?"

I wasn't sure what I was supposed to do with the information, but I wouldn't say that to Johnny, who'd made such a production of getting me to rush over here to listen to him. "Thanks for telling me this, Johnny. I'll keep it under my hat for now."

"But you're not wearing a hat, Seneca." His gaze rose to study my hair.

"Just a saying." I shrugged.

He pointed at me. "Hey, I like that one. Think I'll use it later today, see where it gets me."

I was sort of glad I wouldn't be around when Johnny used that very old saying on someone, thinking it was some new revelation. And I wasn't sure why he decided to tell me about Wiley's insurance woes, but with Johnny, it didn't always make sense. Easier to just let him say what he felt like. I started to get up from my seat.

He reached out and tapped my arm. "Oh, wait. There was one more thing."

Much to my chagrin, he motioned me closer to his onion smell. "What was that?"

"I heard Wiley recently had to look for a new job."

"Oh, because Yolanda died, and he'd been working there? I wondered if they'd close the company down now that she, the founder's wife, was no longer there."

"Actually, no, Wiley got the axe right before Yolanda died."

I shivered, trying not to imagine anyone getting any kind of axe. Then I waited, hoping whatever Johnny needed to tell me wasn't anything to do with his tweezers.

"Shortly before Yolanda met her unfortunate, or fortunate ending, depending on who you ask, she fired Wiley."

That would explain at least part of Wiley's financial strain. "Was there anything else?" I wanted to speak to Wiley on my own. "Do you happen to know where he works now? That is, if he got another job after all?"

"If what my source told me is correct, Wiley's doing some part-time work at a tiny accounting firm over on River Street. I can't imagine that would make him enough funds to dig himself out of his financial hole anytime soon, though. The company is so small, the employees are all part-time, like Wiley. They're not given any benefits. And the wage is quite low."

"That's too bad. You'd assume that if you got a new position, it would at least give you what you needed, even if the job wasn't what you'd hoped for."

"Quite true."

I waited for him to elaborate. But when it seemed Johnny didn't have more to tell me, and was now eyeing his food with interest again, I stood.

"All right. Thanks so much for the information, and enjoy the rest of your sandwich. It looks delicious." I imagined it would be, minus the onions, but kept that to myself.

"Trust me, I will. Murray is a chef extraordinaire."

"That, he is. See you later."

I glanced around, looking for my cat. She was hiding behind a large potted fern in one corner of the café, but her long orange tail and a tip of her butterfly wing gave away her location. She probably thought she was a master at hiding, using her kitty ninja-like movements and cunning. But she'd be wrong.

I gave a low whistle, one I was sure would get her attention as it was the method I used at home to get her to come out for dinner time. It didn't always work, but I was used to that. She had a mind of her own. There were days she tackled me at the door when I entered the house because she was wasting away from hunger. On other days, I had to do a thorough search to find her. If she came out of hiding, she always made sure I understood that she did it of her own choosing, and not because I wanted her to.

As I walked toward the door, I waited for Winifred to follow me and catch up. She must have decided it was indeed her idea, because she slunk out from behind the plant and trotted after me, her tiny claws making rapid scratchy noises against the floor.

Once outside, I picked her up and went the short distance toward my house. She knew what that meant and squirmed a little, but soon gave up and hung limply in my arms, dejected at having to be put inside the house and miss all the fun.

I cuddled her close, hoping she'd forgive me for locking her away for a while. "Winifred, I'm not sure what to do with Johnny's revelation about Wiley, but I'm going to hold onto it. Sometimes the pieces don't make sense until the puzzle is all put together. You just never know when information might come in handy."

She agreed with a meow, but I could tell she was still miffed. A few extra treats before I closed her up in the kitchen should take care of that. Her special salmon mini-bites usually improved her mood, and in turn, mine. I fed her, then closed and pulled the door shut.

As I dug my truck keys out of my purse, I thought about Wiley Snare. Was there a connection to Yolanda aside from having been her employee?

Chapter Twelve

Now that I knew the location of Wiley's current workplace, I headed out to see what I could discover.

My reason for being there would be my invoice for the wedding butterfly release. It was supposed to have been prepaid, but hadn't been. And no one had mentioned it to me the day of the ceremony or even shortly afterward.

Under other circumstances, I would have waited a month or so, then sent an invoice. But I'd use it now as an excuse. Since I didn't know Wiley well, it would hopefully at least get me in the door. Even if he didn't want to pay for it yet, I would not, of course, push it. But the invoice would still hopefully allow me to speak to him. Otherwise, I couldn't come up with a reason to just drop into an office I'd never visited before.

When I reached the address Johnny had supplied, I was underwhelmed. Compared to where Wiley used to work at Yolanda's company, it was like a castle would be to an outhouse. The roof was missing several shingles, the paint was peeling off in sheets, and the parking lot was paved, but had so many potholes that Winifred would have fallen in and yelled for me to rescue her.

Johnny hadn't been kidding when he'd told me that Wiley was having financial woes if this was where he'd landed, probably out of desperation for any job he could find. It was scary being in financial distress. There'd been times I'd experienced it too, so my heart ached for Wiley and his family.

I climbed out of my truck and carefully stepped across the potholed lot, walking past the only other vehicle parked nearby. When I got to the glass door, I reached for the handle, which jiggled a little. A quick tug got me inside. I was glad that a piece of the door hadn't stayed in my hand as an unwanted souvenir.

Once I was in the reception area, the ambiance wasn't much better. There was no music playing, and the only sound was a sporadic hiss from an ancient radiator heater in the far corner. It wasn't a cold day out. Why would it be on anyway? I pushed up my shirt sleeves, hoping to cool off. From the heater's ancient appearance, I wouldn't have been surprised if it was stuck in the on position. Would the employees just have to dress accordingly to deal with the high temperature?

A tiny desk, which looked more like an old Formica table my grandmother used to have, with no one sitting behind it, was situated near the front of the room. A chipped plastic name plate which read Jane Arthur, Receptionist, perched on the desk's edge nearest me.

My glance around the area didn't produce the receptionist or anyone else. A tiny bathroom, with the door standing wide open, was empty as well.

Well, shoot. Should I wait for Jane to return? I glanced at my watch. It might be a lunch break for the people who worked here. I should've timed it better. And I wasn't sure when I might have the opportunity to come back here again. Along with taking care of my monarchs, training Edward, helping Evie, and being a cat mom, checking out possible leads for who had killed Yolanda Steele took a ton of time.

A shuffling sound from behind a closed door in a corner room caught my attention. When I squinted, I could just make out Wiley Snare's name on a tiny plaque that hung crooked on the door. I headed toward the room. It could either be Jane or Wiley in there right now. Or possibly another employee. Although as small as the place was, I couldn't imagine many people working here. Either way, I'd come this far, so I might as well see what I could find out.

I reached into my purse, where I had the invoice for the butterfly release. I wanted to appear prepared when I gave my reason for being here. When I knocked on the door, the name plate shimmied. Now I understood why it was crooked in the first place. A gruff, "Come in," followed.

I jumped at the loud words. Unless Jane had a very deep voice, it must be Wiley in the room. And he didn't sound thrilled that someone wanted to speak to him.

When I opened the door, the sharp squeak of the hinge startled me. I took a deep breath. I needed to calm down because I was acting like Winifred when she was startled. At least my tail wasn't puffy like hers. If I'd had a tail. I forced a smile when I focused on the man sitting behind the desk. "Hello, Mr. Snare?"

He blinked, then recognition crossed his face. "Ah, yes, Seneca James, right?"

"Yes, that's right." I glanced around the room, which was sparsely decorated, to put it lightly. A desk, a filing cabinet, and a couple of chairs were the only furnishings. It closely resembled someone's college dorm room. Namely, mine.

Wiley set aside a piece of paper he'd been holding. "How can I help you today?"

"I'm so sorry to be a bother, but I have your invoice for the kids' butterfly release at the wedding reception." I lightly waved the paper in my hand.

His gaze focused on it, then he gave a slow nod. "Oh, right. I assume I owe you some money?"

"Yes, I'm sorry to disturb you, but it was set up to be prepaid and..." I shrugged.

"Don't apologize. It's not your fault." He held out his hand, making a 'give it to me' gesture with his fingers.

I stepped forward, placing it in his grasp. He sighed when he looked at it. The amount wasn't high, but if he was having issues, any amount wouldn't be welcome. "Listen, it doesn't have to be paid today, Mr. Snare."

"Call me Wiley."

"Sure, Wiley. I'm not in a hurry. I just happened to see the invoice on my desk, was coming in this direction anyway, so decided to drop it off instead of mailing it. I hope that's okay."

"It's not a problem. But I might take you up on waiting just a bit to pay you, if that works."

I waved away his comment. "Yes, it's fine. No problem at all." Now that my reason for being here was established and apparently accepted by Wiley, I glanced at the two pictures on his desk. One was of his wife, Judith, the other was what looked to be a recent photo of Devan and Kinley. Possibly their engagement picture?

I pointed to it. "That's a nice shot. Their wedding was lovely. And Kinley was beautiful. The whole day was perfect, wasn't it? Well, except for..." I watched his face as my words trailed away.

Wiley closed his eyes briefly. "Yeah, what a terrible way for the kids to start off, with something like that happening to Mrs. Steele."

Since he'd worked for her previously, maybe he didn't feel comfortable using Yolanda's first name like I'd heard other people do. Or maybe he was still so angry with her for firing him, it was difficult to even get her name out.

The other possibility, that he'd gone so far as to kill her because of what she'd done to him, had me watching Wiley very closely. "I hope Kinley and Devan are doing all right, under the circumstances. That must have been such a shock."

He ran his hand through his short hair. "They're hanging in there. It was difficult news, not only that Mrs. Steele had been...smothered, but that Sheriff Bales informed them they'd have to stay local for now."

I remembered how bad Cody felt at having to tell them the news about not leaving town. And how embarrassed he and the rest of us had been at the mention of honeymoons.

"I hate that they couldn't go on their trip. They saved up for it. But I assured them they could go later. Still, I understand they must be disappointed." He raised one eyebrow. "Especially since they're staying at my very own house right now. They didn't want to use the money to stay at a hotel, and the apartment they're going to rent is being painted this week."

"At your house? Uh, that must be a little uncomfortable. Right after they've gotten married. All that togetherness, and not much privacy?"

"We're all making the best of it." He forced a laugh. "At this point. I figure, why not? Everything else has gone downhill. We might as well all be miserable together."

"I'm sorry to hear that." And I was. A wedding should be a time of joy and celebration, not disappointment and death. "Sounds like things are tough right now. I know you used to work for Yolanda. That must have been alarming when that happened to her at your daughter's wedding."

"You have no idea. Yes, it was quite a jolt." He waved his hand to encompass his new workspace. "Along with that, this is where I've ended up. Since you found me here, you obviously heard I wasn't working at her company anymore. I'm sure word is getting around."

"Yeah, I did hear that." I kept my focus on him, not looking around the sparsely decorated room, like I was about to do. I still couldn't get over the difference in the two buildings. Like opulence compared to drudgery. I came to a quick decision. "Listen, don't worry about paying for the butterfly release. Consider it a wedding gift to Kinley and Devan."

He frowned. "That's not right. You have a business to run, too. I couldn't let you do that."

"Of course you can. Devan has been a huge help to me in his job at the hardware store. He and I are friends. Please, I'm glad to do it."

"But…"

"I insist." I reached down and slid the invoice across the desk toward me, then slipped it into my purse. "There? See?" I smiled.

He released a relieved breath. "Thank you. That will help."

"You're welcome. Just wish there was more I could do."

He closed his eyes briefly. "At this point, I don't think anyone can do much." He glanced toward the open doorway, then back. Was he afraid the receptionist might return and overhear him? "You see, unfortunately, Yolanda didn't just fire me."

"Oh?"

"No. Before that even happened, she decided she was no longer going to provide or support our pensions, retirement plans, or even health care. She even plainly stated that no one would receive any benefits at all." He looked down at his hands, which were clasped together on his desk. "At least, as long as she was still alive."

I watched him closely to see if his expression might betray guilt for having killed his former employer. "That's awful. Especially since I assume that was your deal when you hired on, to receive benefits?"

"Yes, it was. And what a terrible blow it was when that news came out. I was so angry." His hands curled into fists. "It changed my entire life, my future." He glanced down, then relaxed his fingers. "And I'm still angry, as you can probably tell."

"I can't say I blame you. That's something that would cause stress in your life."

"Yes, a lot. It's affecting my whole family, as well."

"So, what will happen to Yolanda's company, now that she's gone?" I peered inside my purse as if looking for something, trying to seem interested in his plight, but not too nosy.

"It's all a jumble, lots of details up in the air since her death wasn't, uh, planned."

That much was true. No one ever planned to be murdered.

A tiny smile lifted one side of his lips. "However, her nephew, Tyrone Steele, is going to take over the company. He's actually a friend of mine."

"That's great. Is there a chance you could be reinstated?"

He spread his hands. "That's my hope. I have a meeting with him later today. I realize I'm placing a lot on our friendship, but I can't imagine he'd let me down if it's at all possible to help me out of this hole." Wiley checked his watch. "Tyrone's not like his aunt. He'll do what's right and fair for his employees. But even if it all works out, it will be some time until he has it up and running. Until then, I'll be sitting right here." His index finger tapped the desk a little too loudly.

Wiley was obviously wound tight. He'd given me some information, but I didn't want to make his anger cross over to me by staying too long. Time to go.

I stood. "Thanks for seeing me today, Wiley. It was nice speaking with you, and I wish you luck. I hope it all turns out the way you want it to."

"Thanks, Seneca. And thanks again for the gift of the butterfly release. Kinley loved it, and I know Devan did too. It really made their wedding more special."

"You're welcome. I'm glad they loved it. I consider it an honor to do the releases, as well." I waved, then made my way out of his office, through the small, still-empty reception area, then dodged potholes as I returned to my truck.

Things might work out better for Wiley with Yolanda gone and her nephew suddenly put in charge. Wiley seemed to think there was a chance for that in the future. That his life would improve with a new owner at the helm of the company.

Could Wiley have gone the extra mile to make sure his friend would have the chance to be his new boss?

Chapter Thirteen

During my daily check-in at the Painted Wings Café, I noticed that the twins, Nora and Flora, were once again in a heated debate. Those two might have shared a womb, and were obviously identical in appearance—thank goodness they didn't dress alike—but their personalities were as different as Evie's sweetness compared to Murray's gruffness.

I was going to pass by and just give them a wave, leaving them to their squabble, but the word 'murder' made me stop beside their table. I wanted to know more, but knew that Nora might get catty if I simply asked.

Instead, I'd check on them as the café owner. "Hello, ladies. Is there anything I can get either of you?" Knowing Nora would say no, even if Flora might want something, I looked directly at Flora. "Some of Murray's cheesy fries, maybe? Refills on your drinks?"

She gave a quick nod. "That would be lovely, Seneca, thank you. And won't you join us?"

Just the opening I was hoping for, knowing Flora's kindness. I also wasn't surprised at Nora's scowl, although I'd come to realize some of that might be a reflex of her years of protecting her twin, who used to be bullied as a child and was still shy as an adult.

Evie, who was passing by, took the order, then hurried to the counter. The café was filling up with its daily customers, and lunch time was always super busy.

I took the seat nearest Flora, knowing she wouldn't mind. In her hand was a napkin, which I assumed she'd shred into tiny bits, a compulsion she had whenever she was in the café. And, I assumed any other establishment where she could get her hands on one. I purposefully ignored the napkin, knowing it upset her to have it pointed out, even though her sister probably would before their visit was over.

Evie brought our drinks. "Just a few minutes on the fries, ladies."

I smiled. "Thanks, Evie."

"You're welcome." She hurried back across the café, stopping to chat with an older couple who'd just taken their seats.

I took a sip of my drink. "How're you two doing? I hear you have a new pharmacist now where you work."

Flora's expression was pleasant, a tiny smile and crinkles at the corners of her eyes. "Yes, he's quite nice."

"Nice?" Nora's palm smacked against the table. "He definitely is not."

I frowned. "He isn't?" Even though George had been away from Maple Junction for years, I remembered him as being kind and thoughtful in high school. Maybe that was the way I thought of him because he was dating Evie at the time, and he'd made her happy.

Nora pulled her glass toward her, but didn't take a drink. "I'm honestly not sure what to make of that guy."

With Flora's napkin shredded, she reached for another from the dispenser. "Now, Nora, he is our boss. Should you really be saying things like that about him?"

She held out her hands. "What did I say? All I said was I didn't know what to make of him."

"But I know you." Flora's eyebrows lowered. "You meant something else when you said that."

After the sisters had glared at each other for a few seconds, I figured it might go on like this for a while unless I interrupted. "What did you mean, Nora? Has George said or done something to make you not trust him?"

"Well, he's an outsider, isn't he?"

Under her breath, Flora muttered, "So were we."

And Flora was right. They hadn't been in town all that long, either.

I stirred my drink. "Is that all? I mean, just having moved here doesn't seem so bad. Everyone has to come from someplace, right?"

Flora bobbed her head in agreement. "You're so right, Seneca."

I gave her a smile, already knowing Nora wouldn't like her sister agreeing with me over her.

This time both of Nora's palms laid flat on the table. "All right, then what about the fact that he was holding a pillow, the actual murder weapon, when that rich old lady was snuffed out like a burnt out light bulb."

With a gasp, Flora dropped her napkin on the table. "Nora, honestly. How you talk about people sometimes is embarrassing."

"Maybe you need to stop being such a delicate doily, sister."

Flora pouted. "Well, maybe you need to stop being such a…meanie."

A sputtered laugh came from Nora. When she finally calmed down, she took a drink from her glass. Thankfully, Evie arrived with the food right then, which I hoped would be a welcome distraction from the catfight currently forming at the table.

A low hiss came from the location of my feet beneath the table. I knew that particular hiss. Winifred had entered the open doorway. She obviously was giving her opinion on the human catfight, too.

The way these two sisters were going, nothing good would come of it. I was relieved when Evie laid out an empty plate in front of each of us, then a platter in the middle of the table with the fries.

Flora's eyes opened wide. "Those look wonderful."

"Please, go ahead." I pointed to the fries. When neither woman moved, I grabbed a plate, used my fork to stab some, then covered them in ketchup.

Flora glanced at her sister, shrugged, and helped herself as well.

When we'd all had a minute to eat, I edged my plate to the side. "Now, what you mentioned about George and the pillow?"

"Yes?" In Nora's eyes, there was a challenge. But I was used to her and wouldn't let it bother me.

When I got a napkin from the dispenser to wipe my hands, I noticed Flora's gaze following my actions. Maybe she was longing for another napkin, too. "Cody has already questioned George and so far hasn't found a reason to arrest him."

"Ha." Nora pointed at me. "So far. But isn't your sheriff still investigating?"

My sheriff? "Yes, of course. He's investigating everyone who was there."

"But you'd support your man because of, well…" Nora's shoulder went up in a shrug.

My man? What was up with her?

"Sister, don't." Flora's voice came out as a low hiss.

From below, Winifred pawed my ankle, again upset about the catlike noises happening above her.

"Don't what?" asked Nora. "Everyone in town knows about the kiss."

I blinked. "You haven't even been in town that long. What happened, um, actually, what didn't happen, was way before you moved here."

"Nevertheless, from what I've heard, it was something passionate."

Flora sighed. "Like from Gone With the Wind."

Nora's eyebrows lowered. "Do you have any idea how old that movie is?"

She reached for a coveted napkin, caught her sister's disapproving glare, then snagged more fries instead. "If love is at the center, how does it matter how old the story might be?"

I nodded at Flora, in total agreement with her assessment, then held up my hand. "No matter what people are saying, Cody and I didn't share a kiss."

Nora's eyes narrowed. "But…"

"Or anything, for that matter." I gave her a pointed glance.

"How sad." Flora's lips turned into a frown.

"It's okay." I patted her hand. "Cody is my best friend. And we get along well. It's all good."

Nora huffed out breath. "I don't understand what's going on in this town. Love affairs that aren't real. People killing others with pillows." She grabbed a fry and popped it in her mouth.

I needed to redirect things. "Yeah, okay, back to George. I've known him for a long time."

"But he just moved here," pointed out Nora.

"True, but he actually grew up here."

"Really?" Flora's eyes widened. "That might make a difference, sister, whether we can trust him. Why would he come back if he didn't already like the town? And its people?"

Nora huffed out a breath. "Still don't feel comfortable around him yet. I mean, the pillow… That's substantial evidence, I'd say."

Even though it wasn't my job to convince her of George's probable innocence, I still hated the thought of them all working together and the twins feeling distrustful. "George is a great guy. As a matter of fact, he used to date Evie."

"But not anymore?" asked Nora.

"We'll see." I shrugged. "I hope so."

"I hope they get back together, too." Flora closed her eyes. "How romantic."

I eyed them, first Nora, then Flora, hoping to get my point across. George would need people he could trust, who also trusted him. "With the way you two feel, do you think it's affecting you at work?"

Nora sat up ramrod straight in her chair. "We are professional pharmacy technicians, Seneca. We take our duties quite seriously."

I held up my hand. "I didn't mean anything bad by that. I have no doubt that you're both quite capable and great at your jobs."

"Thank you." Flora smiled.

"You're welcome. What I meant was, I know from experience if something is on your mind, it might be harder to concentrate on your job. Aside from the pillow incident, is there anything George says or does that bothers the two of you?"

The twins glanced at each other. Flora's forehead scrunched together. "I guess nothing specific. It's more that my sister has qualms about our boss that makes me take pause about him a little bit, too."

Nora rolled her eyes at Flora, then turned toward me. "All right. I'll give you something to chew on, Seneca."

"Okay. What's that?" Winifred again batted at my leg, but I ignored her. I didn't want Nora to feel as if I wasn't paying attention to what she wanted to say. She could be very snippy, and I didn't want to send her in that direction.

"The man sings." She watched me, like her proclamation about George was scandalous, and she was waiting for my reaction.

I thought for a second. "Oh, that's right. He was in the school choir in high school. Really good, in fact. He was in a lot of plays, too."

"That's not the point, is it?"

"It isn't?" I took a drink, hoping Nora wouldn't get too rowdy with the other customers sitting around us. As it was, she was a loud talker anyway.

"It's not professional." Nora tapped the table. "Honestly, I can't imagine being a customer, entering such a fine establishment as our pharmacy, and hearing a man sing show tunes. It's humiliating."

Flora ripped apart a new napkin. "But Nora, some of the customers seem to like it. I've even heard a couple of them sing along with him."

"Those are just silly women who have a crush on our boss."

"He is handsome." Flora propped her chin in her hand, her eyes wide and dreamy. "You must admit that."

"I'll admit nothing." Nora turned her head away.

"All right." I reminded myself that Nora was never easy to deal with. "So about your boss, we have that he's new to town, even though he used to live here. He likes to sing, and has a good voice, and happened to be unfortunate enough to have been holding a pillow after someone had been killed that way. However, everything Cody has found out so far hasn't shown George to be any kind of a threat."

Nora crossed her arms on top of the table. "Really? Not a threat? How about the fact that our new pharmacist was accused by someone in his other town of attempted murder?"

I held in my gasp. This was new information. Had Evie heard about it? I moved to one side to view her. She had her back to me and was conversing with Mike Larsh, who sat alone at a table, his paperback book lying in front of him.

From Evie's body language, she didn't appear to have heard Nora's words over the other conversations going on in the café.

Good. I wanted to check things out before telling her about this latest revelation. But I found it hard to believe George would have done anything so terrible. There must be some explanation.

I glanced back to our table. Flora seemed to be in shock, as she switched her gaze from me to her sister. She grabbed two napkins and began to shred them. Poor woman. Her OCD was in high gear today.

Nora was glaring at me with narrowed eyes. She gave a quick nod, and a slow smirk appeared on her face. It was as if she'd won something. Proved her point about her boss.

"Nora, whatever happened, or didn't happen with George, I'd need to hear it from him."

"You don't believe me."

At the risk of making her even pricklier, I looked directly at her. "Did you see this happen? Or hear it from George?"

"No. But let me tell you, the rumor mill between pharmacies, even those in other towns, is going strong. If someone in that town who worked with George said it was true, then that's good enough for me."

I looked at Flora, who appeared ready to cry. She tapped on her sister's shoulder. "But…"

Nora gave her sister a look that could have melted iron. "You know I'm right."

There was a barely noticeable shake of Flora's head, but she didn't say anything else.

But I wasn't going to give in so quickly. I would need more than a statement from an argumentative woman who listened to gossip, bossed her twin sister around, and disliked most everyone she met, to believe that about George. No, I needed to talk to him about it myself. And very soon.

Because the more people talked about George and possibly believed him to be guilty, the more it affected Evie. And that was something I couldn't live with.

Chapter Fourteen

After speaking with Nora and Flora, a trip to the pharmacy was in order. I went the next morning after I'd checked on the butterfly larvae in my greenhouse, fed Winifred for the second time, and checked through my personal supplies to see what I might buy at the pharmacy.

I entered the building, admiring the pleasing way products were displayed near the front, and the cleanliness and orderliness of the store. If Flora oversaw the appearance and neatness of the place, I wouldn't have been surprised. She seemed nothing if not attuned to details. I felt sorry for her to have to deal with severe OCD, but admired her all the same for refusing to let it stop her from living her daily life.

Since the twins were nowhere in sight, I approached the back counter. George was there, standing at a station with a computer, his head bent down as he typed. Perfect, since he was the one I wanted to speak with anyway. On my way there, I spotted the item I'd come in to buy, sensitive skin hand lotion, something I really did need anyway, and a brand our grocery didn't always carry.

I placed my purchase on the counter and waited. George, who stood a few feet to my right, hadn't noticed me yet, so I took a moment to watch him. Until the wedding, it had been a long time since I'd seen him. The years had been good to him. He'd been cute in school, but now, with maturity and an air of confidence in his job, he was even more attractive. I so hoped he and Evie were truly going to get back together. My cousin wore her heart on her sleeve, and George was the guy she had her eye on.

I turned around to check a clock on the wall behind me. I only had a short time to be here before I'd need to head back to the farm.

"Oh, hi, Seneca."

I jumped and whipped back around.

"Sorry." He chuckled. "Didn't mean to startle you."

"Not your fault. I'm a little jumpy sometimes. Probably because I spend so much time with Winifred."

His eyebrows rose. "I know it's been a few years since we spoke, but I don't remember hearing anything about you having a daughter."

"What? Oh, no." I smiled. "Winifred is my cat."

He blinked. "Let me guess, she was the one who helped out with the wedding ceremony."

"Yep, that was her. Trust me when I tell you that her actions were not authorized. She has a mind of her own."

"I can see that. Although personally, I thought it added to the experience of the day."

"Thanks. I'm glad to hear that, because I was mortified at the time."

He shrugged. "I think people got a kick out of it and some might have even thought it was planned." He glanced at the counter in front of me. "How can I help you today? Need to make a purchase?"

"Yep. Just this." I nudged the bottle of lotion farther across the counter.

"No problem." He grabbed the bottle, checked something on the label, and typed on some computer keys. After I tapped my credit card on the machine, George printed out my receipt. "Anything else I can do for you today, Seneca? I have a little time. As you can see, it's not busy right now."

I looked over my shoulder. "Where are your technicians? Are they off today?"

"No, I just sent them on an errand, since things are slow."

I remembered a time when I'd heard they both had to take the store's deposit to the bank, and how odd it seemed that they'd both need to go. "They do seem to do everything together. If one is in Painted Wings Café, the other is there too."

He rubbed his hand through his hair. "Yeah, I find it a little odd too, but then, I'm not a twin. How would I know what it was like to have been with a sibling literally my whole existence?"

"Good point. How are you enjoying being back in Maple Junction?" I waved my hand toward the counter. "And working here? I hadn't realized until I saw you again at the wedding that you'd trained to become a pharmacist. Very impressive."

His cheeks turned pink. "Thanks. I love it. Both the job and being back here."

"And seeing Evie again? Was that weird for you guys?"

"Not at all. I was afraid she might not want to see me since my family moved away senior year of high school."

"But that wasn't your choice, right? I mean, didn't your dad get a job offer in another town?"

"Yeah, he did." George winced. "Believe me, I didn't want to leave here. But what's a seventeen-year-old guy supposed to do?"

"Exactly what you did."

"I just wish… I wanted to stay in touch with Evie, but my mom got sick right after we moved. I ended up doing lots of things around the house and running errands, things that she usually would have done, and was so wrapped up, I didn't contact anybody from here for a long time. Thankfully, my mom got better. But by then, I was too embarrassed to call Evie, afraid she'd think I was a jerk for waiting so long. Plus, as sweet and wonderful as she is, I was sure she'd have another boyfriend by then."

Evie hadn't dated anyone else at the time after George left. But I wouldn't tell him that. It might make him feel worse for not contacting her. "I'm glad your mom is okay. Evie would never think that of you. Have you told her what you just told me? About why you didn't call right away?"

"Not yet. But I will. We, uh… We're going out tomorrow night, after she closes the café, which I need to go visit. I've heard great things about it."

"Thanks. And yes, please do tell Evie what you told me. Soon."

"Trust me, I will."

I really hoped he would, because knowing that and keeping it from Evie was something I didn't want to do.

Now for the questions I'd come in here to ask. "Listen, I was really sorry you had to find yourself in that predicament at the wedding reception." Although I wanted to come right out and say it, asking someone why they held a pillow in their hands next to a dead body who'd been killed by it would come out sounding nosy. I was nosy, of course, but didn't want it to come across that way to George.

He hung his head. "It was terrible."

"I'm sure it was. And shortly after you'd moved back, too."

"I'd only just come back to town a few days before. Up until the wedding, I'd been busy finding an apartment and meeting the pharmacy owner in person."

"So you had only spoken to them on the phone?"

"Yes, and through Zoom. That was how we did the interview."

"Are you doing okay? I mean, with the shock of finding Yolanda like that."

"Sometimes it seems like I dreamt it. It was so unreal."

I waited, wanting to ask how it happened. But I'd rather George came out and told me himself. Thankfully, my patience paid off.

George tapped his phone, the top of which stuck out of his pocket. "I'd returned to the back entrance of the chapel to send a text to my family back home. I wanted some privacy, so I left all the noise of the reception for a little bit."

"That makes sense."

"It was my first time going in that way, since I'd entered through the front doors when I came early before the wedding."

"You didn't have to go in there to change into your tux before the ceremony?"

"No, I wore it to the chapel and brought more casual clothes with me. Since some of my clothes were still in boxes from moving, it was easier to grab a few from the nearest box, toss them in a duffel bag, and put on the tux I had hanging from my closet door."

I raised one eyebrow. "To be fair, guys don't need all that time in the dressing area for the wedding, like the girls do."

He fluttered his eyelashes. "But what about my mascara?"

"It's lovely." I giggled.

His smile fell. "I got turned around a little when I went into the back area behind the chapel."

"It is like a maze. I've gotten confused in there before, too." Which was sad, considering I'd been in there several times when having been at weddings and funerals for previous monarch butterfly releases. "Is that when you found Yolanda?"

He closed his eyes briefly. "Yeah. My phone rang. It was my mom, checking in on me after she got my text, so I stepped into a side room to answer. If anyone else was around, I didn't want my conversation to bother them. Though under the circumstances, I doubt it bothered Yolanda."

I frowned. "No, it wouldn't have. Are you doing all right, you know, after finding her like that?"

His shoulders bunched together. "I'm trying not to dwell on it, though that's difficult. But it's been on my mind, if you can imagine."

"Yes, I can, actually. Like when I walked into my greenhouse to discover my attorney's body on the floor. Or entered the café to find a body in front of the ordering counter." I wouldn't tell him the part about what Evie had gone through. I'd leave that up to her when she thought the time was right.

"Gosh, sorry to hear that you've been through it too." He tilted his head. "I guess I have a lot to catch up on, being gone so long from Maple Junction."

"Thankfully, not everything you missed out on was bad. Some things are wonderful. Like you and Evie."

His eyes crinkled at the corners. "Right. I can't wait to go out with her. Spend time with her…"

"Without a room full of people around?"

"Exactly."

"I'm sure Evie is looking forward to it too." Even though she hadn't told me about the date yet, I had no doubt she was floating around the café, her feet barely touching the floor as she served her customers. And she wouldn't even need Winifred's wings to do it.

George crossed his arms over his chest, as if unsure what to do with them. "I hope so."

"I have no doubt about that at all."

He glanced down at the floor. "It was also traumatic for me, what happened with Yolanda, because I'm friends with her nephew, Tyrone. We were in some college classes together."

"Oh. That would add another layer to all of it. How's he doing?"

"Not good, I'm afraid. Not only did he lose his family member, now he'll have to take over running the company."

"He isn't ready to do that?"

"I don't know. Everything has run together for him, and he's at a loss where to start."

"I can understand how he might feel that way." Maybe it was time to change the subject. "Hey, listen, we'd talked about Nora and Flora earlier. I'm starting to get to know them since they moved here a while back."

"They keep things interesting, that's for sure." One side of his mouth rose. "And while they have such different personalities from each other, and Flora is… Well, I shouldn't discuss that."

"It's all right. She and I have talked. She's very sweet."

"Yes, she is. They both are wonderful at their jobs. I'm so glad to have them here."

"That's great. I'm sure they'd like hearing that."

"I need to make sure I let them know. I haven't been here long, but I can already tell they know their stuff."

"One thing they did tell me recently was that you like to sing."

His face reddened. "Um, yeah. I don't do that on purpose. I guess it's like when some people hum when they're doing something they enjoy. I end up singing without realizing it."

"You must like your new job then?"

"I really do. And I love being back in town, since of course, it wasn't my idea to move away in the first place." His brow furrowed. Was he thinking of when he'd had to leave Evie?

"I will say that I heard something recently. I won't say from who."

"What do you mean?" His eyebrows shot up. "About me?"

"Not that I put much stock into it. Just wanted you to know."

"Okay. Go on." I could hear his foot tapping the floor on the other side of the counter. Did he already have an idea about what I was going to say?

"It was something I heard. Just that whoever the person was,"—I didn't want him to know it was one of his workers—"had learned of you being accused of something in the past."

He rubbed his hand down his chin. "That didn't take long. I knew it might follow me here, but hoped it would take longer."

A bell sounded from the front door, and an older man entered. George waved. "I can help you back here." He looked at me. "Sorry, Seneca. Need to get back to work. But it was so good to catch up with you. We'll have to do it again soon."

"Yes, we will. Thanks." I turned and walked through the store, then made my way out to the sidewalk.

What had George been about to tell me?

Chapter Fifteen

The next day in Painted Wings, I was talking to Murray when Gretchen came in with Camry and Marla. It was around noon, so I assumed it was a lunch break for them, but it seemed strange that Marla and Camry, who both worked in the same shop, could get off together. Maybe Betty Rollins took over the front counter at the flower shop so her employees could do that.

I waved to Murray and walked across the cafe toward them. They'd chosen a table in a back corner and huddled together, shoulders hunched, bodies pressed close to each other, as if wanting to discuss something that no one else needed to hear.

I didn't let that stop me from approaching the table. "Hey, all. Can I get Evie for you to take an order?" I'd do it myself, but I was notorious for getting everyone's order wrong, or if I was lucky enough to get them right, gave them to the wrong customers. Thank goodness Evie was so remarkable in her memory of what her customers liked.

The girls looked at each other, as if it was a monumental choice to say yes, no, or wait. Gretchen drummed her fingers on the table, and Camry shrugged her shoulders. Finally, Marla looked at me. "How about we check out the menus first?"

"Sure." I grabbed some menus from a nearby shelf to hand them out. But when I returned to the table, all three were scrunched even closer together, giving cheesy grins while Gretchen snapped a photo of them. I waited until they'd moved their chairs apart again before placing the menus on the table. "That will make a good picture." I pointed to the cell phone.

"Thanks." Gretchen grinned, although it had morphed from happy to scheming, as her eyes narrowed. What was she up to?

She tapped something on her phone, then laughed. "There. Let's see how long it takes her to—"

A ding sounded on the phone.

"No way!" Marla's eyes widened. "That was fast."

Camry's eyebrows rose. "When you sent Tonda the picture, did you add a message?"

"You bet I did," said Gretchen.

"What did you say?" Camry leaned closer, trying to view Gretchen's phone.

"Just that the three of us were having an awesome time together, having so much fun and laughing at all the weird people in here."

I took a step back, hoping I wasn't being lumped in with the so-called weird people.

"Did you add, wish you were here?" asked Marla.

Gretchen snorted a laugh. "Of course not."

"Did she answer?" asked Camry.

"Yeah, what did she say?" Marla pointed to the phone.

"There's a sad face emoji." Gretchen held up the phone with the screen pointed toward them. The phone dinged again. "Oh, now the little face has tears." She giggled. "So very sad."

Camry turned and angled more toward Gretchen. "Maybe we shouldn't have sent her the picture. You never know what someone might do to get back at you. You need to watch your back."

The expression Gretchen gave her was scalding. "No, she deserves this."

I hated how they were all reacting. And how the friendship between Gretchen and Tonda was now threatened. Those two had been friends for years. My heart hurt for what they'd once had. And I hoped they could get back to how they used to be. Relationships were hard to cultivate and even harder to keep. It seemed that whoever of them was together, they made mean comments about who wasn't there. Very catty.

I watched Gretchen for a few seconds before taking a step closer. The movement reminded the girls, who'd been so caught up in their conversation, that I was still here.

Marla's eyebrows rose. "Right, um, guess we should order?"

I waved to Evie, who gave me the thumbs-up sign.

She hurried toward us, giving her customers a big smile. "Hey, there. What can I get you today?"

They took a moment to view the menus, then when Marla said she wanted a strawberry milkshake, the other two immediately agreed. Were they all that tuned into one another, or was it a case of high-school-like efforts of trying to fit in? They seemed a little old for that, but maybe the tension lately of the snubbing that Gretchen felt because of Tonda was rubbing off on everyone.

I did feel sorry for Tonda, though. Being stuck at work when your friends were out doing something fun would be hard to take. Especially when she'd received that text with the picture of the other three out having fun together. That had to sting.

Once Evie had taken the orders and returned to the front counter, I said goodbye to the other three and went to speak to Karen Blain, who was waving me over.

"Hi Karen, how are you?"

She peeked behind me, then focused again on me. "I saw you speaking to those young women over there."

"Yes."

"I'm concerned about them."

"You are? Why?"

"I'm friends online with Gretchen. I used to see her when I was a teller at the bank, and she'd come in with the checks from the funeral home. Anyway, my phone just dinged with something to check out online. It was a picture. Of those girls over there."

"Yeah, I happened to be standing close by when they took it."

"It's a cute picture of them."

"Right, I'd told them that at the time." I waited for more. "Was there something about the picture that bothered you?"

"No, it's not that. It's the caption she used." She held up her phone so

I could view the screen. The picture of Gretchen, Marla, and Camry was indeed a good picture. I wished I was that photogenic. But the post had tagged Tonda's name, and the message was, "Sorry, not sorry!" With a mean emoji face.

I let out a breath. "I wish she hadn't done that."

Karen set her phone on the table. "I agree. How rude to tag her like that. I bet that would make her feel awful. I know it would me, if my friends had done it."

I hated how the spite and competition among the young women seemed to be escalating. The old saying of words can never harm you wasn't true. They could wound a person deeply, and were sometimes hard to get over. "Thanks for showing me that, Karen. I've been worried about them. All four of them and the mini-feuds they seem to be having."

"I'm glad you're keeping an eye on them, Seneca. Friends are hard to find."

"You're right about that."

"I'm glad you and I are friends."

I touched her shoulder. "So am I."

Movement caught my attention from the counter. Murray was waving me over. "Oh, sorry, I need to go get an order from Murray to take to the girls."

"No problem. I have to get back to work anyway. It was good to see you. As usual, I had Murray's cheesy fries for lunch. You know they're my favorite."

"Indeed, I do." I grinned. "See you later." I waved goodbye as I headed toward Murray.

He pointed toward Evie, who was speaking to Mable, who, as usual, had her fingers tightly wrapped around Evie's wrist so she wouldn't escape until Mable was finished talking to her. "Thought since you're still around, you might want to help your cousin out."

"No problem. Thanks, Murray."

He rapped his knuckle against the counter. "Gotta watch out for my girls, now, don't I?"

"And we appreciate it."

As I walked past Evie, who was still held hostage by Mable, she gave me a grateful smile when she noticed the three milkshakes on a tray I carried. I took them over toward Gretchen's table.

When I got closer, the young women were once again bunched close to each other, but I could hear them talking.

Gretchen tapped the table with her fingernail. "I'm telling you, there's something up with her."

"Maybe it's a guy?" Marla shrugged.

"What makes you say that?"

"I saw her talking to some man the other day in the grocery."

Gretchen rolled her eyes. "It was probably just a customer. She does talk to everyone who comes in, you know."

"Maybe, but the way Tonda was smiling at him, I don't think that's all it was. Then she winked."

"Winked?"

"Yep. No doubt about it."

Gretchen's eyes widened. "She only does that when she's really trying to get someone's attention."

"Right, I thought the same thing," agreed Camry.

"Wait, though." Marla waved to get their attention. "Wasn't there something else you wanted to tell us? About another picture Tonda had taken of Yolanda?"

I'd stood to the side of the table a few feet away to listen, but stepped closer to hear them better. The tray with the milkshakes tilted a little, but I righted it before a wet, milky catastrophe occurred. How did Evie constantly carry these trays of food and drink around, often, heavier than this one, without dropping them?

But the three at the table were so intent on their conversation, they didn't look my way. Even when I placed the milkshakes in front of them, they barely seemed to notice me.

"That's right about the picture." Gretchen stirred her milkshake with a straw. "I meant to tell you. So, you knew that Tonda had taken a photo of Yolanda when she walked past us down the aisle at the wedding?"

The other two nodded.

"According to Tonda, she'd taken a different picture of Yolanda."

"From the wedding?" Camry's eyes widened with interest.

"Nope. This one was from a while back. Tonda said it might come in handy down the road."

"Handy for what?"

Gretchen crossed her arms over her chest. "I don't know. But Tonda was excited about having taken it. She sure has been acting weird, for whatever reason."

I wanted to stick close by to hear more, but needed something to make it appear that I wasn't doing what I was doing, which was eavesdropping.

The nearby counter, where we kept some of the menus, napkins, and silverware, needed restocking in the cubbyholes where the knives, forks, and spoons were kept for easy reach. I took the few steps over there, bent down to open the cabinet door at the bottom of the counter, and removed a plastic tub with clean utensils.

While it didn't normally take long to fill the cubbyholes, today, I went at super slow speed, hoping to hear more about Yolanda.

Slow footsteps approached, along with a thumping sound. I turned around to see Mable with her cane.

She looked me up and down, then pointed toward the counter. "You don't normally work in here, do you?"

"Nope. Just helping out today."

Mable placed her cane-free hand on her hip. "You're working very slowly."

"Oh, I, uh…"

"Don't you realize you'd get much more accomplished if you stepped it up a little?"

"Stepped it up?"

"I can tell you for a fact that I'd run circles around you doing that job. Even with my cane." She thumped the bottom of it on the floor for emphasis.

"Well, see I was…"

She moved closer, then studied my face. "Maybe you need some help."

Oh no, was she offering to stand here beside me, to restock supplies? What would I tell Evie about that? When my cousin found out the reason I was doing this, and that Mable and her cane wanted to assist, I'd never hear the end of it.

"What you need is caffeine, my dear."

"I do?"

"You're moving slower than a sloth. A young, healthy girl like you shouldn't be in turtle mode. You should be dancing around, enjoying your youth."

I glanced down at the restocking I'd done so far. I was sure that to Mable, seeing me move slowly, I was either being lazy or suffered from a lack of sleep.

Mable thumped her cane again, then stared at me over the top of her glasses. "Do yourself a favor, Seneca."

"What's that?"

"March over to the counter and grab a cup of coffee before it's too late." With a decisive head bob, she walked toward the exit and left Painted Wings.

Worried that Gretchen, Marla, and Camry might have heard that embarrassing exchange, I whipped around. But they were still huddled close together. I heard them mention Tonda's name, so hopefully they hadn't noticed the mini lecture I'd received from Mable.

With her elbow propped on the table, Marla put her chin in her hand. "I still wonder about her talking to that guy in the grocery, though. You know how she is when she likes somebody. Weird is the word for it all right. It kind of takes over."

"You're right." Gretchen looked first at her, then at Camry. "Last I saw her, she was talking to some guy on the phone, but wouldn't say who."

"I'm dying to know." Marla sat up straight.

"Me too," said Camry. "Why do you think she's holding out on us?"

Gretchen waved away the comment. "I don't care about any of that. The guy's probably a jerk, for all we know."

The waves of jealousy and anger were flowing off Gretchen. I tried to remember the last time I saw her with a guy, or heard her mention someone special. Nothing came to me.

When Gretchen excused herself to go to the restroom and left the table, I stayed where I was in case the other two kept on talking.

Camry took a drink of her milkshake. "You know where Tonda will be Thursday night, right?"

"If she's still doing the same thing, she'll be at the park. But I never did hear what's so exciting about going there by herself. What happens there?"

"It's so boring. But since it's her normal evening off, she likes to collect rocks from the stream. You know, close to that covered bridge?"

Marla tilted her head. "Yeah, I know where that is. But rocks? You're right. That's boring. What does she do with them? Throw them at people?"

"No, she paints them." Camry laughed.

"Like different colors?"

"I guess. She told me she paints pictures of flowers on them, then puts them in her terrarium."

"You're kidding."

"Nope. She talked about it the other day. I heard her."

"I think that woman needs a man in her life."

Camry's eyebrows lifted. "You might be right."

I checked the counter and then the empty bin at my feet. I was officially done restocking, and there was nothing more keeping me here close to their table. Even though I'd been going as slow as a sloth or turtle, according to Mable, I had nothing else to do.

Just then, Gretchen came out of the short hallway where the café's restrooms were situated. Wanting to talk to her before she went back to the table, I hurried toward her as I dodged people, tables, and the occasional shoe of someone with their foot sticking out into the walkway.

When I reached her, I tilted my head in the direction of the table. "Hey, I wanted to ask you something."

"What's that?"

"When I was working over close to your table earlier, I overheard something about a picture of Yolanda."

Her hand landed on her hip. "What about it?"

"You'd said the picture was one Tonda had taken, and that it might come in handy later. What did you mean?"

"Huh, you're really good at eavesdropping."

"For your information, I was helping Evie out by restocking some things." She let out a snort. "Okay, fine. So you weren't eavesdropping."

I was, but wouldn't correct her. "Have you seen the photo?"

"Yeah. And let me tell you, what she posted was brutal."

I gasped. "Brutal? What do you mean?"

"My friend"—she bent her fingers like they were parentheses—"took a picture of Yolanda Steele yelling and shaking her fist at what looked like a homeless guy outside of her house. Tonda posted it online from a separate account, trying to discredit her. The comments Tonda left were hateful and said that the world would be better off if Yolanda was dead."

I realized my mouth had fallen open, and I snapped it closed. "But you said it was a separate account. Does Tonda have a lot of different ones?"

"I'd only known about her original account, but I saw some wording in the post that made me think of Tonda. Plus, in the picture, at the very edge of it, was a corner of what I was sure was her purse. It's unique. I was with her last year when she bought it at a craft vendors' show. That sales lady had told us it was one of a kind."

"So she and Yolanda were together at the time?"

Gretchen smoothed some hair away from her face. "I don't know. It was like she was farther away from Yolanda, but maybe crouched down? I wondered if she was sitting at a table or something, and crouched down, and that maybe her purse was on the table? Just a hunch. But I have no doubt it was Tonda who posted that picture. She takes photos all the time. Of everything. And everyone." She tapped her chin. "And that picture of Yolanda…"

"What about it?"

"There was something about her. Like she reminded me of somebody."

I leaned closer, hoping she'd know something important about the murder victim. "Who was that?"

"I'm not really sure." She waved her hand. "It's probably nothing. Well, better get back to the table."

Rats, that wasn't helpful. I thought about Gretchen snapping the picture of the three girls today. Would the fact that Tonda loved taking photos be an extra punch to the gut when she not only received this one, but it was of her friends without her, and then, according to Karen, Gretchen had also posted it online with the snarky comment?

There was one thing I knew for sure, when the following Thursday arrived, I'd be ready to check out the park and see if I could catch Tonda for a one-on-one private chat.

Chapter Sixteen

Sure enough, when I reached the park in the late afternoon on Thursday, Tonda's car was already there. I recognized it from all my years of shopping in the grocery store where she worked. There was no doubting the olive green shade and dented rear fender of her small car. This was my chance.

I left my truck in the lot, parked at the far end behind a grove of trees, where it would be partially hidden from view. Then I made my way to the bridge that crossed over the stream. If Tonda's three friends were correct, Tonda was up to things she shouldn't be. And some of them might just be centered around Yolanda's death.

Having reached the bridge, I doubted Tonda would be able to see me in the shelter the covered bridge provided. Nevertheless, I stood back in the shadows and held as still as possible. I didn't want any movement to catch her attention and blow my own cover. I doubted I'd get another chance like this one.

As I waited to see what she'd do, Tonda carefully made her way to the stream's edge, bent down, and seemed to study something beneath the water's surface. Then, she stuck her fingers into what I was sure would be cold water. I curled my fingers into my palms as if I was the one with chilly fingers now. Realizing how silly that was, I forced myself to relax as I watched her.

Tonda thrust her hand in the stream several times, coming out with small, smooth stones that she examined closely. Some, she tossed back into the water. But the ones she approved of got dropped into a plastic bag taken from her jacket pocket. Was that all she was going to do? Get her hand wet for a few rocks to take back home with her? Even though I'd overheard the girls saying it was Tonda's normal activity, I still hoped for more. I mean, after a while, how many rocks could a person put in her terrarium before it filled it to the top?

Maybe the stones weren't all for that purpose. Would she throw them at her friends when they did mean things, like send her that selfie of them from Painted Wings Café?

No, probably not. Tonda could be annoying when I went to the grocery because I'd run out of Winifred's food, again. But I'd never known her to be mean or violent. Still, people changed if certain circumstances forced them to do things they might not ordinarily do. And since I was already here, it might be a good opportunity, as any, to speak with her when she wasn't at work, or with her friends.

Just as I was ready to leave the bridge and head down to see her, I stopped. Because Tonda had reached into her other jacket pocket and removed something small, she held in her hand. After staring at it, she threw the item into the water. It landed in the middle of the stream with a small splash.

My mouth dropped open. What had she just tossed into the water? I highly doubted it was a rock, since ones she discarded a few moments ago were put back near the water's edge. No, whatever this was seemed to have upset Tonda, who now sported a frown and bunched up, tense shoulders. Now, I wanted more than ever to go talk to her, maybe ask about what she'd gotten rid of. Could she deny having done it if I'd witnessed it with my own eyes from the bridge?

I turned, ready to go see her, but vehicle tires on gravel from the parking area stopped me.

Oh great. Now who was here? I stayed where I was, still in the shadows of the covered bridge, to see who might have shown up. Footsteps came from my right. It took a minute or two for the person to reveal themselves as I waited.

It was George.

Was he just here to find some quiet time, like I did every so often, and to be alone? He wouldn't have the chance for that now, with Tonda. Maybe if George saw that another person was close by, he would get back in his car and try somewhere else. But to my amazement, he called out Tonda's name and waved.

What?

Had he already known she'd be here? I hadn't been aware they even knew each other. It wasn't as if George had been in town all that long. He only knew Evie, Cody, and me because of going to school together. And he'd been in the wedding because he was Devan's cousin. Maybe he just recognized Tonda from being in the grocery store? Everyone had to stop in there at least once in a while.

I watched in amazement as he walked toward her. Then he reached out his arms. And gave her a hug.

I blinked hard, trying to change the image before me. How was this happening? What was going on? Were they seeing each other? Tonda would be a few years younger than George, but it could happen anyway.

But what about Evie? She'd be heartbroken if George were seeing another woman.

I took a deep breath and let it out. *Calm down, Seneca. It might not be that at all.* Maybe they were just friends. There might be a reasonable explanation. I did tend to overthink things sometimes. Okay, most of the time.

Determined not to jump to conclusions, even though I'd already leaped and landed in the deep conclusion pit, I clasped my fingers around the edge of the bridge railing and waited to see what would happen next.

An enormous rock sat on the ground a few yards away. It didn't surprise me when George and Tonda walked to it and used it as an impromptu bench. I'd done the same thing before, and had seen others use it too. Tonda and George were far enough away that I couldn't hear their conversation very well. Just a few snippets here and there. Some disjointed words that may or may not mean anything. I did pick up the words, uncle, Yolanda, and grandmother. I'd keep those in mind, just in case.

I frowned. Not being able to hear them clearly would make it harder to find out what I needed to know. It wasn't as if I could simply trudge down there and interrupt them. Too bad, because that's exactly what I wanted to do.

After five or so minutes, George stood, helped Tonda up from the rock, and they walked to the parking lot. When they turned my direction, I ducked down behind the stone wall below the railing, waiting until I heard their vehicles start up.

When all that remained were the sounds of birds singing, frogs croaking, and stream water trickling across rocks and reeds, I stood, dusted off my pant legs, and checked to make sure George and Tonda had both left. My truck sat alone in the otherwise empty parking area, so I exited the bridge.

What should I do next? I'd wanted to have the opportunity to speak to Tonda alone, but that wouldn't happen, at least not now. And why was she with George? They couldn't know each other very well, since he just moved here. But the way he'd hugged her told me they'd met before, and were more than casual acquaintances. George was a sweet guy, but I'd never known him to go around hugging people. There had to be an explanation of why he'd done that with Tonda. And I hoped it was a good reason, if it turned out I had to tell Evie about it.

I'd lost out on my initial reason for coming here, to speak to her, but there might be something I could still do. I glanced down to where Tonda had tossed the object. The sun reflected off something shiny in the water. Would I be able to reach it where it lay near the middle of the stream? Time to find out what she was trying to get rid of.

I hurried down from the bridge to the bank, trying to locate what I'd seen from higher up. I tried to approximate where she'd been standing when she'd thrown the object into the water. It took a couple of minutes of searching, but when the sun came out from behind the clouds, the shiny item was visible again.

It was small. Now I was amazed that I'd even been able to see it from the bridge. But I was glad I had. Something told me Tonda wouldn't have tried to get rid of it unless it would get her into trouble if she kept it. Or if she wanted to cover up a secret it was connected to.

Whatever she had pitched into the water was, of course, right in the center of the stream, where it wouldn't be quick or easy to get to. Why couldn't it have been closer, so I could reach down and swipe it from the water, or at the very least, fish it out using a long stick?

But no, that would've been too easy.

I eyed the large, flat rocks between me and where I needed to go. There appeared to be a sort of rock trail leading toward the prize I sought. However, not all the stones were close together. What were the chances I could recover it and not fall in? I bet that water was super cold.

I'd never been accused of being graceful. However, aside from getting a fishing pole and trying to catch what I could now see was gold in color, and possibly had a chain attached, walking across the stones was my best and quickest bet.

In no way did I want to still be standing out there if somebody else showed up to enjoy some time here in the park. Explaining that away might take some doing. Not wanting to leave my purse lying on the muddy ground, I made sure its strap was firmly looped around my neck, and prepared for my hopefully dry journey.

A tiny squeak came from behind me. Had somebody else shown up at the park and I hadn't noticed? As I whipped around, I tried to quickly formulate a reason for doing what I was doing. But there was no one there.

No one human, at least.

It was a squirrel.

I waved my arm at it, hoping it would go to another part of the stream. "Hey, you. Mr. Squirrel. I'm kind of in the middle of something here."

He stared at me, his tiny black eyes unblinking.

"Oh, come on. This is something I need to do. And I don't know how much time I may have if another person happens to come here and…"

Why was I explaining this to a squirrel? But was that so strange? I kept up running conversations with my cat daily. Sometimes she answered, but often not.

I took a step toward the squirrel, hoping that would be enough to convince him this wasn't the best place to be.

Not only didn't he leave, the chattering sound that came from his impossibly tiny mouth sounded like a scolding. If he'd shaken a miniature fist at me or tapped his toe, um, claws, on the ground, I wouldn't have been surprised. But Mr. Fuzzybutt simply gave me an earful for, I assumed, being in his part of the park, where I obviously was not supposed to be.

"Okay. I understand you're upset. I mean, if you came into my house, I doubt I'd just let you stay. Especially since Winifred wouldn't like sharing our living quarters with a wild animal."

He glared at me.

"No offense intended."

His answer was a sneeze. Was that acceptance or rejection of my apology?

I groaned. Either way, I needed to get into that stream, retrieve what Tonda had left there, presumably so it would float down to another part of the water, not to be found by anyone else. And I needed to do it without the supervision of a tiny, judgmental, fluffy-tailed mammal. I frowned. Gosh, I'd just described Winifred.

Determined to get on with my quest—because after all, what was the squirrel going to do, tattle on me to the other squirrels in the park for interrupting his very important nut-gathering duties?—I turned my back on him and concentrated on my current task.

The first rock wasn't as close as I would've preferred. But to get to the others, I had to conquer this one. With determination, I held my arms out to the sides for balance and stretched my leg out as far as I could without falling to one side.

With my first step, my tennis shoe slid across the rock's slick surface. I windmilled my arms, finally able to catch my balance. After a few seconds to catch my breath, I made my way to rock number two. This one went without a hitch, so I felt a little more confident to keep going. I still wasn't close enough to grab the object, but I could just make it out. It looked like a necklace or locket. Why had Tonda thrown it away?

Now I was more intrigued than before, and moved quicker, anxious to grab the necklace. Another two steps on the rocks had me almost there. With my arms held out to the sides for balance, I took what turned out to be a longer step between two rocks.

And slipped.

My foot splashed into the colder-than-expected stream, and I yelped. Thankfully, my foot was the only body part to make acquaintance with the water. The next rock got me to my destination. My shoe, sock, and foot were soaked. And yes, it was icy cold. But I tried to ignore all that and focus on why I'd done this hairbrained thing in the first place. I also refused to acknowledge the squirrel's rapid chatter behind me. As if he was laughing.

Carefully, I bent down and wrapped my fingers around what was indeed a gold chain. But it was caught on the edge of a smaller, sharp rock. I gritted my teeth together. I hadn't come across the stones and gotten a wet shoe, sock, and foot, just to be denied getting the necklace.

I crouched down slowly and tried again. The freezing water stung my hand, but I kept at it. Finally, the chain pulled free. But the rock that had held it hostage dislodged, popped out of the water, then landed right in front of my face with a splash.

I let out a sigh and wiped drops from my face with my dry hand. Then, I could finally see what it was I now held. Not only was it a necklace, but it was a locket. I wiped off my other hand on my still dry shirt, then popped open the latch to open the locket. Inside was a picture.

Of Yolanda Steele.

I gasped. Why would Tonda have something like this? But I'd need to figure that out later. For now, I needed to get safely back to the stream bank without giving myself a totally icy bath.

I gently placed the necklace in my pants pocket, reversed my course from my stream entrance, held my arms out to the side for balance, and carefully placed my feet on the stones. I was glad Sir Laughing Squirrel had taken off, so I wouldn't have to feel more humiliated than I did for dousing my foot. Once on dry land, I hurried back to my truck.

But I couldn't stop thinking about Tonda. Why did she have a picture of the murder victim?

And why had she tried to get rid of it?

Chapter Seventeen

y chef, Murray, who loved romance books, the kind showing a bustle-wearing woman clinging to a bare-chested man on the cover, was too embarrassed to go to the bookstore and pick up his own copies. It was a small thing I could do for him since he was my friend and the best chef around.

Since the shop was only a few blocks away from my farm, I hoofed it to downtown. I was a half block away from Bodacious Books when the door opened, and a young woman stepped inside. It was Marla.

When I reached the entrance and opened the door, I was enveloped by one of my favorite smells—books, with their fresh papery pages and the ink used to print all those fabulous words, and the photos for the covers.

Linda glanced up and waved. I waved back, then pointed to the display of new arrivals on a table just inside the front entrance. With a nod, she went back to speaking to Marla.

I checked out the titles in front of me, but nothing sparked my interest.

How to Gently Discipline Your Child.

Being a Mom in a Working World.

How to Breastfeed Successfully.

I glanced down at my chest. Definitely not.

Even though none of the books were for me, I bent down over a couple of them, acting like I was interested, while listening to the two other women.

"What can I help you find today, Marla?"

A heavy sigh came, and then, "I need a book."

I raised my eyebrows. *A book? Really?*

Linda cleared her throat. "Yes, of course. What sort would you like to read this time?"

"Well, I like some fiction…"

"Okay, we have—"

"Hey, I wasn't finished yet. If you'd let me talk, you just might make a sale today."

Poor Linda. Dealing with a testy customer was never enjoyable.

"I'm sorry. What sort of book do you need?"

I glanced up at Linda. She had her hands on the top of her counter, firmly clasped together, something I did when a person was acting a little like a testy feline.

Marla's back stiffened, and her right foot tapped furiously. "It has to be about money."

"Money?" Linda tapped her chin. "I have several different types. Can you be more specific?"

"Money is money, isn't it?"

It was getting gnarly up there. I'd be sure to buy some books today to help Linda out. I glanced down. But definitely not these.

"I'm sorry, Marla. I'm trying to understand. Maybe something on how to manage your finances? I know there are several of those back in the—"

"I don't need anyone telling me how to take care of money. You know why?"

Linda's eyes were wide as she shook her head.

"Because I don't have any! I need a book to tell me how to do it."

"To do…what?"

"To make money."

Linda slumped against the counter, seeming slightly deflated. "You mean a book about finding a job?"

Marla snorted out a laugh. "Not on your life. I'm not talking about a job. I have one of those. A lot of good that does me."

Linda opened her mouth, then closed it. Maybe she was at a loss as to how to help Marla. I didn't blame her. Finally, she pointed to her left. "Why don't you and I go to that section of the store. Maybe if you see the titles, something will jump out at you?"

Smart move, Linda.

As they left the counter, I ducked my head, pretending to be checking out some other titles. But *Being a Better Mechanic* and *Having Sexier Hair* really didn't do it for me either.

Linda walked briskly across the back of the store, with Marla slogging behind her. I hoped for both of their sakes Marla spotted something she could use.

Once they were looking down at books on the shelf, I gave up my false interest in the ones in front of me. Linda pointed to a middle section of a shelf. "All right, Marla. Here's what we have. Anything seem like what you wanted to read?"

Marla placed her hands on her thighs as she studied the titles. When Linda glanced up, I caught her gaze and showed her a thumbs-up in encouragement. She gave me a half grin, probably knowing I'd understand the customer is always right saying, too, even though it didn't always seem fair to the shop owner.

Finally, Marla's eyes gleamed. "That's it! I found it!" She pointed to her left.

Linda moved over a little to view it. *"How to Get Stinking Rich Before You Die."* Her brows scrunched together. "Uh, okay. This is the one, then?"

"That's right. I want it, and I want it right now."

Linda eyed me again, giving me a raised eyebrow.

Yep, business owners unite.

They made their way back across the store and to the counter. As Linda rang up the book—which from the size of it would cost a lot, depleting Marla's already low bank balance—Marla pressed her hand to her middle. "Oh! My stomach's growling."

"Skip breakfast?"

"Yeah, I guess. But I'll make up for it tonight. Can't wait to go to More Than Just Bread."

Linda put the purchase in a Bodacious Books sack. "I love their food. Do you go there alone?"

Marla took the receipt from Linda and stuck it in her purse. "Nope. I always meet one of my friends. Because eating alone is so pathetic."

I narrowed my eyes at Marla's back. I'd eaten in a restaurant before and didn't feel pathetic. I always took something to read when eating by myself. Books were great company. However, I liked mysteries, and couldn't imagine an interest in getting rich quick.

"Well, enjoy your evening. And enjoy your new book." Linda handed the sack to Marla. "I hope it's what you wanted."

Marla peered down into the sack. "Don't worry, it will be. And even if it's not, I'll just return it." She pivoted around and was now facing me. When she saw me, her eyebrows lowered. "Hi, Seneca. Been there long?"

"Um, no, not really. Just wanting something new to read." I grabbed the nearest book and held it up. Thank goodness it was only the title about being a mechanic and not the breastfeeding one. I didn't need that little rumor getting spread around town with all the others surrounding me and Cody.

Marla watched me for a few seconds, as if deciding whether to say more. Finally, she tucked the bag beneath her arm and marched away from the counter without thanking Linda or saying goodbye. Then, she sailed past me as if we hadn't even spoken.

Once the door had closed behind Marla, I went to join Linda by her counter. I pointed my thumb over my shoulder. "Um, that was…"

She let out a long breath. "Yep. That girl is wound super tight."

"And apparently wants to make money fast." I bit my lip. "Sorry. I could hear your conversation from up by the entrance."

"Don't give it another thought. It's a small building, and you had every right to be here as much as she did."

"Thanks. Don't want you to think I just came in here to eavesdrop."

"I know you better than that, Seneca." She tapped my hand. "So, how can I help you today? Need a new mystery to read to Winifred?"

"I'll need one of those, yes. I might even look at that one." I pointed toward the stack of new arrivals Linda had partially unboxed. "But I also wanted to get Murray his favorite kind of read."

Her eyebrows scrunched together. "I don't think I've had an order from him this month. I hope I didn't miss it."

I held up my hand. "No, this will be a surprise from me. His birthday is coming up."

"Oh, how sweet. He's lucky to have a friend like you, Seneca." She tilted her head. "So you'd like something like what he normally orders, right?"

"Yeah. And since I don't read that genre, and haven't kept track of what he's bought and hasn't bought, I knew you'd be the one to ask."

"No problem. Let me check his account real quick to make sure I don't get one he already has."

"Sure. Thanks." I waited as she jotted down some titles on a notepad.

"Okay, I have the last several books he's ordered. He has three authors he likes.

"Great. I'll let you help me decide which to give him."

She motioned toward the shelves of books. "Follow me. Let's go see what we have. And if you want a different one, I can order that for you. How soon do you need it? I'm not sure I know when his birthday is."

"Not for a couple of weeks. Just wanted to check on it early in case you did need to place an order. After that, you can show me the newest mysteries. For me, of course."

"Of course." Linda placed her hands on her hips. "You and I have the same taste in what we like to read. I read so many books every week. But never get tired of it."

"Neither do I. And Winifred is hooked on those cozy mysteries. They're great stories, but not gory, so she doesn't get scared."

Linda loved Winifred and always paid attention to her when she came into Painted Wings for her takeout. Although my cat, with her moods, may or may not reciprocate the love. Thankfully, she didn't normally take a swipe at people while in there. We didn't need anyone getting injured while in the café.

Or killed.

I thought back to a previous murder, which had taken place right in front of our order counter. The body, face-down, lying in a pool of blood.

No, Seneca. Let that go. I had a whole new mystery to solve now, and needed all my focus to find the killer, so George could be found innocent.

When we reached the romance section, I stood behind Linda. She waved her hand at many titles to choose from, all with covers that promised stories of love, drama, and lots of bedroom scenes.

She held up her pad. "We'll steer clear of what he already has."

I gazed at the overwhelming number of romances, that to me, all looked very similar. What if I chose something he didn't care for? I rubbed my chin. "Um, gosh…"

Linda watched me for a second. "I can either order a new one, or…" She studied the ones in front of us. "Okay, I see a couple of titles here that he hasn't ordered before. And it's by an author I know he loves. Want me to choose for you?"

I checked out the multitude of historical romances lined up on the shelves. "Yes. Please." I let out a relieved breath.

"No problem." She reached to the far left and snagged a book. "Here it is."

"Great. I'm sure he'll love it."

She bobbed her head. "I think so too. Murray is the only one of my male customers that I know of who enjoys reading romance. But good for him. Everybody is different. Thank goodness for so many writers and all the different genres, right?"

"That's for sure." I shrugged. "Romance just isn't for me. Well, in books anyway." Although romance of the actual kind might be nice. A thought of Cody flashed in my mind, his brown eyes, dark blond hair. And I'd been hugged enough by him over the years that I knew exactly how that felt. The fact that there'd been that not-a-kiss-but-very-close told me it could have easily turned into a full-fledged smooch, at least on my part, if Cody had been inclined. And, if half the town hadn't been watching.

"Seneca?" Linda waved her hand in front of my face. "You okay?"

I jerked. "What? Sorry. Got off track there for a minute. Now…what have you got for mysteries?"

She watched me for a second. "Right. Follow me. Although you know where the mysteries are." She lifted her eyebrows.

"That's for sure. My favorite part of your whole shop."

"Mine too."

I perused the titles, mentally checking off the ones I'd already read, which was a whole bunch of them. Once I chose one I wasn't familiar with, but knew and liked the author, I was ready to check out.

Linda edged behind the counter and placed the books in front of her. After scanning them into her cash register, she took my payment and placed them in a bag with the store's smiling-book logo on the front.

"Thanks so much." I put my credit card back inside my purse. I tilted my head toward the front entrance. "Is Marla a regular customer?"

"She doesn't come in very often. It's hit or miss. But she comes in enough that I was surprised at what she purchased today."

I glanced over my shoulder and back. Maybe Linda might know things about Marla that I wouldn't, since she was a customer. "I'm afraid I don't know Marla all that well. Except when I see her in Painted Wings or in the flower shop."

"She's okay. Maybe a little moody at times."

"Yeah, so I've noticed."

Linda pushed a stack of books to one side of the counter. "I can only go by how she is when she shops in here, though."

"When I'm in the flower shop, Betty is always so friendly. But if Marla is the one I'm talking to…" I glanced away, as if not wanting to finish my thought out loud.

Linda placed her elbows on her counter. "I get it. Customer service might not be Marla's best trait."

"But maybe she just hasn't had the training or opportunity to perfect those skills. She might improve, as she gets more experience."

"That's possible."

"I know she and Tonda from the grocery are friends. Sometimes Tonda will mention her, but nothing in detail. Just that they like to hang out sometimes. They've been in the café together before."

Linda pointed toward the bookshop's entrance. "As you probably heard, Marla likes to go to the More Than Just Bread restaurant, too. Maybe Tonda is who she's planning to meet? I'm in there some Tuesday evenings for supper, and she always seems to be there. They have specials on Tuesdays to get customers in since it's their slowest night.

I filed that bit of information about Marla and the restaurant away. It might be a good opportunity to check her out further. Plus, I wouldn't mind going to More Than Just Bread for dinner myself. Win-win, at least for me. It wasn't as good as Murray's cooking, but the food was good and filling. It was a plus that I could also do some snooping, uh, checking things out, at the same time.

Chapter Eighteen

I'd called Evie, but before I could ask her if she wanted to have dinner with me, she chattered nonstop about her date with George. That was good news. I loved hearing my cousin sound so happy. When she finally took a breath, we agreed to meet at the restaurant.

As Evie and I arrived at More Than Just Bread, I was relieved that there were seats available, and that Marla was indeed there, and was sitting with Tonda.

Evie nudged my shoulder. "Seneca, I think the seats across that divider from them are open. Maybe we could ask to sit there."

"Good plan." The young women sat next to a half-wall with potted plants on top. I hoped we'd be able to hide behind the plants and not be seen.

Evie, normally working at Painted Wings until early evening, convinced Murray that since it was a slow day at the café, she'd take off for an hour or so, but promised to return to do all the cleaning and closing up.

Murray had grumbled, but gave in when I told him I'd come back to help her out.

A sign requesting, *Please wait to be seated* was positioned to my left. I looked around, then waved at the woman who stood behind a wooden podium, with a tag that read 'hostess' pinned to her blouse.

She ended a phone conversation, then came forward. "How many are in your party?"

I looked at Evie, then behind us, making sure the hostess wasn't including anybody else. But we were alone. "Two, please."

"Fine. If you'd like to follow me?" She turned and quickly headed toward a table very far away from Tonda. I nearly tripped as I half-jogged to keep up with her. I hoped if someone came in who had difficulty walking, she might slow down for them.

When we caught up with her and stood in front of the table she directed us to, I pointed across the restaurant. "Would it be possible for my friend and I to sit over there? Maybe the one on the end closest to the kitchen?"

Her eyebrows lowered. "Well, I…"

I tilted my head toward Evie. "You see, my friend here has an issue with lights that are too bright. It's a little darker in that corner." When I eyed Evie, she gave a slight nod as if having gotten my hint.

Evie closed her eyes, nearly shut, and placed her hand above her eyebrows as if shading herself from the desert sun. "So bright!"

The hostess sighed loudly. "Fine. Follow me. Again."

We scurried to keep up with her—how did she walk so fast in those spiky heels and not trip, fall, or otherwise embarrass herself?—and reached the row of tables in the section across from Tonda and Marla.

Thankfully, they had their heads down, concentrating on their food, and didn't notice us. We'd kept quiet as we hurried past them, hoping to successfully sit close by without them knowing.

Once we were seated, the hostess, after telling us our server would be with us soon, placed menus on our table and let out a huff, the sound of her heels emphasizing her annoyance as she stomped away.

"Gee, guess we're not her favorite customers," whispered Evie, as she placed her purse on the bench seat beside her.

"Guess not," I whispered back. "But sitting where she wanted us to would have defeated the purpose. I doubt we could have heard anything from them."

"Yeah, you're right."

From across the divider, an arm waved in the air, then Tonda rose up in her seat halfway, still waving. Evie and I slid down in our seats, getting as low as possible so Tonda wouldn't spot us. I wanted them to speak freely at their table, and if they knew we were here, they might not do that.

"What is she doing?" asked Evie.

I shook my head.

Footsteps sounded from the other side of the divider. Tonda asked for more napkins. More footsteps followed, then retreated, as Tonda called out, "Thank you."

I rolled my eyes. I'd slid halfway to the floor because Tonda was a messy eater? Something nudged my shin. I really hoped it was Evie; otherwise, some large creature was down there that I didn't particularly want to meet.

This time, the nudge turned into a kick. I frowned at her and mouthed, "What are you doing?"

She tilted her head to the right, causing me to look in that direction.

It was the server.

Evie and I shuffled upward until we were seated like normal adults were supposed to. I waved at him.

"Good evening." No smile. No warmth. Was that because he wasn't normally friendly, or because his opinion of us was already that we acted like imbeciles?

I saw our table had glasses of water in front of our places. Good grief. So he'd been there long enough to do that, long enough to see us halfway to the floor and whispering to each other. "Uh, good evening." I kept my voice low. Evie and I would have to whisper everything to each other and to him to keep our anonymity intact.

He scrunched his brow as if confused. "Are you ready to order?"

I briefly glanced at the menu, looked at Evie, then whispered. "Yes."

He narrowed his eyes. "I'm sorry. Didn't quite get that."

"Yes."

He touched his ear. "Are you saying yes?"

I nodded.

"All right. What would you ladies like?" He grabbed a pad and pen from his shirt pocket, poised the pen above the paper, and waited.

"I'll have a chocolate shake and a cheeseburger with crinkle fries."

He narrowed his eyes. "I'm sorry, miss, you'll have to speak up."

"Choc-o-late shake. Cheese-bur-ger. Crink-le friiiies."

He closed his eyes briefly. "Perhaps I should come back later?"

This wasn't going well. Maybe I should just point. I tapped the menu.

His eyebrows rose, but he bent over slightly to view the menu better. "Fine. I think I have it." He jotted something down. He turned toward Evie, "And for you, miss?"

Evie eyed me, then picked up her own menu and pointed to her choices. I was glad she hadn't tried to whisper like I had, because I doubted it would have gone much better than my attempt had.

The server wrote on his pad and whisked the menus from the table. Was that to keep us from changing our minds and putting him through it all again? Not that I blamed him.

As he walked away, I let out a breath. "That was brutal."

"Totally. I'm sure it was for him too."

"Yeah, I imagine so. If somebody had come into Painted Wings café and tried to order like we just had, I'd have thought they were nuts. Good chance our waiter was having those very thoughts."

From the next table, there was shuffling, like one of the girls was getting situated in her seat. "Hey," said Marla, "Have you spent much time with Camry and Gretchen lately?"

"Off and on, I guess. But you probably see Camry a lot since you're roommates, right?"

"Not as much as you'd think."

"Really?"

"Our schedules don't always mesh. Sometimes I go a couple of days without really seeing her except in passing. That's not always a bad thing."

"It's not?"

"I wished I lived there alone. Don't get me wrong, it's great to share the rent, but…"

"But what?"

"Camry talked me into letting her live with me."

"Why'd you let her do that if you didn't really want to?"

"Um, the night she asked me, I'd had a beer or two. I mean, I was really tired. I guess my defenses were down." There was a pause, and then, "I've wondered if our boss, Betty, does that on purpose, schedules us at different times."

"Why would she do that?"

"I don't know. Sometimes when Camry and I are both at the shop at the same time, I'll catch Betty watching us."

"Really?"

"Yeah, like maybe she doesn't trust us."

"That's weird."

"Doesn't that ever happen to you at the grocery store, Tonda?"

"No, not really. My boss is rarely up front by the checkouts, so I'm by myself."

A sigh, then Marla said, "Must be nice, not having people spying on every little thing you say or do."

I bit my lip as I glanced at Evie, because spying was exactly what we were doing.

"But Marla, is there a reason why your boss doesn't trust you or Camry?"

Right then, our waiter showed up again, this time with plates of food. "Does everything seem to be to your satisfaction, ladies?"

Startled at his sudden appearance, Evie and I both slid partway down in our seats. I gave him a thumbs up, getting only an eyeroll from him before he left again. Once he was gone, we cautiously sat back in our seats. I glanced over at the next table, but the other young women hadn't seemed to notice us.

And I missed whatever Marla's answer to Tonda might have been about there being a reason for Marla's boss not to trust her or her roommate.

Evie's eyebrows lowered when she pointed down at her plate. "Hey, was your order right?" she whispered.

I'd been glancing around the restaurant and hadn't paid attention. But when I did, my expression probably mirrored Evie's. "Not even close." On my plate was a fish sandwich, Cole slaw, and apple juice. How had the waiter gotten that from where I'd pointed to the menu? "No, mine's all wrong." I shrugged. "Good thing I like all of this, even though it's not what I wanted."

Her lips turned down at the corners. "Mine too. I'd feel awful if I got a customer's order that wrong. I even cringe when I get one thing wrong, and always make it right for them."

"Well, I don't think we can exactly blame him, though. We didn't make it easy."

"You're right about that."

We ate mostly in silence, since we were trying to be quiet. Evie ate all her food except the Brussels sprouts, which I knew she despised. She hated them so much, they weren't even on the Painted Wings Café menu.

"Here, have some of my crinkle fries. They're good. Not Murray-good, but…"

She grabbed a few and smiled. "Thanks."

Once we were finished, we moved our plates toward the end of the table where our waiter could retrieve them. Marla and Tonda must have been finished as well. I could no longer hear forks scraping against their plates. Now that they were done eating, maybe they'd start talking and—

"Listen," said Tonda. "I've been wanting to say something."

Evie caught my eye, then edged toward the potted plants. I did the same, hoping to get as close as possible to listen in to their conversation.

"What?" asked Marla. Then came the sound of a straw slurping the bottom of an empty glass. "I'll need a refill of my drink."

A sigh, then Tonda spoke again. "The other day, when I was stuck at work, and you, Gretchen, and Camry were together…"

"Yeah. I remember."

"I got a text with a picture. Of you guys."

"Okay. So?"

"Um, it kind of… I was…"

"Spit it out, Tonda."

A sound came like a hand smacking against the table. "It hurt my feelings, okay?"

"That there was a picture?"

"And what Gretchen sent along with it. It was sort of mean."

"That was Gretchen's idea. All of it. I didn't even know she'd done it until afterward."

Silence.

My eyebrows shot up as I looked at Evie.

"What?" she whispered.

"Marla knew about the picture and what Gretchen sent. I was standing right there when she did it."

Evie frowned, as if siding with me.

"Okay," said Tonda. "Sorry if I blamed you for something you didn't know about."

"No worries. By the way, are you and Gretchen still friends?"

"Yeah, sure. Why? Have you heard something?"

"Not so much, heard, exactly."

"What do you mean?"

"Look," said Marla, "I don't want to get in the middle of you guys. Better not say anything."

"But…" A sound like a sniffle came from Tonda. Was she starting to cry? "Um, yeah, okay."

"Why don't we talk about something else?"

"Fine…like what?"

"Um, let's see…the wedding? How wild was that?"

Tonda let out a loud breath. Was she switching gears from what Marla had implied about Gretchen? "Yep, pretty wild. Seeing Yolanda there was a shock."

"I couldn't believe what she was wearing."

"Actually, I was thinking more about the fact that she was murdered."

Footsteps sounded, but not to our table. A clanking noise. Had the waiter removed their dishes?

"Excuse me," said Marla. "Could I have something more to drink?"

"Certainly," said the waiter. "You'd like a refill?"

"How about a glass of red wine for me instead?"

"Of course. Be right back." He stepped away.

"Marla, do you really need that glass of wine?" asked Tonda.

"Why not? I'm old enough."

Silence.

"Why?" Marla asked again. "Got a problem with wine? I've seen you drink it before."

"No, I like it. Just sometimes, well… Don't you think you drink a lot?"

Marla snorted. "No, I don't. What's the deal?"

"I just want you to be careful, that's all."

"What's the fun in being careful?"

"Never mind."

The waiter returned with Marla's drink, then left.

"Personally," said Marla, "I think the old witch Yolanda got what was coming to her."

"You mean that she's dead?"

"That's right. Don't tell me you liked her?"

"Not at all. Couldn't stand her. I honestly think she deserved an even worse death. I'm just surprised you'd say it out loud."

A few seconds passed before it started. Giggling. The two young women were laughing about Yolanda, each making suggestions of how she could have had a more painful ending.

I looked at Evie, whose eyes were opened wide. I agreed that it was getting grizzly at the next table.

Their laughter subsided when the waiter brought their bills. Sounds like those of purses being unzipped, followed. After footsteps indicated the waiter had left again, Tonda said, "There's something I wanted to tell you. About Yolanda."

"Really? What is it?"

"I found something. In my mom's dresser."

"What did it have to do with Yolanda?"

"I…well, the item was something I couldn't believe my mother had. Yes, it must have been Yolanda's. But it's gone now."

"What happened to it?"

"I got rid of it. No one will ever find it now."

"But what was it? You never said."

The waiter returned. "Here's your change. Have a lovely day, ladies."

They both thanked him.

"Oh," said Marla. "I need to go now. I told Camry I'd be home soon to help clean around the house." She chuckled. "Yeah, as if that's going to happen. But hey, I should probably show up anyway, right?"

There was shuffling as they slid across the bench seats. Once they stood, I could see them clearly. Evie and I scrunched down in our seats again until we could no longer see them.

"Whoa." Evie waved her hand in front of her face, like she was overheated. "That was close."

"Yeah, it really—" I whipped around to my left when a shadow appeared over the table.

It was our waiter.

His eyebrows rose as he took in our position halfway under the table again. He laid our bills on the table. "Will there be anything else for you this evening?"

"Uh, no. Thanks," I smiled. "We're good."

"That's debatable," he muttered as he walked away.

I pushed myself back up onto the seat. As I laid money on the bill to cover the cost and a generous tip, I thought about Tonda's final words to Marla. Had she been referring to the locket she'd tossed in the stream at the park?

Then I remembered George had been there too. Had met Tonda there. Had put his arm around her in comfort, and they'd appeared to be in deep discussion while sitting by the stream. I had a gnawing pain in my middle, knowing I should tell Evie about George and what I'd observed. But the last thing in the world I wanted to do was hurt her.

She was so happy to have him back in town. In her life. I didn't want to be the one to bring it crashing down around her.

No, what I needed to do was find out for myself what George was doing with Tonda and why, even though they couldn't have known each other long, they seemed quite chummy with each other. It didn't make sense. But I had a feeling it might be important.

Chapter Nineteen

There was a knock on my greenhouse door late the next morning. I knew who it was without turning around. Edward had a very particular way of announcing himself. Instead of using his knuckle like in a normal knock, he drummed his fingers on the wood. It wasn't very loud, but since I had the inner door open and he did it on the screen door, I could hear him.

"Come on in, Edward."

When the screen opened with a squeak, Winifred, who'd been napping in a corner, bolted upright, eyes opened wide, and leaped to the floor. When she spotted Edward, she raced across the greenhouse and sped past Edward's legs before the screen even had a chance to close.

He watched her run across the parking area and disappear into the open café doors. "Huh. Guess your cat was ready for lunch? Hope she didn't leave because of me."

Even though Winifred probably had left because of Edward, I wasn't going to share that. "Don't worry about her. She can be moody. Probably just startled when you walked in."

Although Edward made it sound as if he was upset my cat had left the building, I knew better. He wasn't fond of animals, butterflies, and most humans. I was sure, since he now worked a few hours at the vet's office along with working for me, it was a challenge for him to be around all the furry creatures when he was there.

At least here at my farm, Winifred was the only furry one in the greenhouse or café. The butterflies were another story. They were anywhere they wished to be here at Majestic Monarchs, since it was their home. And the fact that they could take flight was a definite advantage if they wanted to visit the inside of the café, fly around the inside of the greenhouse, or land on people's heads when they were walking close to the farm. Edward didn't stand a chance.

He took a few hesitant steps toward me and touched his ironed, denim shirt-covered chest. "All set for duty, boss."

"Great." Edward was a good guy, and I liked him, but we'd have to work on his aversion to the butterflies and larvae. They were, after all, the stars of the show here, and the sole reason I ran this farm. Even the café, Painted Wings, had been named in their honor. Without them, the farm would cease to matter, or possibly even exist.

I put down my broom, grabbed a pair of disposable gloves, and handed them to Edward. "Here ya go. Why don't you get started on cleaning out the larvae pens, then I'll join you when I'm through sweeping."

"Sure." He snapped on the gloves with a surgeon's precision, making sure they fit properly. But his expression wasn't one of confidence. However, he'd known what the job entailed from the time of his interview, so I hoped he'd get more acclimated to the position soon.

It was never fun to have to do a job if it made you uncomfortable. My brief stint as a teenager working at the recycling center attested to that. Why couldn't people rinse out their food containers before taking them for recycling?

To take my mind off my old job and Edward's mind from his present dilemma, I'd get him talking about something else. Even though the subject would be centered around his other job, he might have some insight on Drew.

I finished sweeping and set the broom aside. Unlike Edward, I went without gloves and stationed myself in the larvae pen next to the one he worked at. I loved seeing how the little larvae in their cocoons, or what some people referred to as their tiny sleeping bags, were growing and progressing. Even though I saw them and their adult versions of the monarchs in the milkweed fields, it never got old. My grandmother instilled a love in me for monarch butterflies, and for that, I would be forever grateful.

"Listen, I've been meaning to ask how things are going at the vet's office."

"Um, it's fine. Lots of people I know come in, so that helps pass the time. Thank goodness for that."

Hmmm, if you had to pass the time too much, it said something about the job. "Do you help Penny at the front desk? Or mostly Drew in the back." When I said, 'in the back', a shiver rippled over Edward's shoulders.

"I do a little bit of everything. Cleaning up following a creature's appointment, though, is the absolute worst." His upper lip curled in revulsion.

"Sure, I get it." Winifred made some icky messes sometimes. Hairballs happened more than either of us would like. And cleaning her litter box, although necessary, wasn't exactly a joy. But because I loved her, I did it gladly. "I'm glad their office was able to fix your hours around working here. That helps me out a lot."

"Me too. It's good for me financially that I can do both part-time jobs. We close the veterinary office to humans and animals from twelve to one so we can take a lunch. Penny likes to go to the bookstore to browse, Drew takes his lunch to Pines Park. And I…well, Mother sends my lunch with me."

Ah, yes. What would we do without the Superman lunchbox? But my ears perked up when I learned where Drew went during his lunch hour. There had to be a reason why he'd suddenly changed. How he was now angry and seemed confused. Plus the fact that he'd mentioned something about Yolanda that he couldn't remember. That'd sent up a major red flag for me.

Maybe I could accidentally-on-purpose run into him. "Are you liking it there? Working with Penny and Drew?"

"Penny is very nice. I like working with her."

"Yes, she's sweet. I'm sure she makes it easy to go in there for your shift."

"That's true." He scrunched his face in concentration and probably extreme distaste of the larvae, but didn't say anything more.

"What about Drew? Do you guys get along okay?"

His left shoulder rose briefly, then lowered. "I guess so."

'I guess so' didn't sound all that positive. "Are things not going well?"

Edward leaned away from the cage and focused on me. "It was awkward. Drew got very angry when he received a payment from Yolanda Steele's account."

That seemed odd. "Was her payment sent a while back, or more recently, after she was…"

His eyebrows lowered. "You know, now that you ask, we got it in the mail the day before she died."

"Why would a payment upset him?" I'd said it more to myself than to him, but when he answered, I jumped.

"I don't know. Usually, when a pet parent sends money, it's good. Penny's always glad to receive them. It helps her balance the books, which I'm sure is a positive thing. And, of course, there are bills to pay in any office."

"But you'd said usually it's good when money comes in. Not this time?"

"Definitely not. Drew's face had turned red. Then he mumbled something about Yolanda, but I couldn't make it out."

"Did he do anything else?"

Edward glanced up as he thought. "He took the check and crumbled it in a ball before throwing it in the trashcan, which I thought was very strange."

I had to agree with him there. "He actually threw money away?"

"That's right. But after he walked away, Penny rescued it and posted it to Drew's office account without him seeing her do it."

"Well, that's good at least." This whole scenario was getting weirder by the second. "Was there anything else that was worrisome to you? Or upsetting?"

He opened his mouth to speak, then his gloved hand flapped away my comment. "No, nothing like that. I mean, I don't think he meant it to me personally. He didn't at first, anyway."

"Did he say something to upset you?"

"I didn't, he uh…" Edward's face turned pink. "First, he was just moody. Kind of snappish with me, and even with Penny. Although who could ever say a bad word to her is beyond me."

I was in total agreement. She was the nicest woman. I worked for a minute and then looked over at him again. "But you said that at first, Drew didn't mean it personally to you. What happened after that? Did something change?"

Edward let out a deep sigh. "When I first started working there, Drew was kind and considerate. But a couple of days ago, he said something about…" Edward glanced toward the doorway and back. While there might have been people outside the nearby café, there wasn't anybody currently standing outside of the greenhouse to overhear us.

"You don't have to tell me, Edward. It's your decision, of course."

He gave a quick shake of his head, then his shoulders slumped. "I feel as if I should say it out loud. That is, to someone other than my mirror reflection."

I had no desire to imagine him talking to his mirror, but the mental picture was already there. Was it something he did on a regular basis? Maybe it was more pleasant to talk to himself than to listen to his mother. "All right. Whenever you're ready."

"Drew very rudely told me I was a Mama's boy." Edward gave a haughty sniff. "Me!" He rolled his eyes. "Yes, all right, I will admit that Mother is very controlling. And I do have a difficult time telling her no. Maybe I am…what Drew said. But I still think it was rude of him to say that to me."

My eyes widened. Partly because I couldn't imagine Drew saying it, and because it seemed to be true and Edward might not have realized it before Drew pointed it out.

"Sometimes it's hard to spend that much time with family." Although I had no issues being with Evie and had spent tons of time with my grandmother, I hoped my words would help Edward.

He blinked. "Yes, that's true. Mother's set of rules are often difficult to abide by. She and I do seem to clash. Even more since I reached my forties. Growing pains, I guess."

I bit my lip. What must it be like to live with his parent for that long? I supposed if a person's family member was sweet and helpful, and gave you your space, it might be all right. But Edward's situation sounded horrid. A tiny house and no privacy. I'd met his mother once, when she dropped off Edward's Superman lunchbox, yes, really, because he'd left it at home that morning. She was large and in charge, taking no prisoners and not taking backtalk from anyone.

She'd scared me, that was for sure. And Winifred had been so terrified, her fur had puffed completely out on all sides, and when she opened her mouth to hiss, nothing came out but a puff of air. I could understand why Edward might have trouble getting along with her.

He finished cleaning the larvae pen he was working on and stepped to the next one. "You know, Seneca, there are times I…" He glanced toward the back of the greenhouse, where there was a set of windows. Was he wishing he was outside? No, that didn't make sense. Edward didn't strike me as the outdoorsy type.

"What is it?" I stopped my work and turned to face him.

"Even though Drew said some hurtful things, I think he may have a point."

"You do?"

He tapped his gloved hand lightly against the pen. "It's time for a change. I'm tired of being a Mommy's boy."

I inwardly cringed at him referring to himself as a boy, but tried to hold in any negative expression. "Do you have a plan for how you might do that?"

"Not exactly. It's more a dream. I'd love to see it happen, but not sure how to go about it yet."

"That's all right. Change doesn't always happen at once."

His face brightened. "You know, you're right. Thank you. That makes me feel a little better."

"You're welcome." Although I wasn't sure, I'd given him any words of wisdom. Still, I was glad it helped.

Edward went back to cleaning the pen, and I did the same. It was quiet for a few minutes, when suddenly, he stood up straighter and declared loudly, "That's it! I need to man up!"

I gasped at the noise. If I'd had fur like Winifred's, it would have puffed out. I took a deep breath, let it out, glad that Edward seemed to be finished with his startling proclamations.

As we finished up the larvae pens and got ready to go out to rake the milkweed stalks, I decided to check on Drew again. Something was off with him. Could it have to do with the murder? Were Penny and Edward in danger working in that office with Drew?

Chapter Twenty

I'd stopped by our local convenience store on my way to lunch the next day and bought some strawberry yogurt and a drink. Normally, I headed over to Painted Wings during that time, but today, I wanted to scout out Drew. And I knew if I stopped into the café, I might get caught up in a conversation or two, and miss my chance to speak to him before his lunch hour was over.

I drove slowly through Pines Park, trying to locate him. Edward had said Drew liked to use the picnic tables, so I drove past one of the areas with shelters that housed tables.

I could've asked Edward for more specific information, but I didn't want to make it obvious I was so interested.

The first two areas were empty, but the third, set inside a grove of maple trees, was where I spotted a vehicle. I wasn't sure what Drew drove, but took a chance it might be him. I pulled into the tiny gravel lot and parked.

It took a few seconds for my eyes to adjust to the dimmer light here in the shade, but I spotted a man sitting with his back to me, eating his lunch. When he turned his head to his right, I was sure I'd found my guy.

Grabbing my yogurt and drink, I hopped out of my truck and walked toward the shelter. When I got closer, I heard his voice. He was on the phone. Should I wait until he was finished with his call to sit close by?

No. It might make it easier to sit there if he was distracted by his call. I chose a seat at a table directly behind him and placed my food, drink, and purse on the table. As I sat down, he jerked, as if he'd heard me, but continued to listen to whoever was on the other end of the line.

Drew talked for another minute or two, but his words were low. I couldn't quite make them out. Maybe he'd been aware someone might have walked up to the shelter even though he hadn't turned around. By the time I had my yogurt open and straw in my drink, Drew was finished with his call.

He set down his phone and turned. "Oh. Hey, Seneca. I thought I heard somebody come in here."

"Hi, Drew. I tried to be quiet when I came in. I hope I didn't disrupt your phone call."

"No, you didn't." He glanced behind me. "Are you here alone?"

A quick stab of fear went through me. With how Drew had been acting, should I really be here alone with him? But it was daylight, and other cars drove by every few minutes. Plus, I needed to do this for George. And for Evie. I forced a smile. "Yep, just stopped in for a quick lunch." I held up my yogurt.

"Would you like to join me? It seems silly for us to both be here and not share a table, doesn't it?"

Good. I'd been hoping he'd ask, so I wouldn't have to suggest it. "Sure, sounds great." I carried my items to his table and sat across from him. "It's always nicer to eat with someone than alone."

"That's true. I guess I'm still new enough in town that I haven't made all that many friends yet. Too busy with work."

"I get it. It does take time to figure out who you might like to spend time with. But hey, you can consider me a friend, so let me know if you ever want a picnic table lunchmate." I really hoped that was a smart thing to say. But now that the words were out, what could I do?

"Thanks. I might do that." He took a sip of his drink, then set it down, giving a glare toward his phone, which sat next to a pill bottle.

"Everything okay? I pointed to his phone. "Not a pet emergency, I hope."

He closed his eyes briefly as he let out a low groan. "No, it's definitely not okay. And it's not about anybody's pet."

"I'm sorry you're having trouble. Anything I can do to help?"

He watched me for a few seconds. "Maybe just listen? Would you mind?"

Even though Drew might say something upsetting, like he had to Edward,

I'd take a chance on listening to him. "Of course, I wouldn't mind. Please, go ahead." I pushed my finished yogurt container to the side and set my drink beside it.

Drew glanced at his food, then seemed to decide he was no longer hungry as he pushed it away. "This goes back a few weeks. See, I started taking a new medication." He tilted his head toward the pill bottle. "For anxiety." His face reddened.

"Hey, that's nothing to be ashamed about. I know lots of people who take meds for that."

"Thanks. Um, yeah, so do I. It's just…"

"You never thought you'd be one of them?"

"That's right. I guess I always thought it would never happen to me. That I'd need pharmaceutical help with a problem like this. Like I should be able to gain control of my anxiety without help. But it wasn't working. And, I finally caved and spoke to my doctor about it."

"I think it's good you talked to your doctor. I understand it can feel foreign to have a medical issue you can't control on your own." I thought about my grandmother and her high blood pressure. The day she started taking medicine for it was tough for her, having always been strong and self-sufficient, but I'd been glad at the time she did, because it helped keep her healthy for many years.

"Thanks for understanding. That's it exactly, about the control issue. And…, I owe you an apology."

I frowned. "You do?"

"The other day, when you were in the office, and I got upset…" He ran his hand down his face. "I was so embarrassed later when I'd realized how I must have sounded. You probably thought I'd completely lost it. And to think Penny had been there to hear it too. I hope she's not sorry I took over the practice from her dad."

"It's okay, Drew. Really. I could tell you weren't yourself, and that there was a good explanation for it. And Penny is the sweetest, most understanding person I know. I'm sure she knew whatever was going on wasn't the way you normally acted, considering you've been working there for a while now."

"Thanks, I appreciate that." He stared at the pill bottle. "The problem with the medication is I'm having trouble adjusting to it. It's making my moods shift like crazy. Some thoughts aren't normal." He pointed to his phone. "That was the nurse at my physician's office just now, telling me the doc wants me to stay the course and keep trying this dose for a bit longer. Even though I told her I wanted to try something else."

"And that's not working well, obviously."

"That's right. When you were there the other day in the office, I think I said something about Yolanda, didn't I?"

I nodded.

"And it might not have made much sense? I'm not even completely sure what I said."

"I knew something was up, but didn't know what. So your medication causes you to say things you normally wouldn't?"

"Unfortunately. For some reason, I seem to have developed a fixation on Yolanda. The drug also distorts my thinking. And…I don't know if they're hallucinations or what, but it's like I have these memories. I'm not sure if they're really my mind playing tricks on me, or events that took place. It's scary."

"That's rough. I'm so sorry. Does your doctor feel these symptoms will go away?"

"That's what he says. Just tells me to be patient. I will say that the time span between those episodes seems to be lengthening. So maybe he's right. Maybe they will go away. At least I hope so."

"I hope so too, for your sake. Feeling out of control is awful." I glanced to my right when a pair of robins hopped near the table. Were they checking for dropped crumbs? "Was there something that you haven't been able to pin down? A thought or possible memory that's especially bothering you?"

"Yeah. Again, it's about Yolanda. I keep associating her with death."

Death? I watched him for a few seconds. "But it sounds normal, under the circumstances. It was so recent, after all. I've been thinking about it a lot, too. Probably lots of people are."

"True, but this…" He tapped his temple. "When I remember it, if it's truly a memory, it's like whatever happened, didn't happen at the wedding."

I latched my fingers together on the table. "Then where do you think it happened?"

"There are just pieces of things, like,"—he framed the area in front of us with his hands, as if looking through a camera lens—"in my mind, I see a couch. A fancy, expensive-looking chair. And Yolanda. But she wasn't wearing the outlandish dress she had on at the wedding."

"What was she wearing?"

"It was more casual. Not a robe. Not a dress, really. Kind of in between?" His brow scrunched as if he was confused.

I thought back to spending the summers with Gram. "Well, my grandmother used to wear what she called a housedress when she wasn't going to be leaving the property, and just doing things inside the house or right outside in her garden."

"A housedress? What's that?"

"It was more common a long time ago, but women might wear them if they were staying home, not going into town. It was to put on when they did housework, mainly. My grandmother's housedresses were ones she made herself. Nothing fancy. Sort of like a smock, but it covered her up like a dress."

His eyebrows rose. "You might be onto something, Seneca."

"Was Yolanda's dress like that?"

"Sort of." He tilted his head. "Hers didn't appear homemade, though. The fabric looked expensive, but it wasn't as frilly as the one she had on at the wedding."

"I would've been surprised if hers had been homemade, as wealthy as she was. She could've purchased dresses to wear at home. Or if it was handmade, I'd guess she would've paid a seamstress to make one especially for her."

"That'd make sense, since she rarely left her house."

"That's true." I turned to the side to see him better. "So the furniture you described... I can't identify it, since I've never been to Yolanda's house. Have you ever been there?"

"Once."

It surprised me that he'd been in town such a short time and had been there, when I'd lived in Maple Junction my whole life and had never even spoken to her. "Do you think what you remember might've been inside her home? Maybe in her living room?"

He shrugged. "It's possible. I don't normally think about things like furniture, to be honest. My little house is sparse with only the bare essentials. Why should I picture something like what I've described if I don't really care about those things?"

"I don't know. But maybe you saw them in Yolanda's living room. You said you're having trouble distinguishing between what are memories and what might be hallucinations."

"It's possible, I guess."

I placed my forearms on the picnic table. "Drew, do you remember why you went to Yolanda's house that one time?"

"Her dog was sick. But she refused to bring him to the office. She kept calling Penny, who told her the dog really needed to be examined there in the office, so I'd have all the equipment here if I needed it for the dog. But when Yolanda wouldn't give up, Penny finally told me what was going on."

"So you went?"

"Yeah." His eyes narrowed. "I'm remembering more now. I did go to see her dog."

"Can you remember what happened when you got there?"

"The poor little guy was lying on...the couch. That couch." His eyes widened. "Now I remember. She had him on a little blanket there. She kept sobbing and saying, 'He's dead!'"

I gasped. "Oh no, was he..."

"No, that's just it. He was ill, but he had an infection. I was able to give him antibiotics and assured Yolanda that he'd be fine in a day or two."

I studied Drew. How amazing that his anxiety medication caused his thoughts to act so out of character. How frightening to go through that. Thank goodness his doctor monitored Drew closely. "Anything else you can think of? Like about that couch or chair you remembered?"

He glanced down at his hands that rested on the picnic table. "That chair...I feel like…" He turned his head to the side and stared off into the distance. "Wait. Now I know. After I'd gotten there, I felt a little dizzy. I'm sure now it was from the meds, although at the time, I didn't put that together. Because since then, I've had it happen again, and the nurse told me that was one of the symptoms."

We were getting somewhere now. Would Drew be able to remember what happened with Yolanda? "And what about the chair?"

"That's where her butler helped me to sit when I got lightheaded."

My heartbeat sped up. It was all coming together. "What happened with Yolanda's dog? Were you right that he was okay after getting antibiotics?"

"Yes, thankfully. When Penny called to check in a couple of days later, the dog was much better." Drew leveled his gaze on me. "Hey."

"What?"

"That all makes sense now. Why I kept associating Yolanda with death. It wasn't about her. It was her pet." He grabbed my hand and gave it a gentle squeeze. "Thank you, Seneca. I guess I just needed to talk that through. When I tried to reason it out by myself, my thoughts got tangled, and I couldn't make sense of it. But saying it out loud to a good listener helped so much."

"You're welcome. I don't think I did much, but I'm glad it helped." It'd certainly helped me understand, at least a little better, why Drew's personality had changed. And why he'd blurted that out about Yolanda when I'd been in his office.

His shoulders slumped. "I just now realized, I need to check in with Yolanda's butler, and make sure someone will be caring for the dog."

"You're a good, caring veterinarian, Drew. I know that for a fact, since you're so good with Winifred."

He smiled. "I appreciate that."

I returned his smile, relieved he'd figured out that his thoughts about Yolanda and death didn't have anything to do with the day of her murder.

Chapter Twenty-One

I was on my way to run some errands early the following evening when I noticed George headed toward Deli Delights. I really needed to speak to him, and this would be my first opportunity since seeing him with Tonda at the park. It'd been hard not to say something to Evie about finding those two together, but it wasn't my place to tell her. It was his.

I pulled my truck to the curb and got out. After waiting for traffic to pass, which was one whole car, I rushed to reach George when he stopped outside the deli.

"Hey." I tapped his shoulder.

He turned. "Hi. Why are you out of breath?"

I laughed. "Because I ran up the block to catch up to you."

He looked over my shoulder toward the sidewalk. "Well, thanks. Good to know somebody likes me enough to run after me."

I pointed toward the large window. "Going into Deli Delights?"

"That's my plan. I always take a break at lunch, but by the time we close the pharmacy, I'm famished again. And I'm not a great cook, so…" He shrugged.

"So you rely on the excellent food in Maple Junction's establishments to see you through."

"Exactly. Glad to know that doesn't sound strange on my part. I know a lot of people cook, but I'm not one of them."

"I only know this from my own experience."

He chuckled. "So I'm not the only one?"

"Definitely not. My grandmother was a wonderful cook, and so are my parents, but somehow I didn't inherit that gene." I wanted to add that Evie got the gene, but wasn't ready to bring her name into the conversation yet. There were things I wanted to discuss with him first.

He studied the specials posted on the outside of the door, then pointed toward it. "Are you headed in there too?"

"Yeah, I think I will. Like you, I wasn't looking forward to scrounging up something from my fridge at home, or my go-to when I'm nearly out of everything else, a peanut butter sandwich." I tilted my head toward the restaurant. "This sounds like a much better plan."

"Perfect." He held the door open for me, and we stepped inside. It was a good thing I was ready to eat here, because the delicious aromas coming from the kitchen nearly made my knees buckle.

We walked to the counter and ordered, then found a table near the back. It felt odd, not having Evie here while I shared a meal with her love interest. I couldn't imagine asking him the questions I needed to with Evie hearing them as well. If I didn't get the answers from George that I wanted, I wasn't sure what I'd say to Evie. I really hoped after George and I talked, things would be cleared up about his meeting with Tonda.

I grabbed a napkin from the table dispenser, unfolded it, and placed it on my lap. When the waitress brought our drinks, I was grateful to have something in my hand. It was either hold my drink or keep drumming my fingers on the table. And that would have been embarrassing for me and most likely annoying for George.

I took a long sip of my drink, placed the cup on the table, then wrapped my fingers around it. "Thanks for inviting me to eat with you, George. That was so thoughtful."

"No problem at all. Glad for the company. And to get reacquainted with you."

"Same here. I can't believe it's been since high school."

He ducked his head. "Yeah. And I feel terrible about that."

"You shouldn't, though. From what you told me earlier, it was your parents' decision to move. And your mom needed your help when she was sick, right? I doubt you had any choice in the matter, being under eighteen."

"Yeah, but..." He sighed. "I just wish..."

I reached over and quickly touched his arm. "It doesn't matter now. You're here, and I for one am glad."

His shoulders relaxed, as if he'd been a little uncomfortable talking about the past. "Thanks, Seneca."

I stirred my drink, then gave him my full attention. "George, I realize there's an elephant in the room right now."

His gaze met mine. "Yep, you're right. There is."

"If you're okay with it, I'd like to talk about that now."

His eyes widened. "Um, sure."

"First, I want you to know that I don't suspect you in Yolanda's murder."

He let out a breath. "Good. I know I haven't talked about it much, even though I was the one who was found standing there, but it's always on my mind, you know? I've even had dreams about Yolanda. About finding her there." He pointed toward the floor, as if seeing her at the reception area, lying motionless, her face covered with a pillow.

"I can only imagine." I glanced around the room, trying to formulate the words to ask the questions I needed answers to. Even though I'd brought up Yolanda's death, and he'd readily replied, the next part might make him, and me, a little uncomfortable, depending on his answers.

George leaned closer. "Is there something else you want to say? It's okay. With the stress I've been under because of Yolanda, let's just say it might help me to get it out. I know I used to live here, but that was a long time ago. And except for you, Evie, Cody, and some of our other high school classmates, there aren't people I know well enough to confide in."

I gave him my undivided attention.

"People who didn't know me before, or at least not well, are giving me stares when I'm around them, or whispering behind their hands about it. It makes me feel unwelcome. At least by some of them. I guess I can't really blame them if they don't know me. I mean, I was found standing there holding that…" He held out his hand, as if still clutching that pillow. "But it makes me not want to be around people." He focused on me. "And that's tough since I work with the public, you know?"

"I get it. I really do. I've been in the situation where people talked about me." I thought of how people still were when it came to Cody. "Being in that position is uncomfortable, at best. I feel for you. Especially since you just got back to town." I peered down at the table, hoping this next part would come out as I intended. "As for saying something else. Okay, here it is. It's not something I want to say, but something I need to ask. More than one thing."

He took a deep breath, then let it out. "Go ahead."

"All right. The first thing is, I saw you with Tonda the other day. I was at the park."

His face reddened. "You did? Oh, yeah. I was… We were talking."

"I don't want to get into all your business, but since you and Evie seem to have reconnected, and are getting close again, it bothered me that you and Tonda seemed…" I held up my hands, palms up.

His eyebrows shot up to his hairline. "No. Definitely not like that with Tonda. Not at all. I hope you believe me. I care so much for Evie. I'd never do anything to purposefully hurt her. She's the best person I know."

"Glad to hear that. It would do me in if her heart were broken again. Can you elaborate about Tonda? See, Evie and I are like sisters…"

"I remember."

"…and we tell each other everything. It's been so hard knowing what I saw and not being able to tell her. She really likes you, George. I'm not sure I can convey how deep her feelings for you have always been. And I don't want her to get hurt again. She's been through a lot."

George's mouth dropped open. "Oh no. When I met with Tonda, I didn't even think…" He rubbed his hand through his hair. "I won't go into detail, but Tonda needed to see me about a medical matter. That's the only reason I would have met with her in private like that. Believe me, it's not something I would ordinarily do."

I sat up straighter. "Oh. I hope she's all right."

"She's fine. Just had a question about a family member's prescription. Some concerns. I can't go into details for privacy reasons, but honestly, it was nothing. I mean, there was nothing between the two of us, other than that."

CHAPTER TWENTY-ONE

I released a breath. "Glad to hear she's okay. Thanks for telling me that."

The waitress delivered our food. When she'd made sure we didn't need anything else, she returned to the order counter.

George watched her leave, then he gave me the side-eye. "Uh, when you were there, at the park. Did you happen to notice anything else?"

I took a bite of one of my fries, then wiped my hands with my napkin. "As a matter of fact, I did."

He stared at me, lips slightly parted, waiting for what I would say next.

"I saw Tonda throw something into the stream."

"You did?" His hand flexed as if he was nervous.

"You don't need to tell me what it was."

"I don't?" He looked relieved. Like he was off the hook for having to tattle on Tonda.

I ate another fry. "No, because I already know what it was. I retrieved it from the stream.

He blinked. "You did? Tonda thought… Uh, she'd assumed the water would carry it away. And that she wouldn't be bothered by having it around anymore."

"She should have checked closer, because it snagged on a rock. I know it has something to do with Yolanda. That it probably belonged to her. That's why I went down and got it. Of course, under normal circumstances. I wouldn't have bothered. I mean, it has nothing to do with me."

"You're also right that it has to do with Yolanda. And I guess I should thank you for trying to find out more about how Yolanda died. Since so many people think I'm guilty. Every clue you find will only help exonerate me."

"I want what's best for everyone. And when you're proven innocent, that's all the better for Evie." I took a sip of my drink. "I also heard Tonda say a few words when she seemed visibly upset. It was disjointed, but I heard a little bit. About her uncle, Yolanda, and her grandmother?"

He closed his eyes for a second. "I guess it's not a secret since you overheard Tonda. And found the locket." His shoulders lifted in a shrug. "All right, since you already know most of the story, I might as well tell you the rest. Tonda wanted to get rid of the necklace. She did that so her grandmother wouldn't ever have to see it again. It was too upsetting."

I waited while George took a bite of his sandwich and set it back on the plate, before asking, "Why would something of Yolanda's upset Tonda's grandmother?"

"Because Tonda's uncle had an affair. With Yolanda. And that caused a major rift in Tonda's family. She used to be very close to her uncle."

My heart lurched. "That's so sad. She must feel awful. And I can see how it would affect their whole family. That'd be hard to overlook."

"Yeah. And the worst part is that Tonda's aunt had a heart condition. When her husband had that affair with Yolanda and split up his marriage, Tonda's aunt had a massive heart attack and passed away."

Shock rolled through me. "Poor Tonda. And her whole family. What a tragedy."

"I know. I feel terrible for her." He leveled his gaze on me. "Seneca, what are you going to do with the locket?"

"Don't worry. I'm not going to parade it around and show everyone. But with some other things I've heard about Tonda recently, when I saw her toss it into the water, I wanted to see what it was. Whether it was something that could clear her of having done something to Yolanda, or..."

"Or prove she'd murdered her?"

"Right. Even though I don't want to believe that of her." As for the locket, I'd give it to Cody. If it turned out that Tonda was the killer, he'd want that for evidence. And since Tonda had thrown it away, I seriously doubted she'd want it back.

George clasped his hands together on the table. "I don't know Tonda all that well. Just to discuss her family's health issue. But I do want the guilty person to be found. Just like you do."

"Thanks, George. I think it's going to take all of us to find the person responsible for Yolanda's murder."

"And I have a special interest in finding that person."

"I know you do. I'm so sorry you're going through this, having just got to town and all. I'm sure it makes being with people and trying to do your job more difficult."

"You're right. But I appreciate you coming to me like this. And bringing things out into the open. Thanks. It helps to have good friends in my corner."

I smiled. "You definitely have that."

"So, I hope that answered your question about me and Tonda."

"Yes, it does, but…"

He tilted his head. "Was there something else you wanted to ask me?"

"I'm afraid so."

"Go ahead and ask. I'd rather talk about it than have you, and possibly others, thinking things about me that aren't true."

I swallowed hard. "Okay. Here goes. It's something I've heard. About you. We started to talk about it the day I was in the pharmacy, but a customer came in, so I left."

"I remember." He stirred his drink, but didn't take a sip. "Unfortunately, there is something that's been said about me. Not here, but where I used to live. I knew it'd come up again, but was hoping I'd get more established in town here before having to talk about it. It followed me here, faster than I would have imagined."

"I'm sorry. Whatever it is seems to be very upsetting for you."

"It is, but the things that happened didn't have anything to do with me."

"Okay."

"See, I was accused of…it all sounds so ridiculous to say it out loud. But a woman was shoved into oncoming traffic, and some people accused me of doing it."

I sat forward. "What? But why?"

"Because the man who did it looks a lot like me. I've seen him, so I know it's true, not just another person pointing it out."

"That's terrible. What happened with the woman? Was she okay?"

"Thankfully, yes. She was banged up a little from landing in the street and very scared, as you can imagine. But the car closest to her was able to stop before hitting her."

"Thank goodness." I pressed my hand to my chest.

George wiped his brow. "The guy, who really does look enough like me to be my brother, happened to be one of those medical professionals who worked in a nursing home. He thought it was kinder to kill elderly people rather than let them live and possibly suffer later on."

I gasped.

"It was a big reason why I wanted to move away from there. I couldn't take it anymore when people would do a double-take when they saw me. Especially when I was at work. The owner of the pharmacy was beginning to question whether I was really the right person for the job, after a few customers asked about me." He pressed against the back of his chair and crossed his arms over his chest. "When I got the invitation from Devan to be a groomsman for his wedding and to come for a short visit to see family, it seemed like a perfect opportunity to come back here and check out job possibilities."

I patted his arm. "How awful. I've had people talk about me, but I can only imagine what you went through."

"It wasn't the way I wanted to leave the other place." He gave me a hesitant smile. "But I'm grateful for friends like you, Seneca. I truly mean that."

I leaned forward. "And I'm so glad you came back. Especially for Evie."

His face turned pink. "Me too."

We finished our meal, talking about pleasanter things than murder, gossip, and mistrust. As I left the restaurant, I felt lighter. And better about Evie seeing him. At least I knew he and Tonda weren't romantically involved. And, even though I'd known George in school, I felt that, after he'd opened up to me, I knew him better, and could count him a good friend.

It also gave me more insight into Tonda and about the locket. But I still considered her a possible suspect for Yolanda's murder. At least until I found out more.

Chapter Twenty-Two

The next day, I was in my greenhouse when there was a knock on the door. It wasn't Edward's nearly silent one, so I knew it wasn't him. Besides, he wasn't due to be here for another two hours since he was scheduled to work at the vet's office this morning.

I hurried to the entrance. Through the screen I could see Liza. She'd never come here before, even when she'd stopped in just across the parking area at Painted Wings.

Opening the door, I smiled. "Hi, Liza. How are you?"

She tilted her hand back and forth in the not sure motion. "Good and bad, I guess."

"Want to come in?"

"Sure. I've never seen inside here before."

"Well, I think it's amazing in here with the caterpillars, but not everyone sees it that way."

Her eyes widened when she stepped into the small building. "Wow."

"Really?"

"Very cool. Can I look closer?" She pointed to the nearest pen with the cocoons hanging side by side from milkweed stalks I'd harvested from my field.

"Of course." I waved her over.

"So these little creatures here"—she tilted her head toward the pen—"will someday become those gorgeous monarch butterflies?"

"Great, huh?"

"It really is."

I watched her as she admired the caterpillars in their pens. "Liza, when you came in, you said there were good and bad things. Did you want to talk about them?"

"Yeah. I would. And, sorry about Payne disrupting us the other day. I was hoping he'd stay out a bit later."

"Trust me. I'm used to him. No need to apologize."

Her lips curved up. "But I won't have to deal with him much longer."

"Did you find another job?"

"I sure did." Her face lit up.

"Where? Or would you rather not say, since you're still at the law office for now?"

"I can tell you. I've seen how you are with people, how you've been with me, and that you can keep things to yourself."

"Ah, thanks. I mean, I try to do that. So where's your new job?"

"Starting in two weeks, I'll be working at the bank. I'm so excited for this change."

"Wonderful. What will your job be?"

"They were going to start me out as a teller. That would have been okay. But when we had the interview, and they saw the experience I have working with records, working with clients, and my background in college with a math minor, they decided to promote me to a loan officer before I even started."

I grinned. "That's awesome. I'm so happy for you."

"Thanks. I'm happy about it too. I can't wait to get started. Karen Blaine will be my boss, and I really like her."

"I do too. She's a nice woman." I wouldn't tell Liza that Karen could be dramatic and temperamental, but she'd find that out on her own. Karen, though, was a good person, and the bank's reputation and customer satisfaction had increased since she'd taken over.

Liza crossed her arms over her chest. "Now that you've heard the good news, I'll share the bad."

I glanced at the corner where I had a small table with two chairs for when I took breaks or somebody, usually Cody or Evie, stopped in for a bit. "Want to sit down? I can get us some soft drinks from my mini fridge."

Even though Painted Wings was a short trek across the lot and I could, and did, stop in there daily for a snack and my drink, I liked to have some here where I worked. When I visited the café, people stopped me and wanted to talk. That was good, but sometimes I was in a hurry and didn't want to take the time to chat.

"A drink would be great."

I asked her for her preference of soft drink and met her at the table with a can and glass filled with ice for each of us.

Once we were seated, we enjoyed our drinks before Liza set hers to one side. "I'm glad you came in the other day. I'd been wanting to talk to you anyway."

"You have?" It surprised me since we'd never been that close. And since I tried to avoid Payne's office unless necessary, I didn't run into Liza much.

"About Payne. At first, I thought maybe I was the problem when trying to deal with him, and I knew, of course, you had lots of experience with him. I just didn't want to cause you undue stress having to relive any painful moments with your ex while listening to me."

I waved my hand. "Don't worry about me. I'm fine. I'm just sorry you're having trouble with him. And just so you know, it's not you who's the problem. It's him."

She took a sip of her drink. "I finally came to that conclusion on my own. But I appreciate you saying that. It just reinforces it for me. And makes me feel a little better about leaving. I feel sorry for whoever he gets in there to replace me. But I hope he or she will be made of stronger stuff to be able to deal with him."

"Was Payne the bad part of what you wanted to tell me about?" I braced myself to listen to her tales about him. I was happy to help her out, but not actually looking forward to the subject matter.

"Not exactly. When you were in the office, I'd started to tell you about Yolanda Steele."

I sat forward, all ears. "Go on."

"This goes way back to before I was born. You see, Yolanda was a college classmate of my mother's at the University of Indianapolis."

"Amazing that they knew each other back then."

"I know. Since Yolanda wasn't from here."

"Were they friends all these years later?"

She glanced down. "Not exactly."

"Oh, okay. Did your mom know Yolanda's husband before then, too?"

"Yes, but according to her, they weren't close. But you know how it is, small town…"

"Believe me, I do know. Hard to keep private. Everyone finds out a person's business. So, Yolanda and your mom weren't friends anymore, right?"

Liza's eyes narrowed. "No, the opposite. They couldn't stand each other."

"What happened for them to feel that way?"

"Yolanda happened." Liza's mouth turned down at the corners. "And this was back when they were still in college."

"What was the problem she had with your mother?"

"It was more to do with my dad. Mom just got caught in the middle."

I thought for a second. "Something romantic?"

"That's it exactly. Yolanda wanted my dad, but he'd already fallen hard for my mom. Even so, Yolanda decided she would have Dad for her boyfriend, and made my mom's life miserable. They were both in the same sorority, so close quarters."

"They probably saw each other daily, then."

"Right. Meals, parties. And just about everything else. When they weren't in class or at another function, they were all at the sorority house. I can only imagine the forced closeness, especially in cold weather when no one wanted to get out much. And even worse, Yolanda's room was right across the hall from Mom's, and they had to share a bathroom."

I blew out a breath. "Your poor mother. That sounds truly awful."

"From what she told me, it was. Mom tried to switch to a different sorority, but that didn't work out. And when she applied to change to a regular dorm room, they were full up. But she kept seeing Dad, sneaking out of the sorority house to do it."

I leaned forward, not wanting to miss anything she said. "So what happened once Yolanda figured out her plan wasn't going to work?" I pointed to Liza. "Because obviously, your parents ended up together."

A smile appeared on her face. "They were so happy together. In love. But also best friends, too."

"You said were. Are they…"

"They stayed together until they died. Just last year, in fact."

"I'm so sorry to hear that."

"Thank you."

"Apparently, Yolanda gave up. Your parents ended up together, and she married another man. Do you think she was happy with her husband?"

"The only thing I know is, she kept after my dad until the very day my parents got married. She met her future husband, Nathan Steele, right at the end of their senior year. They only dated a couple of months before getting married, too."

"That must have been awful in college, with your parents having to go through that just to be together. And I'm sorry you don't have them here with you now." I thought of Gram every single day. I couldn't imagine Liza having lost both of her parents at a relatively young age.

"It's been rough, but at least Yolanda had stayed holed up in her house on the hill, and I didn't have to see her or speak to her. Until recently." Her lips pressed tightly together.

I sat forward at Liza's change in tone. "You had to see her recently?"

"Unfortunately. Since Payne is the only attorney in town now, she needed him to draw up some papers, and I had to deliver them to her afterward."

"Right, she would've used Payne as her attorney, since the other lawyer was murdered."

Liza edged to her left, taking in the greenhouse. "It happened in here, didn't it?"

"It sure did. The other man was my lawyer. So now, if I ever need something, I have to go through Payne. Which, of course, you know, since you work for him."

She shifted in her chair. "I felt so bad for you when all that went on. Finding your lawyer's body. And then having to see your ex in an official capacity."

"I'll admit it wasn't an easy time. I'm glad it's in the past." A sound came from beneath me, then a soft paw poked at my leg. I leaned to one side to peer under my chair. "Hey, Winifred."

Liza pointed to her. "Aww, your cat."

"She likes to spend time with me in here."

"Is it all right if I pet her?"

How to answer that? "Um, you're welcome to try. She's very moody. So don't take it personally if she backs away."

"Sure. I grew up with cats. I know how that works."

I smiled. "Good."

Liza held out her hand, slowly, toward my cat, who was still sitting under my seat. "Hey, Winifred. How are you?"

Winifred let out a haughty sniff and turned her head away.

Liza angled down a little more. "Look at that amazing butterfly costume. Aren't you just the prettiest cat who ever lived?"

That did it. Winifred gave Liza a slow blink, then sauntered over to her outstretched hand. When she reached her, Winifred gently rubbed her cheek against Liza's wiggling fingers.

No hissing. Or growling. Wonderful. Winifred allowed Liza to pet her for another minute, then moved away. My cat ambled across the greenhouse, found a bright sunbeam on the floor, and began to bathe her paws, as her eyelids drooped in the warmth. For being a good kitty, Winifred would get extra treats later, even though she might not remember why she was getting them. But it would make me feel better to reward her.

Liza looked at me. "Thanks. I needed that today."

"I'm glad she was in a good mood. And that it helped you, too." I tilted my head. "Was there any more to what happened with Yolanda and your family?"

"Yes, there is. I…" Liza glanced toward Winifred and gave a faint smile.

"You don't have to tell me if you'd rather not. But I'm glad to listen if you want to."

"No, I want to. I need to. If it's all right with you."

"Sure."

"Years later, Yolanda was on the committee to welcome new students to the University of Indianapolis. The same one I attended. She must have seen my name on a list or something."

"What did she do?"

Liza drummed her fingers on the table. "Things went fine for a while. I took my classes and got good grades. And I loved being there, not only because it would put me on the path to eventually head to law school, but also because it was where my parents went, and met, leading to them getting married right after graduation."

"I can see why you wanted to go there. You had family history. But you said they were fine for a while. What happened?"

Liza closed her eyes briefly, as if wanting to drive away the bad memories. "Since Yolanda knew I was going there, she set out to torment me like she had my mother. It seemed her hatred of my mom filtered down to me, as their child."

"She did that to you? That's terrible. And seems way over the top after all those years. Yolanda still wanted to be with your dad?"

"I don't know about that. But she sure hadn't lost her hatred of my family."

"I'm so sorry, Liza. She must have been a very difficult person to deal with."

"That's putting it nicely. Which I won't do when it comes to her. That woman was a black-hearted witch. And I hated her." Her fingernails scraped against the tabletop as her hand closed into a fist. Liza's face had gone a deep red, and her eyes had narrowed.

I gasped at Liza's reaction. Not that she didn't have reason to be upset, angry, and hurt by the older woman's treatment of her and her parents, but I'd never heard Liza speak like that before. About anyone.

"You see, that horrible woman took away my whole future. All my dreams. Everything I'd planned and hoped for."

"How did she do that?"

"Yolanda lied. To everyone. About me. She told my professors that I cheated on all my work and exams. And that I'd stolen from the foundation's money that was supposed to help students with the cost of their classes. Then…the very worst thing…"

I pressed my palms against the table top, bracing myself for whatever would come next.

"Yolanda announced, in front of a huge group of people, that I didn't deserve to even be a student there because I'd killed my former roommate."

"What?" My eyes opened wide. I couldn't seem to blink. "Your roommate?"

"Yes, she died while we lived together. It was so awful." She pressed her fingers over her closed eyes.

"Yolanda did all of that to you? Just because of who your mother was?"

She lowered her hands to her lap. "That's right. She did. I wanted Yolanda to die. Even more than I needed my next breath. It was the only way I'd ever get any peace or relief from all I've been through."

I held in a gasp. Liza hated Yolanda more than I could have imagined.

"And to top it off, every year on my birthday, and then randomly throughout the year, I receive a card from someone… The messages taunted me."

"What did they say?"

"Usually, reminding me how I was never going to amount to anything. How, because of my mother, I'd be destined to be a failure my whole life." She swallowed hard. "Every time it seemed like I was getting on a better track in my life, I received another card or message from the same person. It's like they were keeping an eye on me. The handwriting was always the same, just never signed. But I knew."

"You knew?"

"They were from her. From Yolanda. I know it in my heart." She tapped her chest.

"Did you ever show the messages to anyone? The police? That would be considered harassment, wouldn't it?"

She sliced her hand through the air. "No. I burned them. Every last one. I just wanted it all to go away."

"That must have been terrible."

"It was. I'm just glad she's gone now." Liza glanced away. "At least I won't have to endure that anymore."

I reached out and touched her hand briefly. "It was unthinkable for Yolanda to use your roommate's death to make things even harder for you. She would've been a very young woman. How was she killed?"

Liza's gaze lowered to the floor. "Believe it or not, she was…smothered. With my pillow."

I opened my mouth to respond, but just then, Liza's phone rang inside her purse. She reached down to get it, saw who was calling, and groaned. "It's Payne. I'll let it go to voicemail."

"Aren't you off today? Why would he be calling?"

"I only took a half day off. I'm not due to go in for another hour, but that doesn't always stop him from bothering me." She stuffed her phone back into her purse, then stood. "I'd better go, Seneca. But thank you so much for taking the time to listen to me vent. It really means a lot to me." She came around to my side of the table, surprising me with a hug. "I'll see you later, okay?"

"Yes. Sure. Good luck with your new job at the bank. I hope you love it."

"Thanks. I really think I will." She walked toward the door, then left the greenhouse.

My mind swam with all the information she'd supplied me with. Most of it terrible. I really did hope she'd love her new job. Without Payne as her boss, it had to be better, didn't it?

But as I watched her through the window as she got into her car, then drove down the gravel drive to leave the farm, there was only one thought that ran through my mind.

Had Liza hated Yolanda enough to have suffocated her with a pillow? And had Yolanda been her only victim, or had the roommate been the first one?

Chapter Twenty-Three

I left my house after giving Winifred her lunch. As I walked toward Painted Wings to see if Evie and Murray needed anything, someone drove up the gravel drive toward me. It was Cody.

He got out of his car and ambled over in his familiar loose-limbed gait. I never got tired of seeing him, but I couldn't really say that to him without him knowing how much I cared. And if his feelings didn't match mine, it could end up making our relationship rocky.

"Hey." I waved.

"Hey, yourself. Everything going okay?" He pointed to the café, but I knew he meant with me, my life, things in general.

I glanced around, making sure no café customers were wandering around. Sometimes they'd hang out around the low stone wall that surrounded the front of Painted Wings to enjoy sitting in the sun.

Just like Winifred did.

I placed my hand on my hip. "Actually, there's something I'd like you to check into for me, if you don't mind."

"When have I ever minded doing anything for you, Seneca?"

It was true. Cody was amazing.

"So, what'cha got for me?" He crossed his arms over his chest, all business now.

"I spoke with Liza again and…"

His eyebrows lowered. "Did you have to go to Payne's office again to do that?"

"No." Cody was super protective of me, but especially when it came to

Payne. He knew the history of my marriage and how Payne had treated me.

His arms relaxed at his sides. "Good. The less we can see of him, the better."

"Preachin' to the choir." I held up my hand.

"I know. Okay, so you talked to Liza again?"

"Yep. She came to see me this time. That girl has a whole history I never knew about."

"Even though Maple Junction is small and people seem to know all about each other, surprises do come up occasionally."

"Well, this one is a doozy." I told Cody about Liza, her and her parents' unfortunate background with Yolanda. And then the kicker, that Liza's roommate had been murdered the same way Yolanda had been.

Cody rubbed his chin. "That's quite a coincidence. What was the outcome of the roommate's death?"

"Yolanda spread it around that Liza had done the deed and…" I frowned. "Liza didn't say who'd done it. Or that she hadn't been guilty."

"But she didn't spend time in jail, did she? I assume there was an investigation."

"She didn't give any information about that. Just mostly talked about how horrible Yolanda had been to her mother, and then to her later on."

He reached out and tapped my shoulder lightly. "All right, kid, I'll check it all out and get back to you."

Kid? Is that how he saw me? He and I joked around all the time and called each other funny names, but for some reason, this time it felt different. "Um, thanks, Cody."

"No problem." His phone pinged, and he glanced at the message. "Ugh. Forgot a meeting with the Mayor. Gotta go. I'll let you know what I find out."

I waved, then hurried into the café. Hopefully, it was a calm day, and I wouldn't need to stay long. I needed to check on the monarchs in the milkweed fields.

But when I opened the café door, I knew the monarchs would have to wait a bit.

The place was packed. And a few people were standing near the entrance, gazing around the café, wearing hopeful expressions as they searched for seating.

Evie saw me, gave a grateful grin, and waved me over.

I hurried to the recently vacated table and helped her to clear it while we talked.

"Seneca, I'm so glad you stopped in. I don't know what got into people today, but I think half the town came in at the same time."

I looked around. "I think you're right. Anything interesting going on? You and I need to catch each other up on information about the… You know." I gave her a quick, whispered rundown of Liza while we worked.

Evie sprayed cleaner on the tabletop and wiped it down, while I checked to make sure the chairs were clean and that there wasn't spilled food on the floor. "Devan was just in here to pick up an order."

I stared at her. "He was alone? Where was Kinley?" Being newlyweds, I couldn't imagine them being apart for long.

She dried off the table with a paper towel. "I think he said something about leaving her at her dad's house while he picked up their food. He was in a hurry, so didn't stay long to talk."

"Since they just got married, I'm surprised she let him leave without her."

Evie rolled her eyes. "According to Devan, this is the first time they've left the bedroom since the wedding."

"More information than you needed?"

"Definitely. Mental images I didn't ask for. Anyway, I asked Devan if their parents had recovered from all the wedding and reception activity. All the planning and everything. I know from helping serve at weddings how much work it is. And I'm not even involved as a family member."

"I bet their parents are exhausted. What did Devan say?"

Evie tossed the disposables into the trash receptacle, then grabbed some paper towels and the bottle of cleaner for another vacated table. "Devan was upset when he found out about Kinley's dad, that he'd lost his job."

I reached out for a paper towel to help her wipe down the table after she'd sprayed it. "I bet he was. I know how I'd feel if that had happened to one of my parents."

"Especially with the wedding. That's a big expense. Devan had said something to Kinley about waiting to get married for that reason, but she'd thrown a fit, threatening to end their relationship and never speak to him again, so he gave in."

"I can only imagine how disappointed Kinley might have been if they'd planned on getting married when it sounded like it might not happen. But to say she'd end their relationship sounds a little over the top. I bet that hurt his feelings, that she'd break up with him because she didn't get the wedding date she wanted."

"Yeah, I thought the same thing, but didn't mention that to him." Evie collected the used paper towels and spray bottle.

"Probably wise on your part. Did he say anything else?" I knew there must be something, since Evie had seemed frantic that she speak to me before I left the café. Usually, when she was that swamped, I helped her out, then we just exchanged quick waves and texted each other later.

"Yes, he did. He mentioned her dad's pension. How Wiley wasn't going to get it now, since Yolanda had decided her employees weren't worth it. And had stripped them of all their benefits that they'd had since signing on with the company."

I pushed one of the chairs further under the table so no one would trip over its leg. "I did hear something about that. How awful. I can't imagine how worried Kinley's parents must be about money right now."

"Right. It was going to be their retirement fund. He and his wife had made plans for it, had everything mapped out so they could afford to do the things they'd always dreamed of someday. They were planning to retire in a few years, but now won't be able to."

"You know, that might make a person angry enough to do something about it."

Evie had turned toward the trashcan, but stopped suddenly. She turned and stared at me. "Go on."

"Like, maybe if Yolanda's nephew, who's in charge of the company since she's dead, might be a different sort of business owner, and treat his employees right. Then it would be in Wiley's best interest if Yolanda were out of the picture. Forever."

"You might have something there." She waved at someone behind me, then said, "There was also something else."

"Okay."

"Devan said he and Kinley are also worried about her parents."

"In a way, besides their retirement? Because that's bad enough."

"Yeah. Their marriage is on thin ice."

"Oh no. What if they split up? That would mar Devan and Kinley's memories of their wedding." I leaned closer. "But not nearly as much as the murder during the reception."

"You're right about that." Evie's eyebrows lowered. "Hey, are you okay? Kind of spaced out on me there for a second."

"I'm all right. Just hate that all of this is happening to their family."

"I agree. I also heard that Kinley's mom blames her husband for losing his job with Yolanda's firm. She says maybe he didn't work hard enough all these years, and now, because of his laziness, they'll be homeless and starve to death."

I thought about Kinley throwing a fit about not getting married. Maybe she was too much like her mom—a drama queen. And that would make things more difficult for Devan. "Let's hope it doesn't come to that, to the Snares breaking up."

"Right. I wish there was something I could do to help them. That's a lot to go through all at once."

"The one thing we can do is to figure out who killed Yolanda. At least then, the guilty person will be arrested and put in jail."

Evie shoved a chair beneath the table. "I just hope it's not Wiley."

"Agreed. So, Yolanda's nephew?"

"What about him?"

"He might be the key to helping the Snares get back on track."

"True. What do you have in mind?"

I glanced at my watch. Maybe I could spare a little more time to check into things before doing my farmwork for the day. "I'm thinking a little chat with the nephew might be in order."

"That sounds like a good idea." Evie glanced over her shoulder at the long line at the order counter. Then she scanned the room. "All right, there are a few empty tables now that I can seat people at. Thank you so much for helping me out."

"No problem. Always here for you."

"I know. And thank you especially for finding out who the killer is, so George won't have this hanging over his head." Her face fell. "Or I won't have this worry hanging over me either."

I gave her a quick hug. "It will all work out. You'll see."

She forced a smile. "I sure do hope you're right." She waved a group of people over to the table we'd just cleaned, then another couple to the next table. She glanced over her shoulder at me. "Let me know how it goes."

"You got it." I was more determined than ever to clear George's name.

Chapter Twenty-Four

I drove to Steele Industries, marveling as I always had when driving past, at its vastness. The building was ornate, and huge. Even the parking lot looked to be enough to hold vehicles for the entire town.

After finding a spot halfway from the entrance, I parked, grabbed my purse, and trekked the considerable distance to the main entrance. Once there, a receptionist, appearing formidable in her dark gray business suit and glasses perched on the end of her nose, asked if I had an appointment. I fudged a little, indicating I did.

She couldn't find me in the appointment book, but I sort of, kind of, said I was a friend of Yolanda's nephew, Tyrone Steele. But when she got a phone call that distracted her, I zipped toward the elevator that took me to the seventh floor.

Convenient signs with arrows led me to Tyrone's office. The door was open, so I stepped in. The receptionist who was on the phone glanced up at me, but didn't make any motions to indicate I should approach her desk.

I hoped she wasn't talking to the main receptionist downstairs about me sneaking up here. Would they call the authorities?

Wouldn't that be just great, for Cody to get a call to come and haul me off the premises?

The woman ended her call. "Yes, may I help you?"

A glance at a closed door had a plaque with Tyrone's name. "Hello. I'm Seneca James." I pointed toward the door. "I've come to speak to Mr. Steele. Is he in today?"

Her left eyebrow rose. "Indeed, he is. Do you have an appointment, Miss

James?"

The way she eyed me told me she already had the answer.

"Um, I…"

The door to his office opened and he stepped out. When he glanced up at me, his brow furrowed. Then, his face brightened. "Oh, hello."

Did he know me? "Um, hi."

He walked to stand beside the receptionist's desk. "Nan, this is Seneca…" He looked at me, his eyebrows raised.

"James, "I supplied.

"Yes, Seneca James. Remember when I told you about the butterfly release at Kinley and Devan's wedding? Miss James is the one who raised the butterflies."

"Oh." Nan seemed less than impressed. "Sir, Miss James doesn't have an appointment with you."

He waved his hand. "It's not a problem. Please." He motioned me toward his now open door. "Come in."

"Thanks." As I passed by the receptionist's desk, I heard her muttering. Maybe she didn't like being usurped by a commoner who had nothing to do with Steele Industries.

I ignored her the best I could and quickened my steps to reach Tyrone's office.

"Please, sit down." He indicated a row of three comfortable looking chairs which sat facing the front of his desk.

I chose the middle seat. "Thanks for seeing me today."

"I was so impressed by the monarch release at the wedding. But I'm guessing that's not why you're here."

"No, it isn't. First, I wanted to offer my condolences for the death of your aunt."

"I appreciate that, Miss James."

"Seneca, please."

"Seneca. Call me Tyrone. Yes, it's been a sad, tumultuous time, I can assure you, losing my aunt in such a horrible way, and at a wedding of all things."

"I can't even imagine how you must be feeling."

"It's been rough. Also, taking over the company like this. I never dreamed it would happen so fast. And so tragically."

I was glad he brought up overseeing the company, so I didn't have to. "I'm sure you're overwhelmed with new responsibilities now."

"That's true. It's a change, that's for sure. We'd planned that I would take over in the future. But not like this."

"I feel bad that you have to deal with all of this. Also, well, I'm a friend of Devan's. And by extension, Wiley." I wouldn't go into detail that I barely knew Wiley, but Tyrone didn't need to know that.

"Ah, yes. That whole scenario has been painful. Wiley's termination wasn't my doing. That was my aunt's decision. He's a close friend of mine."

"I'm sure it's still been difficult for you, even though you hadn't been the one to let him go."

"It has."

I clutched my hands together in my lap, hoping this next part would come out all right when I said it. "Having heard from Devan recently,"—I wouldn't add that it was Evie who'd talked to him—"he and Kinley were upset when their dad lost not only his job, but apparently, his pension and benefits." I held my breath, hoping Tyrone wouldn't get upset at my boldness in talking about it.

He took a deep breath, then let it out. "That's bothered me so much since Aunt Yolanda did that. But there was nothing I could do to stop her."

It seemed Tyrone wasn't going to toss me from his office for prying into his business, so I took it as a sign to continue. "That's awful. But now, you're in charge of the company?"

"That's right. I am." He held up his hand. "It will take a while, but after I have things up and running again, I fully intend to reinstate not only Wiley's position, but all of his benefits too."

"I'm sure that will make him very happy."

"It's the least I can do. I loved my aunt, of course, but didn't always think her methods were the best."

"I can honestly say that I didn't know her. My grandmother did, but since Yolanda didn't seem to make appearances in town much by the time I came along, I didn't have much of a chance."

"That's my aunt for you. It surprised me she even wanted to attend the wedding, until I discovered that she'd always had a soft spot for Kinley."

"Really?"

"Apparently, Kinley used to be in the office with her dad sometimes. Yolanda took a liking to Kinley when she was little. That's why it hurt even more when she fired Wiley."

Poor Wiley, and Kinley. It had to be painful for both of them. "But I assume Kinley and Devan invited Yolanda to their wedding?" Hopefully she didn't just show up. Although from what I'd heard about her, she was capable of almost anything.

"They did send her an invitation. Kinley had always looked up to Yolanda. But that was right before my aunt fired Wiley. I guess Yolanda thought it would still be all right to attend the ceremony, even though she'd caused major heartache for their family." His eyebrows lowered. "I never did understand my aunt's logic on anything."

I brushed some hair away from my forehead, my dark curls always having a mind of their own. "Even though she didn't come to town much, it sounds like she was active at the plant?"

"In a way. She didn't want anything to do with what she referred to as menial work, but had no problem telling people what to do and making major decisions on everyone else's behalf."

"But wasn't Yolanda the company owner, since your uncle passed away?"

"Yes, she was. But Yolanda, though a very intelligent woman, had no business training at all. When Uncle Nathan died, it shocked me that she wanted to be involved in any way since she seemed to find it all so demeaning."

"Demeaning?"

"A factory wasn't her idea of elegance. But when she fell in love with Uncle Nathan, then married him, her life was set. She never had to worry about money again."

I thought of her fancy, frilly outfit at the wedding and the enormous, expensive looking rings. Plus, at least from the outside, the appearance of her ostentatious house.

Tyrone shook his head. "That lady loved money. The more the better. It's why she didn't want to pay her employees what they were worth, and took away their insurance and pensions. It made me sick when she announced she was going to do that, but it wasn't up to me. I knew from experience that when she set her mind on something, you might as well accept it."

"I feel so bad for Wiley, going through financial strain, especially when his daughter just got married."

"He's a nice guy. We've been friends for a long time."

"I saw recently where he works now. It's quite a bit different from Steele Industries."

He leaned back in his chair. "Yes, it is. Shocking that it was the only job he could find. At least on short notice. As you can imagine, I hadn't planned on taking over the reins of this company quite so soon. But"—he held up his index finger—"I fully plan to hire back Wiley, as well as other employees my aunt so thoughtlessly tossed away as soon as I can. It appalls me the way my aunt treated those poor people."

The door to the outer office opened with a squeak. It was then I realized I hadn't shut the door behind me when I'd entered Tyrone's office. I thought of the snooty receptionist sitting out there. How much would she have heard from our conversation?

It was time for me to leave, if another person was here to see Tyrone. As I was about to say something more to him, a loud voice stopped me. I whipped around, shocked to get a glimpse of Marla as she headed toward the receptionist's desk, fists clenched and body quivering as if at any moment she might burst.

Jumping up from his desk, Tyrone rushed past me and into the outer office. "What's going on here?"

Marla narrowed her eyes. "Ah, just the one I need to see."

Tyrone took a deep breath and let it out. Trying to calm himself? "What can I do for you, Marla?"

"You can pay me what you owe me." She put her hands on her hips.

"Excuse me? Why would I owe you anything?"

I crept closer to the open doorway, but stayed partially out of sight. So far, it seemed Marla hadn't spotted me yet.

She took a step closer to him. "Since you now own this company, and are in charge, from what I hear, you're the one who needs to shell out some cash."

"Listen." He tapped his foot in a rapid beat on the hardwood floor. "I'm not sure what this is all about, and frankly, I have a lot to do. Because yes, since my aunt died, I'm now in charge, as you put it. I've had a lot put on my plate in a very short time. So if you'll excuse me?" He held out his hand toward the main door, a suggestion more than a request.

A crease formed on Marla's forehead. "No, I won't leave until I get what's rightfully mine."

Tyrone glanced at his receptionist, who still wore a startled expression ever since Marla barged in. "Nan, why don't you take a break for a little bit, okay? I'll take care of this." He made it sound as if getting rid of Marla would be like taking out the trash. Not that it was a nice comparison, but I could see why he'd be upset with her bursting into his office and making demands.

Nan rose quickly, grabbed her purse from a bottom drawer, and edged past Marla as if she feared Marla might do something to harm her. Apparently, she was only snooty to non-violent visitors.

Once she'd left, Tyrone crossed his arms. "All right, Marla. Why don't you tell me, calmly, what this is all about."

"Sure, I'll tell you." She mirrored him by crossing her arms. Was she trying to appear intimidating? "Your aunt ordered flowers from the shop where I work every week. I delivered those to her every single time."

He dropped his arms to his sides. "Fine. I didn't know that. But what's it got to do with me?" He waved his hand around the room. "Do you see any flowers here?"

"Normally, her driver would run her errands." Marla huffed out a breath. "You did know that much, right?"

"Yes, I suppose so, although I didn't get into my aunt's personal business much. I still don't understand what it has to do with me."

"Then let me fill you in. Her wimpy driver happened to be allergic to flowers. All flowers. And refused to pick them up. That left me driving them to her every week, personally delivering them to her house, which took time away from the job I was supposed to be doing. And I didn't want to make the stupid deliveries in the first place."

Tyrone glanced at his watch. "Will this take much longer? I really have a lot to do." He peered over his shoulder. Had he remembered I was standing in his office and could hear every word they said? Or was he using me as an excuse to get rid of Marla? I hoped he wouldn't say my name and make me step out from my hiding spot.

"If you'd stop interrupting me, I'll finish." She narrowed her eyes. "So anyway, with all that driving, delivering, and often having to step inside the house while I waited on the maid to go fetch her employer, it took a lot of my time."

"But I still don't see—"

Marla stood up straight, her back stiff, and her hands formed into fists at her sides. "Then I'll state it very clearly for you. My problem is this. I never, not once, received a tip from your aunt."

Tyrone held his hands out to the sides as if to say, so what?

Marla glared at him. "I'm here today to collect back pay for all those times I should have gotten a tip from your aunt. And keep in mind, that with all her fortune, that woman should have been a very generous tipper."

He swore under his breath. "You're here because you didn't get a tip from another person? Marla, I don't have time for this."

"Pay me, or I'm not leaving."

Tyrone took a step toward her. "How about I call the sheriff to come and have a chat with you."

My eyes widened. I didn't want to be here if Cody showed up. He'd never let me hear the end of snooping again on my own.

There was silence, then Marla said, "Fine. I'll leave. But you haven't heard the last of me." She stomped out of the room.

I nearly wilted with relief, so glad Cody wouldn't catch me here, doing what he termed spying. I would've gotten another mini lecture from him.

When I was sure Marla was gone, I grabbed my purse and headed out of

CHAPTER TWENTY-FOUR

Tyrone's office. "Um, thanks for seeing me today. I'll just be leaving now."

He nodded, but didn't reply. Then headed into his office and slammed the door.

Chapter Twenty-Five

The next day, Camry and Tonda were in Painted Wings. I wondered if they'd invited Gretchen, but decided not to ask. That would only inflame the hurt feelings already going on with some of the girls. And I never seemed to know who would be friends this time and who might be on the outs. The whole scenario made me tired just to think about it. And more than a little sad.

Several customers came in at once, slamming Evie with too many to handle. Murray had come in a little later than usual, having gone to a dental appointment, so I volunteered to help them get caught up before returning to my own farm duties.

Since I wanted to speak to Camry and Tonda anyway, I chose that table to get their order first. I edged my way past people standing in line to order and made it to their table. "Hi, is there something I can get for you two today?"

They both ordered cheeseburgers, fries, and diet sodas. But they didn't look pleased to be here, and their faces were more downcast than normal. Most people were glad to come to the café. Murray's cooking was that good.

"Okay, I'll be right back with your drinks." I scurried back across the café, gave their order to Murray at the counter, then headed back to the girls with their drinks. I was relieved there were only two glasses on the tray. Maybe I could manage to get there without dropping it, knocking over a glass, or tripping over something or someone on my way back to them. They, of course, had chosen the table farthest away from the counter. More opportunities for me to end up covered in their diet colas, something

I wasn't looking forward to.

After I got there, and safely delivered their drinks, thank goodness, Tonda tapped the table to get Camry's attention. "Okay, now that she's back, go ahead. Tell Seneca what's going on."

They wanted to tell me something? I could only hope it was useful information, not about how they wanted to critique someone else's new haircut.

Camry, with a sheepish expression, turned in her chair to face me. She cleared her throat. "We decided, since you already know a lot about our friends group and what's been happening lately, we'd keep you in the loop. Is that okay?"

Great! "Of course, I'll listen to whatever you want to tell me."

"It's about Marla."

I pointed to an empty chair. "Is it all right if I sit with you for a minute while I wait for your order to get ready?"

Both girls nodded. I took the seat. "So what's going on with Marla?" I focused on Camry since she seemed to be the one with the news. "Something about your roommate situation?"

"Nope. Well, that comes into it, I guess."

Tonda huffed out a breath. Was she impatient that Camry wasn't getting to the point quick enough?

I waited, not patiently, but at least attempting it, hoping whatever she told me wouldn't take too long. Poor Evie was scrambling as it was. But when I told her why I was seated with Camry and Tonda, she'd totally understand.

Camry grabbed a napkin from the dispenser, making me think of Flora and how often she took one. But Camry didn't tear it to bits, just flattened it out on the table with her fingers, as if that motion helped her gather her thoughts. "Since, like you said, Marla and I live together, I hear a lot of things that go on with her."

Right then, Evie arrived with their food order. I'd meant to go and get the food myself, but she'd beat me to it. I thanked her and tilted my head toward the girls. Evie's eyes widened, then returned to Murray who was trying to flag her down.

I pointed toward their food. "Please, go ahead and eat."

Tonda dug in, but Camry stared at me.

"What did you want to tell me, Camry?"

Once again, she flattened out the napkin. Almost as if she was taking out her frustrations on the poor, innocent paper product. Was she that upset about Marla? She sighed, then left the napkin alone. "It has to do with when she makes phone calls, or when she has too much wine and starts babbling on about stuff."

I leaned forward, placing my forearms on the table. "What did Marla say that's bothering you?"

"First of all," Camry glanced at Tonda and back to me, "Tonda told me how you're really good at finding out who killed people."

"She did?" Tonda had never seemed overly impressed with anything I said or did, and instead took every opportunity to make sarcastic remarks at my expense. And if Camry brought up the subject of murder, this conversation might be a lot more useful than I'd first thought.

Tonda nodded. "It's true. I hear a lot when people go through my line at the grocery store, and word on the street is, you're the go-to person for finding a killer."

Word on the street? She made it sound like I was a TV detective. I bit my lip, hoping not to laugh. "Oh, um, thanks."

Camry waved her hand to get my attention back to her. "Since you seem so good at that, I wanted to tell you something." Her food was still untouched, but Tonda's slurp from her drink straw was loud.

Camry seemed to want to talk to me, but was going in circles. It was obviously something that upset her a lot, so it must be important. I just wished she'd give me more details. I only had so much time to sit with them, since Evie needed me for a bit longer to help out. It was time to get to the point.

"What do you need me to know, Camry?"

She glanced around the café and back. "Tonda and I were talking about Kinley and Devan's wedding, and, well, I remembered something from that day."

I refrained from tapping my foot against the floor, but just barely. "What did you remember?"

"That Marla was arguing with Yolanda during the reception. Right before Yolanda was found…you know."

"Before she was found dead?"

"Yeah." Her face paled. "That's right."

I wished she'd remembered this a little sooner, but had to admit there'd been a whole lot going on with everybody since the murder occurred. "Do you know what the argument between Marla and Yolanda was about?"

"No, but it seemed intense. I couldn't hear them since they were across the room, near the entrance to that place where people change their clothes before the wedding, but I could see it. Their body language. They were waving their arms. And seemed to be shouting. But it was noisy in there, with everyone talking and the music playing. Plus, when people started drinking, they seemed to pay less attention. Like I said, intense."

Tonda scooted forward in her chair. "Yep, intense is the word I would have used, too, the way Camry described it to me. I just wished I would have seen them too. Or heard them. That way it would have been more helpful for you, Seneca."

"Thanks, both of you, for letting me know. All right, so Marla argued with Yolanda. They seemed very upset. And apparently, intense, right? Was there anything else?"

Camry tucked a strand of her long blonde hair behind her ear. "Like I said before, since I live with Marla and hear a lot, there was a night recently, when we were both home. It was kind of late, after the flower shop was closed. Marla got out a huge bottle of wine she'd been saving, and had drunk nearly half the bottle before I realized it."

Tonda glanced at Camry. "I really like Marla. But I don't like how much she drinks, either. The four of us go out and have fun. Sometimes we might have a drink. But we don't need that much. Marla goes way overboard, then gets loud and rowdy. It's embarrassing."

Camry, who'd been concentrating on Tonda, turned to me. "And that particular night, Marla was talking about Yolanda."

I leaned closer. "What did Marla say?"

"I don't know if you'd heard or not, but she used to do some work for Yolanda."

"Yes." But I didn't elaborate on what I'd heard.

"Marla would sometimes crab about having to go to Yolanda's house, but it was a different story when she drank wine." Camry glanced down at her food, seemed to remember she'd ordered something, and finally took a bite of her sandwich.

I waited until she'd set her sandwich back on the plate. "How was it different?"

"She was talking about how Yolanda had done something nice for her."

That was certainly different from what I'd been hearing. I waited for her to go on.

"Apparently, Marla had been in a real tough situation a while back, before I moved in with her, and needed some cash, fast."

"She was in trouble financially?"

"Yes, and she made it sound very bad. Like she might not have a place to live or food to eat."

I'd had some lean times over the years, but I'd always had a roof over my head and food to eat. And cat food, for Winifred—also very important. "Did Yolanda give her some money?"

"According to Marla, it was a loan, and it got her out of debt. The money probably saved her from being homeless, the way she talked about it."

"Then, Marla paid her back?" I could imagine Yolanda not giving her one extra second with which to repay the loan money.

"That's just it. Marla said she never repaid it. Never even intended to. That when she got the money, she had no plans to give any of it back. And then she told me that since Yolanda is dead, she won't ever have to worry about it." Camry stared straight at me, her eyes wide. "The last thing, and this is the bad part, she laughed."

I gasped. From what I'd heard about Yolanda, doing that for someone, helping them out, wouldn't be her normal behavior. But for Marla, to beg for help, receive money, then not pay it back or ever plan to, sounded like horrible logic to me.

Camry pushed her plate away even though she hadn't eaten much. "Now you see why I wanted to tell you this. I hate throwing my roommate, co-worker, and someone who's become a friend under the bus. But the more Marla brags to me about getting one over on Yolanda, the more I feel like I can't trust what she says."

From across the table, Tonda pointed at her. "Tell her the rest. What you told me."

Camry closed her eyes. "Lately, I mean ever since Yolanda was killed, I've felt kind of…"

When she didn't answer and seemed especially upset, I placed my hand on hers. "What is it?"

"I'm a little afraid to go to sleep if she's in the apartment." She grabbed a napkin with her free hand and wiped her eyes.

This sounded bad. Afraid in her own home? "What do you mean?" I patted her hand, then moved mine away. Some people didn't like being touched all that much, and I didn't want to upset her any more than she already was.

Her shoulders hunched together. "Like I said, I don't entirely trust her now. Sometimes I think, I mean I wonder if she…"

Tonda edged closer. "Camry's trying to say she wonders if Marla killed Yolanda. And that maybe Camry might be next."

My mouth had dropped open at Tonda's words, but I quickly closed it. When I sat down to see what was up with the girls, I had no clue it would come to this. "What are you going to do?"

Camry shivered. "I don't know."

Tonda tapped Camry's arm. "If you feel like this, maybe you should come and stay with me for a bit. I don't have an extra bedroom, but there is a couch you could use."

"Thanks, Tonda. That means a lot."

Tonda winked. "I've got your back."

I was beginning to think that might be a good idea, too, for Camry to bunk in with Tonda. I couldn't imagine being scared to go to sleep in my own place. Sure, Winifred made some frightening noises that startled me awake when she was in the midst of nighttime crazies, but that was silly kitty stuff. This was real-life fear.

I looked first at Tonda, then my focus switched to Camry. "Thanks, you two, for filling me in. I'm sorry it's come to this for both of you with Marla. Especially, you, Camry, living with her."

"Thank you, Seneca. Tonda said I should talk to you, and she was right. We needed you to know what was happening with Marla. I hate to think she might be the one who killed Yolanda, but…" She held up her hands.

Seeing that the girls had probably told me all there was to tell, and boy was it a big one, I rose. "I need to get back to the counter. Is there anything else I can get you? Or do for you?"

They shook their heads.

"Okay." I went back to help Evie. When I got to the counter, I quickly filled Murray and Evie in on what I'd learned. I grabbed a tray of drinks to deliver to a table full of men in construction gear, and glanced over at the girls' table again. Tonda was doing something on her phone. And Camry was heartily eating her meal. Maybe she felt relieved after opening up to me about her fear of Marla. I always felt better after talking out my problems.

Marla was fast-moving up the list of who might have smothered Yolanda Steele with that pillow, after her argument with her right before the wedding. And being glad Yolanda was dead, so she didn't have to pay her back. Then going to Tyrone's office demanding money since Yolanda treated her unfairly. Things with Marla were escalating. Would she be so off-kilter, she might become violent again?

Chapter Twenty-Six

I glanced at Evie, who gave me an encouraging nod, before I knocked on Marla's door. What if Camry was here too? I didn't really want to say the things I needed to in front of her. That might make things even tougher for her after what she'd clued me into with her roommate. She might not be able to hide that she'd already spoken with me about Marla.

I jumped when the door opened. Marla looked like she'd just gotten out of bed. And she definitely looked hungover. Her hair was flat on one side, poking out on the other. Her skin was a shade of pale gray, and her eye makeup was smeared below her eyes, some filtering down to her cheeks.

"Hey." Marla blinked several times, as if not fully awake yet. "What's up?" She lowered her eyebrows. "Why are you guys here? Do I owe some money at the café? Sorry, but I don't have it on me just now. You'll just have to wait."

When she started to close the door, I placed my tennis shoe in the way.

"What gives? I told you. I can't pay you. Go away. I...I have a headache."

I didn't doubt her head hurt after what was probably a night of heavy drinking. "We're not here for money." I moved my foot, glad it hadn't been smashed in the door.

"May we come in?" asked Evie.

Between the two of us, my cousin was the sweeter one. She didn't have my temper, that, even though not often, seemed to crop up at the worst times. Her way of putting people at ease was why she was so good at being the Painted Wings Café Manager. Everyone there loved her.

Marla studied Evie, then me. "I guess." She left the door wide open.

We hurried inside before Marla could change her mind. Thank goodness for Evie's gentle, calming voice that got us into the house. Left to me, we might have been literally kicked to the curb.

The place was trashed. I wasn't a neat freak by any means, but I could at least walk through my house without nearly tripping over old pizza boxes and empty wine bottles. Evie's eyes widened, and she gave me the side-eye. I knew how this must seem to her. Because Evie was a neatnik. She wrinkled her nose. After glancing toward Marla, Evie calmed her expression.

Marla tossed some empty food wrappers from the couch to the floor. "You can sit there."

Even though I had no desire to sit where there were obvious grease stains on the couch, I sat anyway. We'd need all the good vibes with Marla to get through this conversation.

When Evie sat next to me, she let out a tiny squeak. But she was a trooper and was all in for why we'd come today. I forced my thoughts away from whatever food had once been placed right where I sat and looked at Marla.

She sat across from us, not bothering to move a wine bottle that was wedged between the arm of the couch and a cushion nearest me. It didn't seem to faze her. "If you don't want money, then why are you here? I do have a life after all."

While it was true she had a life, glancing around the room at the result of it made me cringe. We needed to start this conversation so we could get it over with.

I drummed my fingers on my knee, a nervous habit I had when getting ready to say something I'd rather not. "You see, Marla, we're concerned about you. I've been hearing some things. About you."

"What things?" When she shifted in her chair, her foot crunched against a hamburger wrapper.

When I didn't answer right away, Evie nudged my shoulder lightly with hers. I gave a quick check around, but didn't see or hear Camry anywhere. Good. That would help. "For one thing, I happened to be in Tyrone Steele's office the other day when you came in and demanded money."

Her mouth dropped open. "You were there?"

"Yeah, I was."

"Why were you in his office? Were you two talking about me?"

"No, it was about something else." I wasn't going to tell Marla it was about Wiley being fired.

She waited a few seconds. And must have decided I wasn't going to elaborate, because she crossed her arms over her chest. "So what if you heard what I said. It was every bit the truth. Yolanda Steele, that tight-fisted hag, never gave me what she owed me."

Evie leaned forward. "Why did you think she owed you something?"

Marla switched her glare to Evie. "It's what a decent human being should have done."

"Okay." I held up my hand, hoping to calm her. "But some of your friends have said some things. They're concerned about your…um, behavior lately."

"What a bunch of crap."

I jerked. "You don't even know what I was going to say."

"I can pretty much guess, though. They think I drink too much, right?"

When I shifted on the couch, something crunched underneath my leg. I tried not to cringe. "That's part of it, yes."

"It's like I've told them." She pressed her hand to her chest. "I'm an adult and can do what I want."

"Of course you can. And so can they. They chose to tell me some things that were going on because of their friendship with you."

"They just like to spout off about things. Especially Gretchen." When Marla rolled her eyes, I noticed redness outside of her pupils. "She's ticked off because she doesn't have Tonda all to herself anymore. It's stupid."

I leaned forward, placing my forearms on my thighs. "While you might not understand it, sometimes it's hard for people to give up something that meant a lot to them. Like time spent with a friend."

"But are they my friends, really, if they're telling you and who knows who else, things about me that aren't even true?"

I did see how Marla might feel like she was being dumped on. But from listening to the other three, it sounded as if they'd already tried to reason with her. And not only wasn't that working, she appeared to be sinking deeper into her destructive habits.

"Marla, they weren't just sitting around talking about you. Gretchen, Tonda, and Camry care about you. Are worried you're not doing okay."

"Camry? Oh, perfect. My own roommate said things, too?"

I inhaled sharply. Should I not have said that? But Camry was as open with her comments as the others were. She didn't seem like she was trying to hide anything. "Yes, she told me things. They are all concerned for you."

"So they mentioned my drinking." Marla's eyes narrowed. "What did they say I talked about?"

Evie turned toward Marla. "Yolanda."

Marla's laugh came out harsh and raspy, like her vocal cords needed a rest. Maybe because of her hangover. "You bet I talked about Yolanda. That woman deserved what she got. I only wish it had been worse for her. I wish she'd been more afraid and had experienced worse pain."

Next to me, Evie stiffened. I clasped my hands together on my knees, hoping to stay calm against Marla's tirade. "What makes you say that?"

"Isn't it obvious?"

I shook my head.

"Did you know her?"

"No. My grandmother did, but I'd never actually met Yolanda."

"Lucky you. And I feel sorry for your grandmother."

"But why do you feel that way about Yolanda? That you're glad she's dead, and wish it'd been worse? Those are inflammatory words about someone. Especially a person who's been recently murdered, and we don't yet know who killed her."

Marla leaned forward, mirroring my stance. Was she somehow mocking me, or just changing position? "All right, Seneca. Let me tell you why. Yolanda was rich."

I lowered my eyebrows. "Lots of people are rich. And you think that's a reason to hate someone?"

"Yes. It is. Especially Yolanda, who demeaned me every time I saw her." She waved her hand. "I fought and scraped every day to stay afloat, always looking over my shoulder, wondering who was judging me and saying I'd never amount to anything." Marla bunched her hands into fists. "I hate all rich people. They think they own the rest of us. Own the world. Have no regard for other people who might not be as lucky as they are. So they deserve my hatred. And they will get it, every time."

Evie clasped her hands together in her lap. "That doesn't make much sense."

"It might if you'd grown up the way I did."

I sat up straighter, trying not to touch the back cushions. Who knew what sticky food might be stuck back there? "Why don't you tell us about it?"

"Are you making fun of me?"

"Of course not. We just want to understand better. Understand what you've been through. Can you do that?"

She was silent for a few seconds, then slouched down into her chair. "I guess."

A couple of minutes went by. Was she going to answer us, or had she changed her mind? Evie caught my gaze, her eyebrows raised. I shrugged in return.

Finally, Marla let out a long sigh. "All right. Here's what happened. It's not a pretty story, but you asked. I moved back in with my mom for a while. We lived in a rundown little house just on the other side of the railroad tracks."

Cody had told me on numerous occasions that he got more calls to that part of town about trouble happening than any other place. I felt bad for Marla, having lived there.

She wrapped her arms around her middle. "Our house was always so cold in the winter. On windy days, we could actually feel the breeze through the thin walls. More than once, a glass of water my mom had next to her bed froze during the night."

Hearing about the old house, I was tempted to rub my hands together to warm them. But I held still and focused on Marla. This wasn't about me.

She let out a long breath. "Then, the furnace went out. There was no money to get it fixed. We used all the blankets we had, but it never was enough." She stared at the floor. "Then, my mom got sick. Really sick. It...it would have been different if Yolanda hadn't done what she had."

"What do you mean?"

"My mom used to work for Steele Industries." She gritted her teeth together, making a line of muscle form on her jaw.

"Oh. So your mom would've had health insurance to aid with her medical bills?"

"Wrong. Just before my mom got sick, Yolanda started making changes in some of the departments. Mom worked as a custodian." She huffed out a breath. "I guess Yolanda didn't think Mom deserved to keep her benefits at such a *lowly* position."

Beside me, Evie jerked. "That's horrible. And there wasn't any way you could have gotten the money for your mom?"

Marla blinked rapidly. Was she trying not to cry? "No, there wasn't."

Then I remembered what Tonda and Camry had told me earlier. "Wait, I heard something about you getting some money from Yolanda. A loan?"

"That was different. I needed it for rent. I'd gone to Yolanda's house and threatened to camp out on her porch if I lost my home and she didn't give me the money. I even dragged my sleeping bag with me to her house to make my point. I guess she believed me, because she gave me some cash."

I wasn't going to remind Marla what she'd told her friends. That she had no intention of paying the loan back. And that she was glad Yolanda was dead, so she'd never have to. Maybe Yolanda was angry to never get that money back, and said no the second time out of spite?

Marla peered down at her hands, her nails looking as if she'd bitten them. "I did go back to Yolanda. I asked her for help again with money, even though it nearly killed me to do it. But she refused. Said my mom wasn't worth it. And neither was I."

Evie's eyes teared up. "That's awful, she turned you down the second time."

"Yeah, it was the worst. Because I couldn't get the medicine. So my mom died."

Evie and I gasped.

"I'm so sorry," said Evie.

I frowned. "So am I."

Marla gave a quick nod of acceptance, then went on. "Our house was no more than a shack. Since it was so drafty, there was no chance of ever getting warm enough. I did okay because I was healthy, but my mom had recently had the flu. The virus ended up going into her lungs, and she got pneumonia. That's why she needed the medicine. I stayed with her and tried to help, but there wasn't anything more I could do for her." Marla roughly wiped tears away, as if determined not to appear weak in front of us.

"That's what killed her?" I asked.

"Yes. It was the worst thing I've ever gone through. If she'd gotten the medicine, she might have recovered. And I wouldn't be going through life without her. I miss her every day."

I closed my eyes briefly, so heartbroken for Marla and her mother.

"The day after my mom's funeral, which was the barest form of burial because I couldn't afford to pay yet, and that's all the funeral home would do, Yolanda told me I was less valuable than dirt. That I'd end up like my mother. Living in a rundown old house. And would live a worthless life. And then I would die, still worthless." She turned and faced us straight on. "That was the day I hated Yolanda enough to kill her."

Silence filled the room. That had sounded like a confession to me. I could feel the tension and hate sift off Marla as she sat across from us. Surely she'd been the person who smothered the older woman to death with a pillow.

I waited until Marla made eye contact with me. "With what you've told us, I have a strong feeling you had something to do with Yolanda's murder. Don't you think you need to talk to Cody about all this? He could help you—"

"No. No way. I don't want any part of that."

"But you just told us you were glad she was dead. That you wish it'd been worse. And the reason why you hated her so much." I stared at her. "Marla, did you kill Yolanda Steele because of your mother's death?"

She stood up suddenly. "You both need to leave. Right now."

"But…"

"Out!" She pointed toward the door. "No way I'm getting blamed for this! She got what she deserved!" Her face turned an angry red, and her eyes narrowed to slits.

I wasn't sure about Evie, but I was ready to get out of there. If the quick steps Evie took toward the front door were any indication, she was ready too.

We rushed out onto the porch, both startled when the door slammed behind us. I wanted to talk to Evie about all we'd heard, but as if by mutual agreement, we hurried to my truck, I started the engine, and we were several blocks away before we broke the silence.

Evie let out a long breath. "Wow, just wow."

"My thoughts exactly."

"That was… I hadn't expected to hear all of that. Especially about her mother. That's rough."

"Yeah, that was awful. I can't imagine."

"That whole scenario really does give Marla a strong motive for murder, doesn't it?"

"Yeah, I think so too."

"What should we do now? We heard a lot of things from Marla. I'm not going to go around telling people what she said."

"But there is one person who needs to know."

She glanced at me. "Cody."

"Yep. I bet he'll find all this as interesting as we do. And if he decides to start talking about me getting into things I shouldn't, I know you've got my back."

"You've got that right, cousin." She wrapped her arm around my shoulder.

As I drove my truck up the gravel path that led to my house and the café, Evie's phone buzzed.

She swiped the screen with her thumb. "It's from Cody. Want me to read it?"

"Go ahead." I pulled in front of my house, put the truck in park, and waited.

Her brow furrowed as she looked at it. "Apparently, he contacted the authorities where Liza went to college. Their records showed that Liza had been cleared of her roommate's death."

"That's good, anyway." I wondered why Cody hadn't texted me the info, too. Maybe my phone's battery had run down. I'd have to check it later.

She bobbed her head, but kept reading. "Oh, and the roommate had lots of alcohol in her system when she died. They thought it was possible she turned wrong in her sleep."

"She suffocated herself?"

Evie held up the phone so I could see it. "I guess."

"Okay, thanks."

"Now that we know Liza is innocent of the other girl's death, does it make you feel that maybe she's innocent of Yolanda's, too?"

I thought for a second. "That's where I'm heading, yeah. Because…"

Her phone buzzed. "It's Cody again."

"What does it say?"

"He says he forgot to add that Liza is now cleared of Yolanda's death, too, as far as he's concerned."

I relaxed against the back of my seat. "Very good news."

"But there're still some people to keep an eye on."

I tapped her phone. "You've got that right."

Chapter Twenty-Seven

The next morning after I'd finished working in the greenhouse, I wanted to call Evie and talk more about our conversation with Marla. I looked everywhere, but couldn't find my phone. I'd been distracted the night before and forgot to look for it to recharge it.

It wasn't in my truck, which I confirmed after checking the seats and floors of the vehicle. It wasn't in my house. And I hadn't had it with me when I'd gone to the milkweed fields, so I couldn't have lost it out there. I groaned. Just perfect.

I rushed over to Painted Wings to see if I'd left it there. The café wasn't open yet, but Evie, who started prep work early, hadn't seen it or had anybody turn it into lost and found the day before.

"The only other place I'd been yesterday was to see Marla."

Evie's eyes widened. "So you have to go over there? Now?"

"I'd better. But not even sure if anyone is there. They might be at work."

"Betty doesn't open Precious Posies until ten o'clock. There's a good chance either Camry or Marla might still be at home. I don't think those two get up very early."

"Good point. Okay. I'm heading over there. I'll be back before the lunch crowd comes in to see if you need anything. I doubt I'll be gone very long."

"Good luck. And be careful." Evie waved.

When I returned to my truck after grabbing my keys and purse from the house, I noticed the rear passenger door was ajar. That's the last side I'd looked on when searching for my phone. I must not have latched it all the way.

On impulse, I did a quick check to make sure Winifred wasn't in there. She did, after all, have a history of getting in my truck when she wasn't invited. I didn't see her, so maybe she'd taken my scolding to heart after the wedding debacle. I closed the door, then drove across town.

When I pulled next to the curb in front of their house, I couldn't tell if anybody was there. Some other vehicles were parked on the street, but I wasn't sure which ones might belong to Marla or Camry.

When I opened the door to get out, the warmth of the morning hit me full force, so I left my jacket in the truck. I eyed the sun, bright and warm. It was supposed to get toasty later. Better leave a window down too, so I didn't roast when I got back in. Either my phone was at their house, or it wasn't, but there was always a possibility we'd have to hunt for it in couch cushions, or that whoever was there might want to talk.

I glanced back toward the house. Only one way to find out if anyone was home.

After I walked the short distance to the house, I knocked on the front door. Was it only yesterday I'd been standing right here? And Marla had tossed me and Evie out?

Footsteps hurried in my direction from inside. Through the tempered glass, I could see someone, but couldn't tell which girl it might be. I guess it didn't matter, since all I wanted was to see if my phone was there. If it was Marla, I hoped she'd relent enough to let me look for my phone. Or at the very least, search for it on my behalf if she didn't want to let me back in.

The door opened with a squeak, making me jump. Why was I so antsy? Maybe because if Marla was the one answering the door, and I was certain she'd killed Yolanda, I wasn't looking forward to her wanting a repeat of murdering someone. Especially me.

I let out a relieved breath when Camry was the one in the doorway.

"Hi, Seneca. Um, how are you?" She looked past my shoulder. Was she expecting someone else?

"Hey, sorry to bother you. When I was here yesterday, I might have dropped my phone."

"You were here?"

"Didn't Marla tell you?

"She doesn't always tell me things. And she's been moody lately, so we haven't talked as much." She shrugged. "That's okay, though. Come on in. We can check for your phone."

"Thanks." I stepped inside, glad to see the living room wasn't quite as trashed as yesterday. Maybe Camry was the neater of the two. I looked at the stairway behind her. "Is Marla here too?"

"No, she decided to go take a walk before her shift later today. I'm on in a couple of hours, but we have time to look for your phone." She pointed toward the living room. "Were you guys in there?"

"Yes. I looked everywhere else I could think of, but your house was my last hope."

She waved her hand for me to follow. "Come on in."

I stepped into the living room and took in the changes. The empty pizza boxes and wine bottles were gone, so searching where I'd been sitting might be a little easier. And possibly less sticky.

"I hate to think what you might have come across in here yesterday." Camry waved her hand to encompass the room. Marla isn't the neatest roommate."

"Everyone is different, I guess."

"You're right about that. Good thing at least one of us living here isn't a total slob."

I had no desire to get in the middle of whatever those two had going on. "Mind if I check the couch? That's where I was sitting."

"No problem."

I looked on top of the cushions. Then into the deep crevices in the seams down the center of each one. Nothing. "Mind if I remove the cushions to look?"

"Go right ahead. I'm going to go upstairs to figure out what to wear to work today. Be back in a few."

"Take your time. Thanks."

As Camry's footsteps took her upstairs, I placed each couch cushion, plus a few throw pillows, on a nearby chair. There was no phone visible. Shoot. I really didn't want to reach down inside the couch. Furniture always seemed to collect crumbs and other undesirable things I'd rather not touch. But it seemed I'd have to. I guess Edward and I had something in common after all. The ick-factor.

Glancing behind me to make sure Camry hadn't come back, I reached into a side pocket of my purse where I kept a set of disposable gloves. I doubted most people carried them around, but after getting stuck in the middle of previous murder investigations, I'd found the gloves came in handy. No pun intended.

I snapped on the gloves, tugged up my shirt sleeve to my elbow, and plunged into the depths of the upholstered great unknown.

Ick.

Just as I thought, every time I lifted my hand out, the glove was covered with crumbs, dust, and some things I could guess at but would rather not know. I repeated the action time and time again, all around the couch crevices.

No phone.

Frustrated, I snapped off the gloves, turned them inside out, and stuffed them into my pants pocket. I was hoping Camry would be back by now. Not that I wanted her to see me wearing gloves, but if I hadn't found my phone by now, the next step was to look under the couch. That meant moving it a couple of feet to see if anything was lying on the floor. If that didn't work, the following step would be to tip the whole thing over. I really hoped it wouldn't come to that.

My own couch had been known to swallow phones, remotes, jewelry, and about a thousand cat toys that got stuck and suspended somewhere between the cushions and the floor, squeezed in next to the tight metal frame, like moss on a tree.

I thought about calling up the stairs, asking Camry for permission to go further, but I could hear her walking around above me, getting ready for work. I was probably causing her a delay just by showing up. No sense making it worse. When I got dressed to go someplace, I never appreciated interruptions either, although that was Winifred's favorite time to follow me around, telling me all her kitty problems and expecting me to listen.

After checking out how much space was behind the couch so I wouldn't run into any other furniture or valuables, I shoved the couch back a bit. There was nothing on the floor except some spare chain, a pen, and a couple of paper clips. Rats. Now I'd have to go all the way with my search.

I bent down, got a good grip on the bottom of the couch, and hefted it up. The couch thumped against the floor as it fell onto its back. It looked like a helpless blue turtle, stuck on its naked, cushionless shell.

Unfortunately, there was nothing lying on the floor near the back. I'd hoped my phone might have been lodged against the rear edge, where I might not have seen it when I moved it before. But maybe my phone wasn't here after all. How stupid was I going to feel if I dismantled part of Marla and Camry's living room for no good reason?

Another check behind me showed Camry still hadn't returned. Might as well go all the way in my search before giving up. This was my last hope.

On my hands and knees, I checked the innards of the piece of furniture. I even grabbed the tiny flashlight I kept on my keychain for better viewing. When I'd about given up, the flashlight beam reflected off something. My breath caught. Could it be?

I reached in and tugged the object out. Yay, it was my phone! As I was ready to turn away, the flashlight beam caught onto a second item. When I retrieved it, I could see it was a photo. An old, battered-looking one.

It was of a woman holding what looked to be a newborn baby. I held the picture closer. And blinked. The woman looked like a younger version of the lady I'd watched strut down the chapel aisle. The one whose final breath had been snatched away by a pillow. Yolanda Steele.

Why would Marla and Camry have a picture of the recently murdered woman in their house? Did they know her more than casually, or just having done some work for her? It didn't make sense. And the photo didn't look to be recent. From Yolanda's appearance compared to now, the picture had to be over twenty years old.

Just as I was ready to place the photo on a nearby table, a scratching noise came from a window that faced out onto the porch. I didn't pay much attention at first. Maybe the mailman was shoving magazines into the mailbox attached to the end of the porch. Or a squirrel was stashing a nut in one of the otherwise empty flower pots sitting to one side of the door.

But when a loud howling followed, an all too familiar exasperated meow, I gasped and ran to the door.

Flinging it open, I looked to my left. Sure enough, there sat Winifred.

"What on earth are you doing here?" My gaze flew to the truck with its open window. I tapped my foot. "You did it again, didn't you? You were hiding in my truck? But I checked it and didn't see you. How did you do that?"

My cat's answer was to close her eyes and wash her paw, looking every bit as if she was smiling beneath her long white whiskers. Winifred was one of the sneakiest felines I'd ever met. And I'd known a lot throughout my life. She was like a tiny orange magician with fake wings, always hunting for her next opportunity to perform a trick.

I couldn't just leave her out here. The house was too close to the street, with cars whizzing by. And I didn't want to shut her in the too-warm vehicle with the windows closed. I'd read where that could be dangerous for pets. Maybe I could crack the windows a couple of inches. "All right, Winifred, let's get you back into the truck and—"

An orange blur sped past my feet, the wings of her monarch costume shimmering in the sunlight as she rounded the edge of the doorframe and darted inside the open doorway.

"No! Come back here!"

I ran after her, not finding her at first. But the tip of her tail stuck out from beneath a recliner chair. I took a deep breath and let it out. "Honestly, Winifred, I—"

Footsteps again sounded upstairs. Was Camry coming back down soon? As quickly as I could, I lowered the couch and pushed it to its original spot, then placed the cushions in their places on the couch. Camry's footsteps were now making their way down the stairs.

I turned, ready to give her the good news about my phone, but her gaze was locked on something on the side table. The photo I'd discovered. She lifted her head. And stared straight at me.

Camry was no longer in the pleasant mood she'd been in when I arrived. It was time to go and let her finish getting ready for work. I held up my phone. "Look what I found. Thanks so much for letting me search your couch."

A tiny sneeze came from beneath the chair, but Winifred's tail was no longer visible.

Camry's mouth dropped open. "What was that?"

I forced a laugh. "My cat, Winifred. I'm sure you've seen her at Painted Wings before? She hangs out in there showing off her butterfly costumes."

She didn't comment. Just stared toward the chair.

"Let me just go get her, and we'll get out of your way." I rushed across the small room, bent down, and tugged my cat, who hissed, out from under her newly acquired fort. "Come on, Winifred. Time to go."

When I had her securely in my grasp—not easy while trying to hold onto my phone—I turned and took a deep breath. "I've got her now. Sorry for that. She followed me in, and I didn't know she'd been in my truck so—"

Camry held up her hand, palm out. "Stop talking."

I snapped my mouth closed. She really was in a bad mood. I waited, but when she didn't say more, I took a step toward the front door. "Listen, we'll just leave now and…"

"Where did you find that picture, Seneca?"

I stopped at the change in her tone. "It was under your couch. Where I found my phone. I'd meant to ask you why you had a photo of…"

She stalked to the table and snatched the picture up. When she studied it, her eyes narrowed. But she didn't say anything.

I wanted to leave, but her or Marla possessing an old picture of a recent murder victim was something I couldn't ignore. My bet was on Marla, since she was number one on my suspect list. "That photo. I might be wrong, but is that Yolanda Steele? From a long time ago?"

Her brow scrunched as I spoke. She blinked and then focused on me. "What?"

Maybe Camry had never seen it either. It would make sense if it belonged to Marla. I angled my chin toward her hand. "Is that Yolanda? It might be somebody else, but I thought I spotted a resemblance to her."

Camry whipped around to look at the open doorway as if just now noticing it. She raced toward it, then slammed the door closed.

Winifred growled at the loud noise and buried her head in my armpit. I wished I had an armpit to hide in, too. Well, maybe not that part of a body, but I sure could use a hug from someone nice right about now, because Camry was freaking me out.

She stomped back toward me, halting just a few inches from my face. I tried to step away, but the back of my legs hit the chair where Winifred had hidden earlier. "Camry? What's wrong? Is this about the picture and Marla?"

"Why would you think it's something to do with Marla?"

"I...well, when I was here yesterday with Evie, we talked to Marla and got some bad vibes from her. Some of the things she said were very harsh."

Camry crossed her arms over her chest. "That sounds like my roommate. Moody and hard to get along with."

I glanced at the photo. "So, what I found isn't Marla's? I thought—"

"You thought wrong. I doubt she's ever seen it, or even knows about it."

"Then, it's..."

"Yes, it's mine. Did you get a close look at it?"

"Enough to think that might be Yolanda Steele, holding someone's baby."

"That's not just someone's kid. It's hers."

"Oh." I hadn't realized Yolanda had children. I'd never heard them mentioned. And the way gossip raced around this town, it seemed odd no one had ever known anything about it before. Surely my grandmother would have said something if she'd known back then.

"Yolanda had one child. A daughter." Camry held the picture up next to her face so I could see the front of it. "See a resemblance to anybody else?"

I blinked. "Wait. That's...you?"

Chapter Twenty-Eight

"Now you're getting it," Camry glared at me.

"But why didn't you ever say anything? Your mom just died. I'm so sorry."

"I don't need your sympathy." She finally moved a few steps away, giving me room to breathe.

Winifred turned away from my armpit and glared at the person who'd slammed the door and frightened her. An inaudible growl, that I could feel vibrating in her chest, told me how scared she was.

Camry eyed the photo. "She was never a true mother to me."

"She wasn't?"

Camry blinked hard, like she was fighting back tears, then gave a quick shake of her head.

"I don't know what happened, but I can't imagine not being close to my mother."

"It's not just that we weren't close. She didn't want me. At all. She never wanted me to be born. I was a mistake. That picture was the only one of us together. Yolanda dumped me in an orphanage in Ohio as fast as she could right after that. My adoptive parents, such as they were, told me that."

What was going on? Yolanda was her mother, who didn't want her? I felt like I'd fallen into something I wasn't ready for. Never in a million years would I have guessed that Camry was Yolanda's daughter. "You seem to have a lot on your mind. I should take Winifred and go."

Her eyes opened wide. "But you can't leave yet."

"I really do need to get back to the farm. But I appreciate you allowing me to search for my phone." Since she'd moved a few steps away, I edged a little bit toward the door.

"Are you leaving? Now?"

"Like I said,"—another step—"I need to go. Plus, you'd mentioned you need to get ready for work. I don't want to make you late."

Camry snorted a laugh. "As if I care about that place. She hardly makes it worth my while to show up."

"I thought you liked working there."

"It's almost a waste of my time. But I do need even the measly amount she pays me. Although I do have plans to quit."

I thought about Liza, trying to find a job. It didn't sound like there were very many places hiring. "What kind of job do you want?"

"I don't want to work. I just want money."

"Yeah, well, it's kind of hard to make money. If you don't have a job."

"I don't need one. I deserve what's rightfully mine. Yolanda's wealth. All of it. Since I'm her only child. Now that she's dead."

"Camry, I'm so sorry for what you've gone through. I really am. But I don't think I'm the person you need to speak to about this. Maybe an attorney?" I inwardly winced, realizing if she went that route and stayed with someone in town, it would be going through Payne's office.

"But you're the one I need to talk to. Don't you see?"

I took another step. "All I wanted was to get my phone. And I found it, so—"

Camry closed the distance between us. Her fingers clenched around my wrist, which supported Winifred's back end. Winifred's tail lashed side to side. But Camry didn't budge. I tried to pull away, but Camry's grip was strong.

"Seneca, I need your advice. You're a little older. Have more life experience than I do."

"I still don't think I'm who you need to talk to."

Her fingers dug into my wrist, sending jolts of pain into my arm.

I gasped. "Stop! That hurts. Let me go!"

"Not gonna happen."

Winifred took a swipe at Camry, who dropped her tight grip on my wrist. Dots of blood formed on Camry's arm. Now freed, Winifred leaped down. She ran to hide beneath the couch in a flurry of whiskers, fur, growls, and hisses. All she'd left behind was a clump of orange fur that drifted slowly to the floor in her wake.

Just great. Not only was I stuck here with Camry, who was turning out to be violent, now Winifred was hiding. Again. It wouldn't be as easy to grab her as when she'd been under the chair.

I rubbed my wrist. Red welts formed. "Thanks a *lot* for this." I held up my hand. "Not sure why you thought I deserved that." I glanced over toward the couch. "This time, I'm going to get my cat. And leave your house. Trust me. I won't be coming back." And to think I'd sat and listened to her cry and vent about Marla when we were at Painted Wings.

Her hands smacked against my shoulders in a hard shove. I tumbled backward onto the chair.

I glared at her. "This is insane." I grabbed my phone. "I'm calling Cody Bales. He'll sort this out, and you'll be—"

She reached into her pants pocket and took out a small gun.

I sucked in air so fast, I nearly choked. My phone tumbled to the floor. "Camry, what are you doing?"

"I've been hearing things about you. You know more than you should."

"About what? You mean the picture I found? That has nothing to do with me. I wasn't looking for it in the first place. Just my phone, which you said was okay to do."

"Not just that. You seem to be everywhere. All over town." She pointed toward her front door. "Talking to people."

"So? Lots of people talk to each other. It's not that unusual."

She stepped closer.

"Listen, Camry, you're a…um, nice person, and I'm sorry for what you've been through. But I need to leave now."

"Not on your life."

I didn't like the sound of that. "I'm not going to tell anyone who your mother was, okay? I found that picture by accident. It's nobody's business if you don't want them to know."

"Are you kidding? By the time I'm finished, everyone in this stupid town will know. I want them to."

"Then why are you so mad at me?" I slowly scooted to the edge of the chair. I needed to get out of here. Now.

"Because you're asking questions about Yolanda's murder. About who held that pillow to her face." She gripped the gun in one hand but showed me the picture of Yolanda in the other. "The smaller person in this photo is who killed Yolanda."

Shock rolled through me. "No…but Marla…"

"Stop thinking about my roommate. She may be weird, and drink too much, and have all sorts of issues, but the one thing she didn't do was kill my mother."

This couldn't be happening. Other people in town had motives to have killed Yolanda. Especially Marla. Camry had done a great job keeping her true relationship with Yolanda Steele a secret from everyone. Until now.

She kept the gun aimed at me, but tapped her foot to some rhythm only she could hear. "Right before I killed Yolanda, I told her who I was."

"She didn't know?"

"No. Even though I'd thought deep down that a woman should automatically recognize her child, she treated me like she did everyone else. Like old gum stuck on the heel of her shoe."

"What did she say when you told her?"

Camry ground her teeth together, her jaw forming a solid ridge of muscle. "She laughed."

"Laughed?"

"That's right. Then she said she'd assumed I'd probably died somewhere along the way. Not that she would've cared. And that, she'd hoped I had, so she wouldn't have to think about her dumb mistake of getting pregnant."

My mouth dropped open. Even though my legs and arms were shaking, and my mouth had gone dry from fear, I still felt awful for the way Camry had been treated by her mother.

"That was when I did it. Right after she laughed. It was easy, really. There was a pillow there. A decorative one. I guess someone had left it at one time or another."

I shrugged. "Maybe a bride had used it as a pillow for the ring bearer to carry the ring down the aisle."

"It doesn't matter." She glared at me. "If you'd let me finish?"

"Uh, sure. Please, go ahead."

"So anyway, I was so mad about her laughing, I stole her small purse she'd carried with her."

I thought back to Yolanda strutting down the aisle. "Yes, she did carry a small clutch in her hand. So you took her money?"

"Ha, what money? All she had in there was a stick of gum, a used tissue, and a tube of that awful bright lipstick she wore."

"Then how will you get her money if she didn't recognize you as her daughter?"

Her eyes narrowed. "Gee, thanks for rubbing that in."

"Sorry." My foot tapped nervously against the floor.

"Believe me. I have a plan for that."

Camry didn't say anything else. Was I supposed to ask? "Um, what's your plan?"

"So glad you asked. I got ahold of my birth certificate."

"You mean a copy from where you were born? Like from the county courthouse?"

"No, the one they gave my so-called mother."

"But how did you—"

Camry's hand rose to stop me. "One time when Marla had to deliver flowers to Yolanda, I went along for the ride. I snuck out of the flower shop when Betty was busy waiting on a customer. While Marla was talking to my mother, I crept upstairs."

"How did you know where to look?"

"Marla told me that one time when she was waiting for the maid to bring out Yolanda, she got impatient and started looking herself. She spotted a safe deposit box on a shelf in a study. When I found the box, it was unlocked. How stupid could Yolanda be? When I opened it, my certificate was in there with some other things I didn't care much about."

"So you just stole it?"

"How can it be stealing if it's about me? About my birth?"

It wouldn't do me any good to argue with her. I held still and waited for her to go on.

"With my birth certificate in my possession, I have proof of my relationship to Yolanda. And that gives me leverage to get her inheritance." Suddenly, Camry gave herself a shake, as if needing to get into action. "Enough chatting. Time to get on with it."

Was I the 'it' in that sentence? I didn't like how that sounded. "Why don't I just get Winifred and get out of here. This all has nothing to do with me and—"

"Are you kidding? There's no way you're leaving. Not alive anyway. And neither is your orange furball."

From beneath the couch, Winifred gave a low growl. She must not have liked the way this was going either.

I clutched the arms of the chair. "But I need to—"

"I said you're not going anywhere. You don't listen very well, do you, Seneca?"

Even though she was right, that I didn't always do what other people wanted, I wasn't going to take this sitting down. I jumped up, catching Camry off guard.

The gun wobbled as her hand trembled.

Her hand may have been shaking, but my legs matched it by trembling. Still, this was my only chance to get away from her. To save not only my life but Winifred's.

I took a step toward her, trying not to look directly at the gun. That was hard, though, with the weapon's tiny dark opening where a bullet would fly out, pointed right at my chest. What I wouldn't give for Cody's bulletproof vest right now.

Or even better, to have Cody here.

A tiny squeak caught my attention from the floor in front of the couch. An orange paw had popped out and was tapping the area in rapid beats. My cat didn't know Morse Code, but she was trying to get me to look over there. She'd been with me before when I'd been confronted by a killer. And had been a big help.

As I took another step, my foot bumped against something. My phone. It landed there when I'd dropped it earlier, after Camry shoved me.

A quick glance at the screen showed a text message had come in. Maybe it was someone wanting to know where I was. I'd love to clue them in, but I needed to grab my phone first.

Camry moved closer. That girl didn't believe in personal space.

"All right, Seneca. Enough is enough. I have things to accomplish today. And you're first on my list." She held the gun out so it was now a few inches closer to my chest.

More tapping came from the orange paw. I wish I knew what that meant. Camry's foot moved, and I glanced down. A loose thread hung from where it had unraveled on the hem of her pants.

A dangling thread was pure catnip to a feline. Was that what Winifred noticed?

A few seconds later, Winifred's paw tapped again. Deciding I had nothing to lose, I tapped the floor lightly with my shoe in answer. Maybe she'd get curious and stick not just her paw out from beneath the couch, but her head, too. If she'd dart out for the dangling thread, it might distract Camry.

"Hey." Camry frowned. "What are you doing with your foot?"

"I…have a cramp. In my calf. Don't you hate those?"

She blinked. "I don't care about your stupid cramp."

"Sorry. It just helps to relieve the pain if I move my foot. Otherwise, the cramp might get worse, and my foot tends to leap out. You might end up getting kicked. Really hard. Accidentally, of course."

She huffed out a breath. "Fine. Keep moving your foot around. I have no desire to get a new bruise."

Camry was worried about a bruise, but seemed to have no qualms about putting a bullet in me.

A noise outside caught Camry's attention. She turned halfway toward the door. When she moved, Winifred's face appeared from below the couch.

Her eyes widened as her pupils grew large. I could imagine that beneath the couch, her butt was doing a little wiggle. She was getting ready to pounce on the dangling thread.

I moved away from Camry, just a little, and waited.

Her eyebrows drew together. "Must have been my postal carrier. She makes too much noise when she delivers my mail. It's so rude." Camry's foot shifted as she glared at the door.

Winifred leaped from her hiding place, bounced across the floor, and attacked the hem of Camry's pants. Her sharp kitty canines were on full display, as they sunk into the girl's bare ankle.

"Ah!" Camry jerked and glared toward the floor. "Get off of me, you winged vermin!"

With all my strength, I shoved Camry. She crashed against the floor. The gun went flying out of her hand and landed near the couch. Like an expert hockey player, Winifred smacked the gun under the furniture until I could no longer see it.

Go, kitty, go!

"No!" Camry still lying on the floor, grabbed my leg, and punched the back of my knee. I dropped like a sack of cement right next to her.

A thump came from the porch. Winifred zipped past me and ran toward it. Where was she going? I could use some more help here.

I wrestled with Camry, trying to get her talons from digging into my arms. Winifred let out some yell-meows normally saved for high distress moments. Like me accidentally stepping on her tail. This was definitely high stress—at least for me!

The door crashed open, and loud footsteps pounded toward us. It was Cody! Evie was right behind him.

Cody wrenched Camry away from me, giving me a much-needed break to rub my sore arms. Tiny moon-shaped imprints were in my skin where her nails had dug in.

Evie knelt beside me and wrapped me in her arms. "Are you all right? I was so scared when you didn't show up at the café, and I couldn't reach you on your phone."

"I'm okay." I let out a huge sigh. "Thank you for showing up."

The door opened again, and Cody's deputy, Bud, entered. Cody held Camry while Bud put the handcuffs on her, then Bud took Camry out to the police vehicle.

Cody reached down to help me stand. "Are you hurt?" His gaze roved over me.

"I'm all right. But thank goodness you guys showed up when you did!"

Evie touched my shoulder. "You can also thank Winifred." She picked up my cat and cuddled her close.

"Thank you, kitty. You were a big help distracting that mean Camry so I could get away from her horrible gun."

Evie gasped as Cody said, "Gun?"

I pointed toward the couch. "It slid across the floor when Winifred was chewing on Camry's ankle. Then Winifred did a perfect hockey swipe, and it ended up beneath the couch."

Evie patted Winifred's back. "What a clever kitty." When she kissed the top of the cat's head, Winifred let out a rumbling purr, then squirmed, demanding to be placed on the floor.

With his arm around me, Cody studied me closely. "Sure you're okay?"

"I am now."

He kissed my cheek, sending warmth all the way through me. "I'm so relieved."

I looked up at him. "How did you know to show up here?"

He gave me a final shoulder squeeze, then released me, but stayed close. "It was Evie. She called to tell me about your visit with Marla yesterday, and that you had to run back here today."

"That's right." Evie looked at Cody, then back at me. "When you didn't show up, I was worried about you here alone with Marla. So I called Cody for backup."

He raised his eyebrows. "Backup?"

Evie giggled. "I guess I was your backup?"

One side of his mouth rose. "Yeah, that works too."

"Thank you so much, both of you, for showing up."

Cody glanced toward the doorway, where Bud had taken Camry outside. "Winifred was a big help, too. When I saw her inside the house, cat-screaming at me, I knew something was wrong. Imagine my surprise when I arrived and found not Marla, but Camry."

"Me too," said Evie.

I let out a long breath, as if I'd been holding it in since realizing who the real murderer was. "Yeah, I was kind of surprised too."

Evie blinked away tears. "I'm just glad you're…"

"I'm fine. Really." I nudged her arm lightly with my elbow. Evie wiped her eyes and walked away. Where was she going?

Cody moved closer again. His embrace was tighter and warmer than any hug he'd ever given me. When he kissed my cheek, I felt moisture from his face. Had he been crying? Worrying over me?

"Oh, Seneca, I…" He tugged me closer.

I never wanted him to let me go.

Chapter Twenty-Nine

everal of us met at Pines Park. Since it was such a lovely evening after Painted Wings had closed for the day, we decided to take a picnic outdoors to celebrate the capture of the town's killer and the freedom of those who people had wrongly accused of the murder.

We found an empty park shelter with picnic tables, the same area where I'd spoken to Drew a short time before. I was so thankful this visit was one of joy, instead of sadness, trouble, and searching for answers.

Murray, always concerned about food and its presentation, had a red and white checkered tablecloth, plates, silverware, and napkins ready for us. He'd even brought a lantern to set on the table, because by the time we were finished, it would be dark.

He took his time setting the table as if he were serving high-class visitors for an expensive meal. His love for us may not always have been expressed verbally, but we knew his thoughts by how much he cared for us.

When Evie arrived with George, my heart filled with joy to see them together. It was obvious from the way they walked, arms linked, and the frequent glances and smiles, that they were indeed in love. Evie was such a sweet soul. She totally deserved to be happy after missing George all this time.

Cody arrived five minutes later. It wasn't until his car pulled up that I realized I'd been on edge, as if he might not show up. But I should have known better. Cody always showed up. And always would.

It was one of the many reasons I loved him.

There. I put that thought at the forefront of my mind. Not shrinking away from it anymore. Even though I'd been involved in checking out two previous murders, there was something about the way this one nearly ended that made me evaluate my life and those I cared about. Maybe it was the gun that had been pointed directly at me. The look of murderous intent in Camry's eyes. The possibility of my life being snatched away in the quickness of a single breath.

If Camry had been successful, I'd no longer be here to take care of my grandmother's beloved monarchs. Winifred would be an orphan. I'd leave behind my friends, especially Evie. And…Cody.

I knew how I felt about him. But that didn't mean he shared those feelings. And I was too chicken to come right out and ask.

He cared for me; I had no doubt about that. We'd been best friends forever. But that kind of love was different from what I hoped for. And I couldn't have that if Cody didn't feel the same way. Plus, I wasn't the sort of person who'd settle for a one-sided relationship. I had that with Payne and would never go down that road again.

I let out a sigh, then forced a smile as Cody left his car and walked across the grassy expanse toward me.

He waved. "Hey, you two."

Two? I glanced down. Sure enough, Winifred sat just behind me, staring at Cody. Her whiskers twitched, and her caramel eyes were bright. The rays of the setting sun caught the sparkles in her Painted Lady butterfly costume, making it appear animated, with a life of its own.

I picked her up, but the way she pulled away from my chest told me she didn't want me. She reached out her paws toward Cody. He carefully took her from my arms, snuggled her against his chest, which caused her to purr.

I'd purr too, if it was me.

No, I needed to put those thoughts aside. Cody had held me tight after saving me from Camry. But wasn't that just one friend showing concern for another? Evie had hugged me, too. Maybe that's all Cody's had been.

"Seneca? You okay?"

I startled at Cody's voice. *Must stop daydreaming.* "Sure, fine. Mind was drifting a little, there."

"Nothing new, right?"

I gave him a mock scowl. "Give a girl a break. I've had a rough time of it lately."

He moved Winifred to one side and reached out his free hand. He placed it on my shoulder. "Believe me. I know."

I looked first at his hand, then slowly up into his eyes. His grin was gone. In its place was... Concern? Worry?

I touched his hand, allowing the moment to end. Winifred turned her head toward me. And winked.

Wait. Why had she winked? Did she think she was getting away with something? Probably. She'd had a crush on Cody ever since she was a tiny kitten. I had to admit Winifred had good taste, so how could I blame her?

"Hey, you people," Murray called from one of the picnic tables. "Now that we're all here, let's get this show on the road."

Cody bent closer to me and whispered, "Murray has spoken. We better go."

"Exactly." Ignoring Winifred's huffed out murmurs, I gently took her from Cody.

We walked to the table, taking our places where Murray had set out the plates and silverware. Winifred flipped her tail at me when I placed her on the bench to my right, but turned in a circle three times before curling up in a ball.

The food, as always, looked and smelled amazing. But there was more. A calm sensation. A fullness. Was it because I'd come close to having my life snuffed out, and now I wanted to appreciate my favorite things even more?

A glance to my left showed Cody, who was admiring the plates of food in front of us. Maybe he was relishing life anew, like I was.

I smirked. No, Cody was being Cody—always hungry, always ready to eat, no matter what it was. He even ate food I made, which wasn't often since I rarely cooked, but that had to say something about his eating habits.

However, Murray seemed to have outdone himself this time. Everything on the table looked appetizing, tantalizing, and, as Gram used to say, good enough to eat!

Evie looked over at Murray. "Thanks so much for this. It looks amazing."

He waved her comment away, but a tiny smile formed beneath his bushy mustache. "Go on, now. You're around my cooking every day. I doubt you find it all that appealing anymore."

Was he kidding? I moved my hand to get his attention. "I'll have you know, sir, that your food is the best around. Bar none. And I have it every day too. So you can say what you want, but your food is amazing."

Evie, George, and Cody all nodded. I pointed to them. "See?"

"You people…you're all my family. It's what family does for each other." Murray's face reddened, and he cleared his throat. "But enough of that mushiness. Let's go ahead and eat."

Evie's gaze met mine. She had tears forming in her eyes at Murray's comment. And so did I.

Once everybody had filled his or her plate, and Winifred had a not-so-tiny pile of her kitty treats on the bench next to me, we began our meal, and unwound enough to start conversation.

Murray took a bite of salad, then pointed his fork at Cody. "Have to hand it to you, Sheriff, you've done it again, getting a dangerous criminal off the streets of our little town."

Cody gave a shrug. "Thanks. I did have help, though. From all of you. It takes a village. Or I guess in our case, a town."

I watched Cody for a few seconds, wondering if I'd get another lecture from him about snooping into police business. However, he left it alone this time. I let out a breath. Not that I hadn't heard it all before with the other murders, but tonight was a celebration. I wasn't in the mood to hear about how I shouldn't involve myself in murder investigations.

When Cody turned to me, made eye contact, then winked, I nearly spit out my water. What did that mean? Had he only been kidding when he praised the rest of us for helping him with clues?

Stop it, Seneca. Take it for what it is. A nice gesture.

Or…

Did that wink mean something more? Deeper? Maybe Cody was starting to think about me like I was about him. Maybe…

"…Seneca?"

I blinked. "Huh?"

"Earth to Seneca." Evie waved her hand in front of me.

"Sorry. Zoned out there. What were you saying?"

"We were talking about the murder."

Good grief. How long had I been sitting there like a zombie?

"I wondered if you'd suspected Camry at all before you were at her house and…" Evie grimaced, as if not wanting to mention the gun and what could have happened.

"Maybe a little bit. At times. But only because she was included in the group of the four women, and a couple of them were on my list. I mostly looked past her. She'd seemed innocuous enough. Obviously, I shouldn't have overlooked her." I picked up my glass and took a sip.

"You weren't the only one, Seneca." Cody elbowed me lightly. "Sure, I checked Camry out initially, like I did everyone else at the wedding, but she slipped under my radar too."

George let out a sigh. "All I can say is, I'm so grateful you all were on the lookout for the real killer, since I was the one standing there holding that pillow." His face paled.

Evie grabbed his hand. "I never once thought you were guilty, George. You know that, right?"

"I do know that. Thanks." His kiss on her cheek was so sweet, it nearly made me melt, and I wasn't even the recipient.

I angled forward to see George better. "I didn't think you'd done it either."

Cody and Murray echoed the same sentiments.

"Thanks, everyone." He smiled. "That means a lot. Also, thanks for inviting me to your private party. I know you've all been close for years, so it's an honor to be here with you."

Evie tapped his arm. "Hey, you're one of us now. And you're stuck with us. Sorry about your luck."

George laughed. "What a great place to be."

A soft pat came from beside me. Winifred tapped on my hand. She'd eaten every last morsel I'd brought her. I held out my empty palms. "Sorry, kitty.

That's all I brought." Just great. Not only was I having mom guilt again, I had to experience it with an audience.

A rustling sound came from across the table. Murray picked up a tiny piece of fried chicken from the half-full platter. "This okay, Seneca?"

"As long as there aren't any bones."

"Nope. All clear. Here ya go, Winifred."

At first, she eyed him suspiciously, since she trusted so few people. But she raised her nose into the air and sniffed. Her eyes widened at the scent of chicken. She hopped down from beside me, ran under the table, and popped up again next to Murray, taking the chicken he held out to her. Thankfully, she didn't nip his fingers in the process.

I pointed to Winifred. "Thanks, Murray. I was underprepared with her treats."

"No problem at all. I'm kind of attached to the little orange furball." Murray smirked, then stood up to clean up the table and box up the leftovers. When Evie stood to help, he pointed to her seat. "You sit and relax, young lady."

"But…"

"No, I insist."

"Thanks, Murray." She retook her seat, pressed her shoulder against George's, and let out a contented sigh like Winifred did when I came into the house after being out all day, and snuggled her close.

Murray was so organized when it came to food preparation and delivery, he had everything packed up and tidy in no time. Once he took his seat again, the conversation turned back to the murder.

I wiped my hands on my napkin, then set it on my lap. "I still can't believe it was Camry, all that time."

"And," Evie added, "that she was Yolanda's unwanted daughter. That part made me feel sorry for her." She held up her hand. "But not enough to excuse murder."

Murray pressed his palms against the table. "That Liza Loring must have really gone through it with Yolanda making her and her parents' lives miserable. When she stopped in Painted Wings earlier today, she said she loves her new job with Karen Blain at the bank."

I smiled. "Glad to hear that. She deserves a happy life after all she's been through." And I was especially glad she wouldn't have to see my ex every day at work anymore.

Cody tapped the table with his knuckle. "Oh, before I forget, I ran into Marla today. She's looking for a new roommate if you guys know of anyone who's looking."

Evie glanced at him. "Yeah, I think she'd need a new one now. Hopefully it's someone nice this time. Who doesn't murder anyone. But boy, I really thought she was the one who'd done the deed."

"You and me both, Evie. I was so certain it was her for a while." I peered down at the table. "But I'd also sat right here with Drew when his thoughts cleared enough from his new medication to figure out he'd been thinking about Yolanda, but not about her death. What a relief that must have been for him. And, for me too. I was really hoping he hadn't been the murderer."

George made eye contact with each of us, one at a time. "Thank you all for not thinking I was capable of murder. I have to tell you, I was scared. When I was accused in my former town of pushing an older woman into traffic to try to kill her… Then I moved here and was standing there holding that pillow."

"It's okay, George." Evie nudged him with her shoulder. "It's all over."

"I'm so grateful. It all could have ended so differently if people had believed I'd been guilty in either case. That man who was going around trying to do away with elderly people really did look a lot like me. No wonder people believed I'd done it. Thank goodness he's behind bars now." George wiped his hand across his brow.

Evie watched him for a few seconds, then glanced at the rest of us. "On another positive note, I'm happy to say that Tonda and Gretchen have patched things up and are back to being best friends. They were in Painted Wings and seemed quite happy to be spending time together. They've decided to include Marla, but all three had pledged to stop trying to divide friendships."

I reached over and ran my hand through Winifred's fur. "That's good to hear. I hated it that those four, I guess now it will be three of them, couldn't seem to get along. It was painful to watch.

"Also," Murray glanced at each of us, "good news for Wiley Snare. He'll be heading back to Steele Industries in a few weeks. He's happy and so is his wife."

Cody nodded. "And speaking of the Snares, Devan and Kinley were off on their honeymoon trip to Niagara Falls this morning. Mr. O'Hurley said he couldn't wait for 'details' about what they did on their trip." Cody rolled his eyes, but laughed. He checked his watch in the light of the nearby lantern. "Oh, hey, I need to go, guys. Early day tomorrow. Thanks again, everyone for your help in tracking down another killer."

"And…" I looked at Murray. "Thanks to you for this amazing meal."

Everyone agreed.

We all stood. Winifred yawned, then hopped down onto the nearby grass. She wouldn't go far, since she wasn't familiar with the park. Plus, she'd want to go home with me and have a second supper.

Evie and George left together, holding hands and whispering. Then Cody helped Murray load things into his van before he headed back to the café with the leftovers.

As I bent down to pick up Winifred, Cody walked over. "Would you two girls mind staying for a little bit?"

"I thought you had to leave." I watched the taillights of Murray's van disappear at a bend in the road. "Is something going on?"

"I'd just like you to stay. Will you?"

"Sure. Of course." I tilted my head. "What's up?"

He gazed down at me. "I thought maybe, you know, now that things are quieting down around here, you might have some free time."

"When do I ever have free time? I'm a farmer, remember?"

"But won't you have a little extra? I'll have a quieter schedule, no longer chasing after a killer. I figured since you're not looking for clues anymore, you might have a few spare hours too."

Something was going on. "What's this about, Cody? Are you okay?"

His shoulder lifted, then relaxed. "I'm obviously not very good at this."

"At what?"

Winifred squirmed, so I put her next to my feet on the grass, where she immediately watched a lightning bug with its glowing butt, fly around Winifred's tail in circles.

Cody took my hand. "What I'm trying to say is, maybe you'd like to go out for some pizza sometime, or—"

"That does sound good. I haven't had that for a while. Maybe we could invite—"

"I'm thinking more just you and me."

"Sure, okay. That sounds fun too." I was always up for some Cody friend time.

He closed his eyes. "I'm still not getting through."

"Cody, just say it, all right? I'm tired, still kind of wired from the past few days, and—"

"Then I'll just come right out with it."

I frowned, really starting to worry now. "Okay."

"Will you go on a date with me?"

I tried to blink. Why couldn't I blink? "A…"

"Date, yes." His eyebrows rose.

"With…"

"Me, yes, that's right."

My mouth opened, but nothing came out. I snapped it closed. "I-I wasn't expecting…"

"I know. Sorry to spring it on you like that. But honestly? After what we've been through lately, especially your encounter with Camry and her gun… I don't think my heart could survive not asking you to take our friendship up a notch. Life is short, Seneca."

"Yeah, I get that. It's…" I took his other hand in mine. "I've actually been thinking about…um, feeling like maybe we…" I slowly gazed up into his eyes.

Cody pulled me close, and leaned down until our faces were inches apart. The kiss wasn't a friendly peck on the cheek or even a quick touch of the lips. This kiss was something the town could really talk about. And this time, they'd be right. But holy cow, I was kissing Cody!

When my knees threatened to buckle, I pulled away gently. "Why, Sheriff Bales...that was..." I waved my hand in front of my face, trying to cool off.

He gave a slow grin. "Yep, it sure was. Exactly how I'd imagined it."

I stared into his eyes until Winifred pawed at my leg. When I picked her up, she burrowed herself between Cody and me, letting out a purr so loud it rivaled an outboard motor.

I petted Winifred for a few seconds, then gazed up at Cody. "So...does this mean..."

Cody lifted my chin with his finger, then peered down into my eyes. "What do you want it to mean?"

How I longed to say what was on my heart. And even though he'd kissed me, was it just attraction on his part, or did he want something more?

I wanted more. But could I say it?

"Seneca? You okay?"

"Yeah, um...I want..."

"You can say anything to me. You know you can. That's always been part of who we are."

An urgent desire came over me, not only for Cody and our physical attraction, but for something lasting. Something permanent. "I want...you. I want a family. With you. A life. Children someday." My words hung in the air. Had I said too much? Would it scare him away? He'd never been married. Maybe he wasn't ready to go that far.

He smoothed some hair away from my cheek. "That's good to hear, because I want the same things with you. I love you. Always have. Always will."

I let out a small gasp as joy filled my heart. "I love you too. I can't wait to be a family with you, Cody."

From my arms, Winifred meowed.

I kissed the top of her head. "Yes, kitty, that includes you, too."

When Cody wrapped his strong arms around both of us, my life, and my heart, finally felt complete.

Acknowledgments

To my blog group, Murder, They Write. Their support and friendship mean the world to me!

About the Author

Ruth J. Hartman spends her days herding cats and her nights spinning mysterious tales. She, her husband, and their cats love to spend time curled up in their recliners watching old Cary Grant movies. Well, the cats sit in the people's recliners. Not that the cats couldn't get their own furniture. They just choose to shed on someone else's.

Ruth, a left-handed, cat-herding, farmhouse-dwelling writer, uses her sense of humor as she writes tales of lovable, klutzy women who seem to find trouble without even trying.

Ruth's husband and best friend, Garry, reads her manuscripts, rolls his eyes at her weird story ideas, and loves her despite her insistence all of her books have at least one cat in them. See updates about her cozy mysteries at www.Ruthjhartman.com.

AUTHOR WEBSITE:

https://www.ruthjhartman.com/

SOCIAL MEDIA HANDLES:

https://www.facebook.com/ruth.j.hartman
https://www.facebook.com/profile.php?id=100063631596817

Also by Ruth J. Hartman

The Seneca James Mysteries (Books 1 and 2)

The Mobile Cat Groomer Mysteries (3 books)

The Kitty Beret Café Mysteries (4 books)

Ring of Death (The Dorey Cameron Mysteries, Book 1)